Folk Tales : From the Bard's Mouth

Folk Tales

From the Bard's Mouth

Original in Gujarati by

Jhaverchand Meghani

Translation by

Ashok Meghani

Shree Jhaverchand Meghani
Loksahitya Kendra,
Saurashtra University, Rajkot

PRINTWORLD

Publishers of Indian Traditions

Cataloging in Publication Data — DK
[Courtesy: D.K. Agencies (P) Ltd. <docinfo@dkagencies.com>]

Meghāṇī, Jhaveracanda Kālīdāsa, 1896-1947, author.
[Short stories. Selections. English]
Folk tales from the bard's mouth / original in Gujarati by Jhaverchand Meghani ; English translation, Ashok Meghani.
pages cm
ISBN : 9788124608739

1. Meghāṇī, Jhaveracanda Kālīdāsa, 1896-1947 — Translations into English. 2. Tales — India — Gujarat. 3. Short stories, Gujarati — Translations into English. I. Meghani, Ashok, translator. II. Meghāṇī, Jhaveracanda Kālīdāsa, 1896-1947. Dādājī nī wāto. English. III. Meghāṇī, Jhaveracanda Kālīdāsa, 1896-1947. Raṅg chhe, bārot!. Selections. English. IV. Title.

PK1859.M4A2 2016 DDC 891.4736 23

ISBN: 978-81-246-0873-9
First published in India in 2016

Published by:
Shree Jhaverchand Meghani Loksahitya Kendra
Saurashtra University, Rajkot (Gujarat)

and

D.K. Printworld (P) Ltd.
Regd. Office: Vedaśrī, F-395, Sudarshan Park
(Metro Station: Ramesh Nagar), New Delhi - 110 015
Phones: (011) 2545 3975, 2546 6019
e-mail: indology@dkprintworld.com
Website: www.dkprintworld.com

Printed by: D.K. Printworld (P) Ltd., New Delhi

This translation is dedicated to

Darabar Shri Punja Wala

and

Dr Niranjan Rajyaguru

in grateful appreciation of their expert and affectionate help to my attempt in preserving the colloquialism of the original tales

Contents

The Co-publisher's Statement

The Government of Gujarat has established Shree Jhaverchand Meghani Loksahitya Kendra under the aegis of Saurashtra University at Rajkot. The Kendra is tasked with Research, Compilation and Preservation of oral traditions and folk literature of Gujarat.

Among the many activities conducted by the Kendra, it considers translations to be one of the principal activities. The voluminous work done in various world languages in the field of oral traditions and folk literature will be of tremendous benefit to our scholars and researchers if made available in Gujarati. Likewise, if the best of the work done in Gujarati were translated into English, it could receive its deserved recognition from folklore researchers, both in India as well as abroad. Today, we are glad to see the first step being taken in the Gujarati-to-English direction.

The folk tales in "Dādājini Wāto" and "Raṅg Chhe, Bāroṭt!", two works written by Jhaverchand Meghani (1896–1947), are powerful examples of the oral traditions of Gujarat. The two scholarly treatises included in the two books also point the way to further research on these oral traditions.

At a meeting of the Executive Committee of the Kendra in 2012, Dr Balwant Jani proposed to have these two volumes translated into English. The committee approved the project and invited Ashok Meghani, the author's son, to work on the project. Shri Meghani completed the task in a few months, but expressed the desire to have the translation published by a publisher of International reputation. The eminent publisher D.K. Printworld, New Delhi, was chosen to print and publish the book, with the Kendra being the co-publisher.

We have received much encouragement and counsel for this project from the Saurashtra University Vice-Chancellor, the Registrar, the Chief Accounting Officer, the members of the Kendra's Executive Committee, Prof. Avadhesh Singh and Shri Jayant Meghani. I express my heartfelt appreciation to all of them. I also voice my special gratitude to Shri Ashok Meghani for accepting our proposal and producing a beautiful translation in a timely fashion.

Dr Ambadan Rohadia
Director
Shree Jhaverchand Meghani Loksahitya Kendra
Saurashtra University, Rajkot

Prof. Pratapsinh Chauhan
Vice Chancellor

Accredited With Grade "A" by NAAC

SAURASHTRA UNIVERSITY
University Campus, Rajkot - 360 005. Gujarat. India.
Tel.: (O.) +91 (281)-2577633, Fax : +91(281)-2576802
email : vc@sauuni.ernet.in
email : drpratapsinhchauhan@yahoo.co.in

VC/1.12/2338/2016 23-06-2016

From the Vice-Chancellor's Desk

After perceiving the need for a publication that caters to the readers and scholars of Jhaverchand Meghani in India and abroad, I had put forward a proposition to the Meghani Loksahitya Kendra. In the fruition of this thought, it truly befits that not only selected stories from Meghani's two acclaimed anthologies *Rang Chhe Barot* and *Dadaji ni Vato* but also a discursive essay evaluating the relevance of Meghani's oeuvre against contemporary literary-critical reception has been included in this work of translation.

It gives me great satisfaction and happiness that this work of translation into English has been undertaken by such an illustrious and competent person as Mr. Ashok Jhaverchand Meghani who has the added benefit of having an insider's view of the Meghani family. I express my heartfelt gratitude to him. The publication of this work by the reputed DK Publishers of Delhi would enhance the quality and visibility of this book as a product. I consider it to be a fortunate happenstance that this work could get Professor Balwant Jani's learned advice, and the overall execution was looked-after by the Director of the Meghani Loksahitya Kendra and a renowned scholar of Gujarati Bardic literature, Dr. Ambadan Rohadia.

I wish that many such works are borne by the Meghani Centre on the Saurashtra University campus, making the rich tradition of Saurashtrian folk literature available to a wider and discerning readership.

23/6/16

Dr. Pratapsinh Chauhan

Translator's Note

JHAVERCHAND Meghani explored many areas of life in the Saurashtra (Kāṭhiāwāḍ) region of India in the second quarter of the twentieth century. He traveled throughout Saurashtra and studied traditions, festivals, rituals associated with all stages of life in remote villages and towns. He collected authorless stories, songs and hymns that represented the values and aspirations of folk life. He published these hitherto believed "ramblings of the illiterate" and secured for them a place alongside the so-called civilized literature in the minds of reading populace.

One of those areas of folk literature is tales orally recited in a distinctive and artful style by professional storytellers. Meghani heard these tales from some master storytellers and made extensive notes. He put these in print while making all possible efforts to preserve the original language, style and content. The first book of these stories *Dādāji-ni Wāto* was published in his early writing days, in 1925. Publication of the second collection *Raṅg Chhe, Bāroṭ!* was delayed until 1946, the year prior to his death.

In this work, I have translated a selection of stories from those two books. All five stories from *Dādāji-ni Wāto* and five of the twelve tales from *Raṅg Chhe, Bāroṭ!* are in this translation. Taken together, this selection is a good representation of this class of stories.

According to the current standards, these stories may not be suitable as children's stories. Violence and a casual treatment of the use of opium-based drugs are principal among the objectionable elements of these stories where children are concerned.

I have used diacritical marks to provide the correct pronunciation of many names for people, places and artifacts. Also, the audio effects used in the telling of these stories would be incomplete if the sounds are not properly depicted by the spellings of some words. I hope the reader with find my use of the following diacritical marks to be unobtrusive:

- The overlined vowels *Ā/ā*, for the "aah" sound.
- The underdotted *Ṭ/ṭ, Ṭh/ṭh, Ḍ/ḍ, Ḍh/ḍh, Ṇ/ṇ* for the retroflex or cerebral consonants (Gujarati ટ, ઠ, ડ, ઢ, ણ or Devanāgarī ट, ठ, ड, ढ, ण).
- The overdotted *ṅ*, for *anusvāra* (nasalization) instead of the ISO specified *ṁ*.
- *Ḷ/ḷ*, for the retroflex lateral approximant (Gujarati ળ or Devanāgarī ळ).

As far as the content of these stories goes, some of it may not bear out under strict historical and geographical scrutiny, possibly because the storytellers were people with little education.

I have corrected some discrepancies between the *Raṅg Chhe, Bāroṭ!* Foreword and the text of the stories. These discrepancies may have arisen with changes made to the stories in later editions but not reflected in the Foreword.

At the onset of this project, I had decided that the two treatises (one with each of the two books) written by the author to be of primary importance to any serious student of this oral folk-story form. Close reading of those two treatises convinced me that I should do the stories themselves first and keep the treatises until later. I hope the reader of this book follows that same sequence, i.e. read the stories first and the treatises later. Knowing something about the author's life, I can imagine the time and effort that must have gone into the collection of these stories. However, the task of writing those two treatises must have been even more arduous with the scarcity of reference material available to him in the rural Saurashtra of the 1920s and 1940s. I was able to collect much information – some entire articles – from the internet; in contrast, the author probably had to go to a big city library to borrow a book or two.

Dr. Balvant Jani proposed that I should do this translation project for Shree Jhaverchand Meghani Loksahitya Kendra affiliated with the Saurashtra University in Rajkot, India. Dr. Ambadan Rohadia, who succeeded Dr. Jani at that institution, worked out the final arrangement for the publishing of this book. I thank both these gentlemen for their support of this project, and for helping bring it to a successful conclusion.

I owe much gratitude to three very knowledgeable people for their help. Darbar Shri Punjā Vāḷā, a high caliber storyteller himself, spent long hours very patiently explaining some terms, techniques and references to me. Dr Niranjan Rājyaguru, an authority on folk-lore, very kindly expounded on some other questions that surfaced later. This is the second project on which I have needed help of this nature and these two gentlemen have very graciously come through for me. A new source of information for this project was Shri Prabhudān Suru, a *chāraṇ* scholar, who ran down *hiṅgāraḍi*, the elusive among the fourteen *vidyā*s mentioned in the story "Occupying Someone's Body". My heartfelt thanks go to all three of them.

My family, as always, has helped me in this endeavor. Under the mistaken notion of a self-imposed deadline, I chose to take time out from our Himachal Pradesh vacation to work on this project. My wife Asha tolerated this disruption with good grace. My children Bela and Sagar, like in other previous projects, read and offered corrections to parts of the manuscript. I am thankful to all three for their active and passive encouragement.

I will be grateful for any feedback from the readers.

Baldwin, MD, USA **Ashok Meghani**
ashok@meghani.com

Dādāji-ni Wāto

(*Tales from My Grandfather*)

To my grandson
1945

Foreword
To *Dādāji-ni Wāto*

First Edition, 1927

Written in their original [oral] style, I have read out these stories to students of a few schools and colleges, especially the institution – Mahilā Vidyālay, Bhavnagar – where I have been privileged to test recite all my folk literature writings so far. I believe the teachers as well as the students of various ages have listened to these with joyful absorption. That has convinced me that this family of stories has a soul-deep relationship with the world of education.

These folk tales are a rare part of our legacy from a colorful past. It has made a substantial contribution in our nation-building efforts. And that is the reason it gives me great pleasure to publish them.

* * *

Second Edition, 1927

I had launched *Dādāji-ni Wāto* (Grandfather's Tales) in the field of folk literature as a new adventure. I believe, that adventure has succeeded. Many readers have testified to finishing the book in a single sitting. Children young and old have recited these stories in the forceful *chāraṇi* style and enjoyed giving full rein to their imagination while roaming in the world of clean and enriching fancy.

For a sequel, I have material ready for a collection of tales of even more gallantry and adventure that can further enrich Gujarati literature – stories that are full of fantasy and yet contain sensible lessons. These are waiting only for me to get around to publishing them. But, my young friends, I will not make you wait much longer!

* * *

Fourth Edition, 1932

The Third Edition was sold out two years ago. The hesitation in reprinting centered around the discussion of whether fairy tales and stories of fantasy legitimately belong to children's literature any more. But, our childhood education experts have been unable to adequately answer that question. Not only that, but many of our universally recognized children's authors have continued to publish such literature.

My main objective was, and continues to be, to present these as samples of a special class of stories. I am publishing this edition only with that perspective in mind, and not as children's literature.

* * *

Sixth Edition, 1945

I have recently published another collection of similar stories under the title of *Raṅg Chhe, Bāroṭ*! (Bravo, Storyteller!). I have included a treatise on the subject of folklore in that book. With that book, I have made good on my promise to publish a sequel to *Dādāji-ni Wāto*. I urge those of my readers that enjoyed *Dādāji-ni Wāto* to not miss reading *Raṅg Chhe, Bāroṭ*!

Jhaverchand Meghani

The New World of Folk Tales
A Treatise

LORD Vishnu showed up at the demon king Bali's door in his dwarf (Vāman) form; then, in his vast (*virāṭ*) form, the Lord took three steps to cover the heaven, the earth and *pātāl* (the netherworld).

That same vast power appears at man's door every day – in the guise of tens of millions of dwarf-sized children, and in the form of foot-long infants.

But, this world proves to be too small to satisfy their colossal curiosity. Their aspirations are too big to fit into the narrow lanes of our mortal world; their imaginations want to wrap their arms around the heavens and nether worlds. This insatiable need of these restless children drives their parents to their wits' ends!

Flights of Fantasy

Grandfathers and grandmothers the world over experienced this same frustration for ages. So, they created ever fresh new worlds and turned the children loose to play in those fantasy worlds. Other grown-ups – pragmatic and worldly wise folks, those accustomed to dealing only with the hard realities of life – also felt the pull of this fantasy world. At night, these grown-ups doffed their soiled apparel of worldly respectability, donned the fanciful finery of imagination and, assuming the necessary childlike naiveté, they too joined the game in endless halls of this make-believe world. That is the world of these flights of fantasy, of fairy tales.

And what did these travelers see in that world?

They saw winged horses and chariots that can fly in the sky; cobras that can spread their venom over a 25-mile radius; flames coming out of cold well water; pairs of eagles and swans that foretell human future; diamond-studded rings that turn into snakes; killer hills that collide and crush life; arched gateways that collapse by themselves; human bodies that turn to stone upon revealing forbidden secrets; wooden statuettes telling tales of the past; Goddess Vidhātā coming to write a six-day-old infant's fortune; lions springing to life from their paintings on a wedding canopy's earthenware pots; snakes sitting atop a snake hole with seven urns of gold, assuming human forms and speaking in human tongue; the snake-wives standing in a *vāv*'s crystal-clear water and crying their hearts out just like the mortal women; Dariyāpeer (the ocean god) pulling sunken ships out from the bottom of the sea and Goddess Kāḷkā bringing her dead devotees back to life; divine female swan birds incubating their eggs at the bottom of the ocean; vegetation burning to a crisp with a snake's venomous breath and turning green again with its nectar breath; flasks containing the life-giving elixir, a few drops of which can revive to life the pieces of a dead body.

A World of Hope

Who – not only children but grown-ups as well – would not find that miracleful fantasy world enticing? To find life's sustenance from the fantasy world while plying the real world is a natural human trait; it is a source of hope in the face of uncertainty. A merchant selling his wares by the pound, unwilling to yield an inch, burning midnight oil to account for the last penny, keeping his feelings and emotions at bay for every waking moment of his life is after all a person of flesh and bones; he too often grows weary of his life's clockwork routine. The millionaire expecting to lose even the shirt off his back tomorrow, still hopes and prays for divine intervention today. One who has lost billions today aspires to incredible affluence tomorrow. In his dreams, he handles bags of money, jingles keys to his safe, and builds mansions and palaces. He, too, finds his consolation, blessings and the strength to fight life's battles from his imagination and fantasies. If such is the case with the adults, what other remedy would the nature-nurtured, fantasy-fed children have?

Human Values

Is this world of fantasy nothing but a means of titillating the children's sense of garden riches? Is its purpose only to entertain their curiosity for a few minutes? Do the children that roam this improbable world become superstitious, meek, whimsical and habitually impractical? Watching this imaginary world flow with unearthly accidents, does the young mind learn to be totally submissive to the concept of God's will and divine providence?

No. A contrary opinion exists that says the children can look above and past all the mumbo-jumbo contained in these stories. The brave characters in these stories that use their brains and their brawn to make their way past the forces of good and evil are the only ones that become the young readers' idols. In the impenetrable darkness of the jungles of these stories, it is human heroism that shines like bolts of lightning. A child's heart is bound to skip a beat upon seeing a king lost and lying unconscious in the wilderness while a fire-breathing cobra roams the same jungle; but hearing of Manasāgaro leaping with a naked sword and using his agile mind to save his friend from the cobra's venom, the same child breathes a big sigh of relief, and badly wants to become a Manasāgaro himself. The terrible sadness of Manasāgaro turning to stone pales against the nobility of Manasāgaro's quiet self-sacrifice. The revolting thought of a snake occupying King Vikram's stomach does not survive against the idealism of Vikram giving up opium because that would poison the snake living inside and violate his own principle of hospitality. The Goddess Kāḷkā's fearsome persona is easy to forget in view of her motherly love, especially shown by the compassionate goddess form in which she covers the three dead bodies with her *choondaḍi* and brings them back to life. The young listeners add their own voices to Phoolvanti's heart-rending wailing, and then rejoice upon watching the virtuous woman washing her husband's feet with her tears; they see the hunchback sister-in-law's cruelty and the woodcutter woman's heartless bloodletting overshadowed by the halo of chastity shining around the saintly Phoolvanti's head. When they see the rainbow of sacrifices made by the valiant men and women light up the trial-darkened overcast skies, these young listeners see the triumph of human spirit over the terrors of this fantasy world. The children emerge from these episodes not afraid but idolizing the bravery of their heroes. It is as if Veeroji walking across the *seeṇo*-filled moat and Manasāgaro roaming the impassable forests are describing their exploits and telling the children, "None but the brave deserve the fair", that the garland from a fair maiden must only adorn the neck of the valiant one.

A New Stream

Today we are venturing out in a new direction in the world of folklore.

[Prior to this] common folks had spread true stories of bravery from our past in their own words as we saw in [my] *Saurāshṭra-ni Rasdhār* and other volumes [*Sorаṭhi Bahāravaṭiyā*].

Folks took stories from the epics *Rāmāyaṇ* and *Mahābhārat*, dressed them in new clothe styles and let them flow from one mouth to another, from the tip of one tongue to the next. Through stories about ritual pledges, riddles, humor, wisdom, animals, birds and many other things, the folk-spirit let the milk of its collective experience squirt. The stars above, hidden messages in the birds' chirpings, abnormalities of flora and fauna – all that got associated with episodes of sacrifice, truth or just plain old human emotions; I have collected those stories in my book *Kaṅkāvaṭi*.

An entirely different stream flowed from the folk hearts in the form of folk songs. I captured that in the six volumes of *Raḍhiyāḷi Rāt* and *Chooṅdaḍi*.

An altogether new stream [in documented form] emerges today. Very artistically rendered from the heart, these stories were narrated to large groups of listeners in a highly lyrical style by our mostly illiterate brethren. Countless bursts of laughter, sighs of despair, expressions of praise and tears from the audience have attested to the life-touching qualities of these stories.

Lacking any historical or factual support, these tales of fiction are timeless tributes to the importance of human life and spirit. Who authored these? They were not "authored" at all because no creator's name is associated with them. Mother Nature uses earthquakes to form well-defined bodies of water, beautiful mountains and caves. Similarly, trials and tribulations of the folk life must give spontaneous life to these tales. The "folk" saw examples of friendship and self-sacrifice. Characters like Manasāgaro and Veeroji were crafted from the combination of those attributes. People saw virtuous women falling prey to the suspicions of their villainous family members; from the tears shed by all those innocent women they created the Phoolvanti-like characters. Then, in order to test the truth, chastity and bravery of those heroines and heroes, they created a world full of animals and birds, of forces good and evil.

But, neither those gods and demons, nor the birds and animals have ultimate control over these stories. Those miraculous happenings do not overshadow the humanity of the human characters. The ambience of improbability does not stifle the importance of humanity. Take the miracles away, and you will still see the same heroes and heroines – as full of humanity, as courageous and heroic, as strong or weak. Those miracles actually play a subservient role to the attributes of sacrifice, gallantry and purity.

Roles Played by Birds and Animals

On the contrary, human values get a big boost that way. The evil forces try mightily to torture truth and human virtue, but finally must bow their heads in defeat. Consider the episode of the Sinduriyo Nāg and you find the supernatural powers actually becoming participants in man's adventurous pursuits. Goddess Kāḷkā comes to Veeroji's rescue and Nāg Padamaṇi wipes Phoolvanti's tears. The animals and birds make big sacrifices for the humans, stay awake at nights and feed the hopes and aspirations of human kind. Take the pair of eagles that reveals the six death threats in store for the king, the swan couple that virtually makes Phoolsaudāgar the gift of a son on that Vaishākhi full-moon night, or Nāg Padamaṇi giving the life-restoring *ami* flask to Vikram. All these acts overcome the distance separating the human world from the animal world. The two worlds embrace each other.

Richness of Prose

What the folk tongue has put into these spoken words has now earned its rightful place in the halls of world literature. I have attempted to present these tales here as samples of the folk tongue's artistry in their original spoken style. Examine the unpretentious yet attractive phrasing, stylish descriptions and emotion-filled prose here:

"Pitch black darkness: a dome of thick clouds overhead: *Tram! Tram! Tram!* go the night crickets." This short description creates the exact sense of that atmosphere.

"A moon complete in all sixteen degrees is up. Its brilliance is overpowering." Those words make a deep impression on children in the audience.

"All thirty-two segments of the king's body light up like lamps." The language and aptness of that metaphor are both uniquely effective.

"A hot sun burns overhead. The earth boils. Hot embers seem to rain down from the sky. . . . The bottoms of her delicate-as-roses feet get cut and bruised. Throat goes dry and hiccups set in."

With their carefully chosen words, these crisp descriptions make us aware of the folk tongue's artistic richness. But, amid those short-phrased descriptions, some exceptionally long constructs crop up to describe a royal court scene, dense woods, a bedecked beautiful woman, some armed-to-the-teeth warrior, a *yogi* or a Gāṅgali Ghāṅchaṇ. Even in such extravagantly showy wordplays, lifelike details, elegant metaphors, ringing poetic prose and accurate word usage bear abundant testimony to the power of the folk tongue. Absent from these narratives is the monotonous pedantry of *Kādambari*, as is the stark simplistic prose of *Arabian Nights* or the overt metaphoric opulence of the old classical [Sanskrit] literature. The prose in these folk tales is ever fresh, of infinite variety and has powerful word-pictures – short or long to suit the need – that hit the nail on the head.

This effectiveness of the language is supplemented by the use of words with sound effects. For example, the midnight clocks that go *ṭaṇaṇan! ṭaṇaṇan*!; *zaḷaḷaḷa*! : a bright glow radiates from the hut; the swing goes *Keechaḍook*! . . . *keechaḍook*!; takes to the skies . . . *kha ra ra ra ra*; the horse goes *jhakāk*! *bakāk*! *gham*! *khararara*!; *kaḍaḍaḍa*. . . the whole mansion shakes. These words with their auditory impact add an extra dimension and further supplement the richness of this orally presented story form.

Thematic Development

Just like the liveliness of this language flow in the folk tales, an effortless life-beat throbs in their thematic development. The sequence of events flows at a furious pace. New, unexpected but related events unfold one after another almost spontaneously, and eventually merge together very naturally. The characters portrayed here are not lifeless idols. They are characters that live their lives jumping into adventures at a moment's notice, short on words, laughing and crying, faltering and repenting, live human beings unsure in the face of diversity but finding their way out of their problems. The stories flow along events that weave in humor and irony, shrewdness and intelligence, maturity and wisdom. That shows these stories are about real life, not mere magic. The role magic plays in these tales is that of lush green trees, colorful songbirds and the beautiful hues of dawns and dusks on the banks of a flowing river. All this adorns the river, makes it picturesque but does not stifle its flow.

Virtue in Folk Tales

The value of virtuous conduct is deeply rooted and finds many expressions in these folk tales. In walking through the fire of society's harsh judgments, Phoolvanti proves herself to be the folk system's real Sītā – the classical epitome of virtue. Manasāgaro – who uses his brain and brawn to get his friend the king married, and then invades the privacy of the royal bedroom to save the king's life – is the true Lakshmaṇ, the devoted brother, of folk life. In Padmāvanti – who experiences love at first sight, then pines away and prays for that alien beloved for six whole months, and even then marries him only after following the *svayaṁwar* ritual – we see the chaste vision of a folk Draupadi. The Rajpoot princess – who sees her conditions for marriage being fulfilled by a brave but uncaring warrior Veeroji – and runs after him alone and barefooted, also represents that folk ethic of virtue.

Breaths of Fresh Air

On the other hand, these stories have managed to avoid propagating the stifling influence of scriptural pretentions on folk ethic. The brave men and women of these tales do not docilely follow priestly orders and parade their moral beliefs, lecture others about chastity, hide their faces behind veils nor wait for the solemn chanting of [wedding] rites. The Rajpoot princess seeks nobody's permission before running after Veeroji, jumping onto his horse and riding behind him, scolding him for his carelessness after being trapped in a swindler's house, declaring her accusations against him in front of a full royal court; and then, starting with her wedding night, for spending every night alone for six months waiting devotedly for Veeroji, her chosen husband. Our other heroine Padmāvanti sees no ethical lapse in deciding for herself and making her symbolic declaration of betrothal near those ancient temples. Why not? Because, her ethical responsibilities are pledged only to her conscience, not to any scriptural decrees. Her devotion is to bravery. She puts her chosen hero's bravery to the test of finding

Kanakāvati before formally accepting him in a *svayaṁvar* wedding.

In a similar manner, the loyal minister Manasāgaro of our folk tale does not recite a canto like

I recognize not the armbands,
Nor do I recognize the earrings.[1]

Instead, he sneaks right into his friend the king's bedroom and violates the scriptural dictates in lapping up venom drops from the queen's cheek. His conscience remains clear, his intentions clean. The feeling behind that contact was as pure and sweet as that of a son caressing his mother.

Ethics flowed through the folk life in wafts of such unbridled, fragrant and pure breeze. Life smelled of sweet and spontaneous humanity; it did not wilt under the hot glare of religious decrees. The age that created tales of Phoolsaudāgar's brave exploits across the seven seas must not have been touched by the priestly powers that declared crossing of the oceans as unforgivable sin. People of that period must have felt free to dare the fate and leap into the lap of adventure.

Hailing from those days in the not-too-distant past, and portraying life unaffected by the scriptures-ordered dos and don'ts, these tales were told by mothers and heard by their daughters, elders recited them to young men. None ever felt the slightest embarrassment. Be it the episode of the swan king taking Phoolsaudāgar to spend a full-moon night with his wife, or Phoolvanti's breasts squirting milk when she bares them in the direction of her son, or the night in the palace bedroom when the royal couple faced the last threat on their lives – none of these has caused even a pretense of awkwardness among folk women. Our mothers and sisters have not run scared from these narratives, because these episodes are either about motherhood or clean conjugal relationships. Even if those episodes hinted of sensuality,

---

1 "नाहं जानामि केयूरम्. . .": the Vālmiki *Rāmāyaṇ* canto where Lakshmaṇ claims to have looked only at his sister-in-law Seeta's feet.

such sensuality was a real and natural part of life.

A Treasure Trove

A huge treasure of these folk tales – that give free rein to imagination, teach the value of sacrifice, set ideals for adventure, bravery and chastity in artistically adorned prose – remains buried in the fading memories of many a Saurashtri grandfather. They contain beautiful weaves of myriads of episodes of great variety. There is very little time left before these stories become extinct. My publication of this small sample of stories is only an experiment to gauge the depths to which our prospective readers can delve into. This is the very first attempt to introduce our [Gujarati] oral literature in print form. Even the tales of King Vikram's exploits have never been published before preserving the unique Sorathi narration style and values.

Bengali Tales of Fancy

At least one other [Indian] province – Bengal – has captured and preserved its folk tales in nearly their entirety. At least ten separate collections with possibly different versions of stories have been published. Just like this *Dādāji-ni Wāto* (Grandfather's Tales) collection of mine, *Ṭhākurmār Jhuli* (Grandma's Bag of Tales) is considered to be the version that presents the stories preserving the grandmotherly style intact.

But that is not all. Bengal has also recognized the worth of these tales in the world of research. The University of Calcutta has conferred the honorary Doctorate of Literature on Rai Bahadur Dinesh Chandra Sen and appointed him as Ramtanu Lahiri Research Fellow to write commentaries on Bengal's folk literature. This scholar delivered a series of twelve lectures on folk tales to the postgraduate students of the university [in 1917]. These lectures presented an in-depth study of [Bengal's] folk tales from the perspectives of art, literature, life and antiquity. The University of Calcutta has published these lectures in book form under the title

The Folk Literature of Bengal [in 1920].

In reading the collections of Bengali folk tales and this scholarly study, I realized that our own stories, albeit with some geographical transformations to allow for regional differences, have also surfaced in Bengal and been so completely absorbed in their psyche as to run in the veins of the [Bengali] people. In comparison, these Bengali folk tale versions seem purer, richer of variety and alluring due to their wholesome values and content. I found our own "Phoosaudāgar" tale incomplete and have incorporated some episodes from its Bengali equivalent "Shaṅkhmālā" in my presentation.

What is more, this scholar [Dr Dinesh Chandra Sen] cites examples of Western fantasy tales to postulate a common origin for the wealth contained in Eastern and Western versions of these tales. He goes even beyond that and, on the basis of numerous observations from both domestic and external tales, comes up with the following conclusion. He claims it was these Bengali folk tales that sailed with the ships carrying fine *malamal* and other cotton-silk blends in ancient times, plied the oceans and landed at many foreign ports – in other words, the stories went from the Bengali sailors' tongues and fell on Western ears. The tales put on their Western attire, eventually got published as "Grimm's Fairy Tales" and returned to India as European beauties!

[*1927*] **Jhaverchand Meghani**

To Grandpa's Land!

Buddies, let's go to my grandpa's land.
The-ocean-of-love Almighty God's land;
Yes, friends, let's go to grandpa's land.

Where the sweet wind blows,
The rivers sing all kinds of songs,
And, away the smiling rowboat glides,
In my lord the King's land;
Yes, friends, let's go to grandpa's land.

Through the seven seas our ship will sail,
Past the snake maidens' palaces we'll go,
Pearls will drip from their love-filled eyes,
Friends, let's go to that pearls' land;
Yes, friends, let's go to grandpa's land.

Through the seven winds we'll take our ship,
Three hundred million stars we'll play with,
Moons and Suns we'll pocket a handful,
Friends, let's go to that moonlit land;
Yes, friends, let's go to grandpa's land.

Late in the evening we'll reach grandpa's land,
Climb on his winged horses and we'll fly,
Then fall asleep in the fairies' loving laps,
Friends, let's go to those fairies' land;
Yes, friends, let's go to grandpa's land.

Who cares if the seas are rough?
Let the storms rise up all around us,
We will leave our sanity behind,

And enter our grandfather's land;
Yes, friends, let's go to grandpa's land.

(From the author's poem "Dost Hālo!" in his collection of children's songs.)

Manasāgaro

SORAṬH peninsula's Pānchāḷ region, its *kanku*[1]-red soil, and the Chotilā Mountain in its middle, and the town of Morasar located at the foot of the mountain, where King Magarapratāp holds its reins. The king is about 25 years old – young, dashingly handsome and with wisdom to match. The king has already amassed riches to rival those of the legendary King Jālandhar.[2]

This is a kingdom that is like paradise in every regard . . . except one. The town of Morasar has no garden or park. Gardeners spend the day planting shrubs and trees; at night, a whole horde of boars comes down from the Māndav Hill and mows down all the newly-planted greenery with their sharp tusks. Their habitat is along the shores of the Sāṇḍhasar and Sinḍhasar lakes.

Every morning, the chief gardener would go and complain, "Help, O great king! Help! The big bad boar mows our heavenly gardens down every day!"

The king says, "Let me know the next time these boars show up."

It is a full-moon night. A moon complete in all sixteen degrees is up. Its brilliance is overpowering. Soon the male and female boars arrive and see the freshly planted flower beds.

The female boar warns, "Beware, O my gullible mate! This looks like the king's garden to me. Come morning, he will have no less than 1,200 cavalrymen gunning for you, don't you realize?"

---

[1] *Kanku*: *Kumkum* (turmeric powder slaked in lime), the red paste used by women to put a *chāndlo* on their foreheads.

[2] Jālandhar: The king of demons in Hindu myth who defeated the gods and conquered all three worlds – heaven, earth and netherworld.

And, the male boar replies, "Timid female, tie your litter of piglets around your waist and take them back to the hills! I am not resting until I mow these new plants down!"

Saying that, the wild boar makes "Hook! Hook! Hook!" sounds, lowers his head and charges at the flower beds and the trees, and ravages them with his powerful tusks. The female boar takes her young back, tucks them away safely under a ledge, comes back and now stands watch.

The gardener goes and calls out: "Help! Help! Help!" The king hears the call.

He says, "There are seven score of you warrior Rajpoots sitting here. If that damned boar slips through our hands, I will tie each of you to canons' mouths and blow you away!"

The seven score Rajpoots mount their horses and take off on the boar's trail. Seven score muskets fire as one and their shots rain down on the running boar. But, when the boar takes a hit, he takes a dip in a nearby pond and his wound heals instantly.

When the musket fire gets too intense, the boar slips into a cluster of *jhāḷ* shrubs and hides out of sight. The female boar taunts him:

The male boar naps under a jhāḷ, *the female paces with fright;*
"Wake up, O sleeping husband, horses stampede your abode."

Smitten by those words, the male boar rises and says, "Is that so, you timid female? Just watch me tear them apart!"

Hook! Hook! Hook! Ignoring the fusillade of shots flying all around, the boar runs out with his sickle-like tusks bared. He is surrounded by seven score and one horses, and He thinks to himself about whom he should attack first. *Hell, why aim low! Go for the top!* And, without even looking at the other seven score, he runs straight at the king's horse. His razor sharp tusks take a swipe at the forelegs of the king's horse, and he runs out of the circle of horses and disappears in the hills.

The king says, "Manasāgaro, you let him slip right past you!"

A brief smile fleets on Manasāgaro's face as he says, "If you say so, my king! But, I suggest you take care of your horse's hooves first!"

The king looks down to find blood gushing out of his horse's forelegs . . . *dhakhākh, dhakhākh, dhakhākh*! He mounts another horse, and says, "My warriors, you all go back to your homes. I swear off drinking my city's water until I have slain that boar."

He sets off on the new horse in the boar's trail. *Taḍbaḍ, taḍbaḍ, taḍbaḍ* . . . the pedigreed steed flies through the gap in the hills like an arrow. The king catches up with the boar in no time, and comes alongside him. But, as he leans down and swings his sword, the boar speeds up and evades the strike. When the king shoots an arrow, the boar dodges that too.

The king keeps the chase up through the day and wears the boar out. The evening comes, the sun starts sinking, and its rays start fading. Now, when the boar seems to be slipping out of his grasp, the king pulls his bow's string back to his ear, says a prayer, and lets an arrow fly. The arrow finds its mark and. . . *bhaf*, the buffalo-sized boar hits the ground hard.

The sun has set. The moon's rays begin to fill the skies. In front of his eyes, the king finds:

Impenetrable woods!
The adjoining hills rubbing their mustaches.
Trees with their branches locked together.
The thorny shrubs so densely packed
That even a rabbit will lose its skin trying to pass through!
The heads of sāg[3] *trees peaking out from ninety* hāth[4] *up.*
Monkeys playing oḷāmbo koḷāmbo *games.*
Bears growling.

---

[3] *Sāg*: Teak.

[4] *Hāth*: Unit of length used in old India, about 18 inches.

And, full-maned lions that measure nine hāth *head-to-tail*
Letting out roars loud enough to shake the surrounding hillsides.

All this makes the king feel very lonely. The gaping hollows in the mountainsides appear threatening to devour him. A confused king looks back towards where he came from, only to find someone standing there . . . his minister Manasāgaro!

"Manasāgaro! What are you doing here?"

"What else, my king? Leave you alone and earn a black face for the rest of my life? No way, Sire!"

"Bravo, my Manasāgaro! Bravo!"

Manasāgaro brings out some opium, drips water over it, and the two men slurp that *kasumbo* from their palms. Soon, the Sun-god's rays pierce the darkness. Manasāgaro gathers up some dry kindling from wild *āvaḷ*, *bāvaḷ*, *lapoḷiya* and *jhapoṭiyā*, strikes his flint and gets a small flame going. And then,

Tobacco from the yard of Vāliyā Gābu,
Goḷ from sugar cane buried for a whole year,
Sand from the River Machhu,
And, some river water

are mixed together and then packed into the bowl of a *hoko.*[5] It is lit, but the bowl is packed so well that if turned upside down not even one ember will drop out of it.

Three deep draws from the *hoko* and the king's body goes on a high. He, however, has not had a drop of water in almost a whole day. His throat is parched and hiccups rock his body. The king starts crying out, "Water! Get me some water!"

Manasāgaro climbs a tree and sees some birds swarming in the distance. He figures that must be a place with water. He starts off in the direction of the birds to find water.

Here, the king looks around and sees five ancient temples

[5] *Hoko*: *Hookah*, waterpipe.

nestled among some trees on one side. Soon, he hears a *gha ra ra ra*! sound and a flying carriage arrives from the South. It is pulled by winged horses.

The carriage lands near the temples. A woman as beautiful as an *apsarā*[6] alights from the carriage and seems to fill the surroundings with rays of light. The *apsarā* casts a glance at the king and enters one of the temples. Soon her worship completed, she comes out. She looks directly at the king; dips some rice into red *kanku*; holds a coconut up for the king to see; raises six fingers; unsheathes a dagger and points it to her stomach. Then she gets into her carriage and flies away . . . *gha ra ra ra*!

The king just stands there, "She's gone! She's gone!"

Manasāgaro comes back with water and finds the king just chanting "she's gone! she's gone! she's gone!" The king seems to have lost all other awareness.

Manasāgaro says, "My king! What is going on? What has gotten into you?"

"Manasāgaro, this *apsarā* just flew away in her carriage. She made some cryptic gestures at me. And now she's gone! She's gone! She's gone!"

"*Apsarā*? What *apsarā*? Must have been a witch! You saw a witch and got scared. Spit, my king! Spit and get her out of your memory!"

"No, Manasāgaro! I cannot spit her out. Now I will eat and drink only when that *apsarā* cooks for me."

"If you don't eat, you will go and join my ancestors soon! Just drink some water, my king!"

But the king doesn't want to budge. His whole being is stuck in the "She's gone! She's gone! She's gone!" rut. Manasāgaro is finally convinced the king has not lost his mind. *Something curious has definitely happened here!*

---

[6] *Apsarā*: Heavenly nymph.

Manasāgaro goes into the temple. What is this? *Kanku* and saffron footprints, incense in the air, a lamp still burning, and rice! An *apsarā* for sure! Who else would worship as exquisitely as this? But what was she trying to convey with those gestures?

Manasāgaro is an ocean of intelligence. He takes each gesture individually and deciphers its meaning:

What did the coconut and rice signify? Yes, must mean "O king! In my mind, I am already married to you."

The six fingers? Yes, meaning I will wait six months for you.

The dagger to her stomach? Must mean I will kill myself if you don't arrive in that time.

She singled out Lord Shiva's padma *(the lotus) to worship. Would Padmāvati be her name? Has to be.*

Where does she live? She surrounded the padma *with* kanak *flowers, so she is telling us Kanakāvati is her town.*

Certain that he had found the logical solution, Manasāgaro goes back to the king and says, "Snap out of it, my king! If I don't get you married to that *apsarā* in six months, you can punish me as you see fit."

The king says, "I will take your head, grind it and build its grains into every *kāṅgarā* (merlon) of my new fort's battlement, do you understand?"

Manasāgaro says, "Once you take my head, who cares what you do with it! I am not going to be around to see it!"

So, the king drinks some water, then takes four long drags on his *hookah*. *Dhaṇaṇaṇaṇa* . . . his senses rise to an exhilarated state of headiness, his body feels invigorated. The two saddle up and mount their steeds. *Daṇaṇaṇaṇa* . . . they fling the horses homewards! By that evening, they are back in Morasar.

Days go by, and the king's spirit continues to thresh like a fish in a puddle. Every day, the king begs his minister for news, "Please, Manasāgaro, when can we go to Kanakāvati?"

"Kings, clarions and monkeys are all alike . . . they never stop tooting! All you do is talk about this! It's not like Kanakāvati is just around the corner! Who even knows where it is?"

Manasāgaro has been trying for three long months but has found no trace of a Kanakāvati city. Only three more months to go . . . and the time is flying at the speed of river waters. What was he to do?

One day, Manasāgaro is walking down the town bazaar and sees a *jogi* from the north. Some *nāgadābāwā*[7] – long yellowish locks of hair, eyes clouded like in a trance, whole body covered with thick layers of ash, a long pair of steel tongs in one hand and a *khappar*[8] in the other – is coming towards him calling out "Ā . . . lek![9] Ā . . . lek!".

Manasāgaro greets him, *namo nārāyaṇ, bāwā-ji*! Praise the Creator!

"*Namo nārāyaṇ*, my son! Praise be to Him, but I have no *gānjā*,[10] no dry tobacco, nothing!"

Manasāgaro picks out some weed buds, wets them with water and kneads them in his palm, fills a *chalam*[11] and hands it to the *bāwā*. No sooner he starts a flame with his flint and holds the light to the *chalam*, the *bāwā* starts the invocation:

Āh . . . lek, *my merciful Girnāri Guru,*
Send me a bale of gānjā;
He that casts an angry eye,
May he crawl the rest of his life.
Venom from a dying snake,

---

[7] *Nāgadā bāwā*: Mendicant of the Nāgā Bāwā sect, typically with ash-smeared body and the briefest of loin covering.

[8] *Khappar*: A large shallow bowl used for begging and eating from.

[9] Ā . . . lek: Ahālek or Alakh; the unseen, untraceable God.

[10] *Gānjā*: Marijuana.

[11] *Chalam*: *Chillum*, a straight conical smoking pipe, usually made of clay and used by *bāwās*.

Father of all gānjā *it makes.*
Kāḷkā, my cackling Goddess
In a hot burning cremation ground,
Lord Hanumān of the deserted village.
Let a fierce battle rage
A waft of cool breeze
The boon from a bāwā *sage*
Some inhale the gānjā *air,*
And some drink their poison rare.

The chant finished, the *bāwā* snatches up the *chalam* and takes a deep drag. A flame leaps out of the *chalam*, and the *bāwā*'s consciousness jumps up to the seventh tier. The drug takes its full hold. Manasāgaro grabs the opportunity and starts massaging the *bāwā*'s feet and calves. "Peace, you sage of Ages! Peace!"

The *bāwā* says, "Ask, my son! Ask me for a boon!"

Says, "O great *jogi*, I am lost! All I ask is to please show me the way to Kanakāvati."

"Is that all, child? I have worn out the road to Kanakāvati under my feet! Look, from here to the Baradā Mountain, then Shetrunjā Mountain, then Nāndivelā Mountain. There the road forks. If you go right, Kanakāvati is 14 miles; left, it is 6 miles. But, you must avoid the left, and go right."

Manasāgaro informs the king.

The king orders, "Yes, let the drums roll! Get the chariots and wagons, tents and all our army ready to march!"

Manasāgaro whispers in the king's ear, "Sire, have you already been to Kanakāvati and eaten the ritual piece of *goḷ* of betrothal?"

Says, "No. Why?"

"Then what is all this noise about? No mother-in-law is waiting to ceremonially receive you there. You are more likely to be greeted by blows of iron chains to your back, don't you realize!"

The king grabs both his ears to admit his mistake. The two

friends get into one carriage and set out. *Ṭhananana*! *Ṭhananana*! *Ṭhananana*! The carriage speeds away. They make night stops and eventually reach the fork near the Nāndivelā Mountain.

A confused Manasāgaro stops the carriage at the fork. Which way to go? He forgets the *jogi*'s warning and takes the left. They get lost in an extremely dense forest. They stumble around for about 8 miles and then the king's head starts hurting. Soon he is in extreme agony, feeling his skull is about to burst out of his head. Life seems to be ebbing out from him. Manasāgaro is at his wits' end.

"Please, my young king! We are lost in an alien land. Please be patient!"

But, how was the king to be patient? A malicious and extremely venomous *nāg*[12] roams the forest terrorizing the travelers. And –

His venom reaches out 24 miles,
Seeking out the reigning royalty.

That venom is now spreading through every vein in the king's body. When it is evening, they are close to the venomous *nag*'s *vāv* – a stepwell; the king's life-force is already at the tenth portal.[13] The only sign of life is a faint beating in the roof of his mouth. The extremely nervous Manasāgaro makes his plea, "King, my king! Please say something!" But, the king is in no condition to respond.

Manasāgaro goes to the step well to fetch water. From the top, he looks down the steps. It is a dark *vāv*, deep enough that a pigeon will need to rest thrice to reach the bottom step. Leaves, layers of leaves cover the entire water surface!

Manasāgaro moves the leaves aside to fill a water urn. He sprinkles some water on the king's head, but fails to revive the king. The dark night descends and the king remains unconscious.

---

[12] *Nāg*: King cobra.

[13] The tenth portal: *Brahmarandhra*, the believed orifice in the crown of the head through which the soul escapes the body.

Manasāgaro stands guard with his sword, shield and the quiver of arrows ready.

The night has set in at its blackest. The crickets chirp *tram! tram! tram!* About three hours into the night, a tornado of leaves flies out of the step well . . . *fararararara!*

Manasāgaro thinks, "*This is curious! I have seen tornados in the woods; but, in a well?*"

Thick smoke pours out of the *vāv*. That is followed by flames leaping out . . . *jhaḍaf, jhaḍaf!* All the green shrubs and trees around the tree are burned to soot black. And soon –

Fooṅ! Fooṅ! Fooṅ! The fearsome *nāg* comes out hissing. Manasāgaro is taken aback for a moment, but the longer he hears the hissing the more he thinks, "Shame on me! I, the product of the red soil of Pānchāḷ . . . am I going to die of fear like this? Hell, no!" He draws his sword and charges, "Stop right there, you son of a snake!"

"*Hā, hā, hā!*" laughs out the *nāg*!

"*Hā, hā, hā!*" Manasāgaro laughs back.

The *nāg* asks, "Hey, what are you laughing for?"

Manasāgaro counters, "Then what are you laughing about?"

Says, "I laughed because I saw you draw your sword and make that foolhardy run at me. I can burn you to a crisp with one snort, do you know?"

Says, "Okay, so you can burn me to a crisp. Is that something to brag about? Is that all you can do? Have you ever done anything good for anyone?"

That gets the *nāg* thinking. Manasāgaro grabs the opportunity to deliver a taunt, "Come on, I challenge you! Restore to life all this that you have burnt, and I will kowtow to you. Or else, if I make all that green again, you kowtow to me. What do you say? Do you know what is at stake? People will talk forever about the big Sheshanāg kowtowing to a human!"

The *nāg*'s heart skips a beat or two. *That makes sense! If this lowly human brings the greenery back to life, he will be rubbing my nose in dirt!*

Says, "Is that so? Let me show you!" And the *nāg* chomps down on the sac of nectar in his mouth, and blows on it . . . *fararararara*! And, the stumps of trees and shrubs burnt earlier had buds and branches sprout again. Everything turns green all around.

And . . . the king regains consciousness!

The *nāg* says, "So what do you have to say now?"

Manasāgaro claps his hands and says, "*Hā, hā, hā, hā*! Did I make a fool of you or what? You idiot, do you not know that no mortal human has the power to restore the burnt back to green? All I really wanted was to get my king alive again, and I tricked you into using your nectar for that! What an imbecile!"

Every cell of *nāg* is afire with rage, but he is powerless to do anything. His sac of venom is emptied out! It will take six months to replenish.

The *nāg* rises up and spreads his hood, "Just remember this, boy! When the first drops of rain arrive under the Swāti *nakshatra*, I will catch them in the air, convert them to *haḷāhaḷ* poison, then find you wherever you are and bite you. One bite and you will be nothing but water!"

"*Oho*! In that case, take this! You say it, you pay for it." Manasāgaro springs with his naked sword, and cuts the snake into two with just one swing.

"May your soul find salvation. Why could you not just hold your tongue and go away?"

The two pieces of the *nāg* thresh about for a while. The king and Manasāgaro get into their carriage and drive away. *Ṭhaṇaṇa*! *Ṭhaṇaṇa*! *Ṭhaṇaṇa*!

They reach the outskirts of Kanakāvati and see a garden nursery swing in its full glory. *Kichooḍ*! *Kichooḍ*! *Kichooḍ*! A *māḷi* (male florist-gardener) is working the ox-pulled *kos* to draw water from a well.

Chāṅpali *mālaṇ* – his wife – sporting black soot dots on her cheek, is approaching with her husband's lunch. Manasāgaro figures that staying at a *mālaṇ*'s house in this alien land would be a wise move.

Just as the mālaṇ walks by their carriage, Manasāgaro moans out loudly, *aaaaaah*!

Chāṅpali yells at them, "You good for nothing bums! I hope your people would die so you can mourn them! Don't you cast your sad thoughts at the gate of my green garden!"

Manasāgaro says, "Sister, we are sad thinking of our sister back home who looks just like you. She too puts those soot dots on her cheek. Seeing you reminded us of her. Here, sister, take this gift from your two brothers!"

And, he hands her a fistful of gold coins. Immediately, Chāṅpali is all sweetness, says "Brothers! My brothers!" and performs the *ovāraṇā*[14] gesture on the brothers' temples. She serves the lunch meant for her husband to her "brothers" and tells her husband, "Listen, you bum! My brothers have come to visit". She takes them to her home and showers them with affection.

Manasāgaro asks, "Sister, who do you sell to?"

"Brother, our king here has a princess named Padmāvanti. She worships Shankar – Lord Shiva – and leads such chaste life as to avoid even a masculine-named[15] food grain like rice. I take a basket of flowers for her every day."

"Do you get paid?"

"Heavens, no! We grow vegetables in our garden, and they don't collect any levies from us. And, when the royal court has any festivities, we get to eat there!"

---

[14] *Ovāraṇā*: The feminine gesture of cracking of knuckles on the temples to wish someone well.

[15] Masculine-named: In most Indic languages, the inanimate object names also have genders – masculine, feminine and neutral – associated with them.

"My sister! Back in our land, a *māḷi*'s basket never goes back empty! Let me make something special for you that will help you earn more!"

The *mālaṇ* fetches flowers, and Manasāgaro weaves them into three pieces of garment: a *kānchaḷi* blouse, a *chaṇiyo* skirt and an *odhaṇi* – a short *sāṛi*. He uses a mind-blowing pattern of nine colors, and hides a small paper note in it. Chāṅpali very happily goes off carrying the basket of these garments to the royal palace.

Princess Padmāvanti sits with her below-the-knee-length hair let down. Her forehead is anointed with a saffron-*kankutilak*. And she is chanting:

My head bows to Shiva – God, mother and father in one!
Reciting his name absolves me of tens of millions of sins!

Then the basket of flowers arrives. The princess takes a double handful of flowers and offers it to Lord Shiva. When she changes into the floral garments, the message note falls out of them. She picks it up and reads:

Near temples five, you must recall,
The man with a two horse carriage.
No mere man, a heavenly creature;
Now here, he awaits your answer.

The message sends Padmāvanti's heart racing. She realizes that the guest she has been waiting for had arrived.

Now, how do I send a reply back? This Chāṅpali is not the reliable sort. If she finds out, the world will know. I have to devise a way to scare her and yet get the word back to the guests.

The princess dips her palms into a platter filled with red *kanku* and saffron powder, and then slaps Chāṅpali on both cheeks. That leaves red *kanku* palm-prints on Chāṅpali's face. Chāṅpali goes home crying, and wails, "Throw your special tricks into fire, you bums! Look what they did to me!"

The king says, "Time to make a run, Manasāgaro. Looks like we made a big mistake!"

But, Manasāgaro ignores that; instead, he hands a fistful of gold to Chāṅpali and she is happy again.

The king is taken completely aback, "Listen, Manasāgaro! I fear they are going to put us through the mill and make oil out of us."

Manasāgaro says, "My king! Make yourself comfortable on a mattress filled with a hundred pounds of cotton. Not even a hair of yours is going to be touched. On the contrary, looks like you will wed Padmāvanti soon. Look at the coded message!"

He draws the king's attention to the *kanku* palm-prints on Chāṅpali's cheeks. Now the king grasps the meaning of it.

The princess sends word to her parents, "Arrange my *svayaṁvar*;[16] I am ready to choose a husband."

The king and queen of Kanakāvati have waited long for the daughter to agree to marry. They order up immediate arrangements. The *svayaṁvar* is set up, kings and princes from all over arrive, and from among them, Padmāvanti chooses King Magarapratāp of Morasar and plants the nuptial garland around his neck.

With the wedding gifts of elephants, horses, palanquins and covered wagons loaded with riches, Padmāvanti departs for Pānchāḷ with her husband.

On the way, they arrive at an enormous banyan tree with orange-colored leaves. The king's entourage stops to spend the night under this tree. At night, the king and queen are sleeping in their tent, and Manasāgaro stands watch with his naked sword outside.

It is now past midnight and Manasāgaro is passing his time admiring the bright moonlit night. He hears two birds talking in the banyan tree's canopy above:

---

[16] *Svayaṁvar*: The custom to allow a girl to select a groom from among those present and put a garland around his neck.

"Say, my eagle queen!"

"Yes, my king!"

"This king and his queen are our guests tonight, but their kingdom will be without their master tomorrow!"

Says, "Why so?"

Says, "The king faces six lethal perils tomorrow."

Says, "What perils?"

"The first: when their carriage picks them up here and departs, a huge branch of this banyan tree will crack and fall on the king and the queen and crush them."

"Can someone not save them?"

"Yes, if the carriage goes a different way, the couple can survive this. But, a short distance from here, they will come to two mountains. Any living being tries to pass between them, the two mountains converge on them and collide. There the king and the queen will be flattened."

"And if they survive that?"

"A diamond-studded gold ring lying in their path will tempt the king; when he picks it up, the ring will turn into a *tamboḷiyo* snake and bite him."

"What if he somehow gets by that peril?"

"His horse arriving with the receiving procession back home will throw the king and crush him to pulp."

"What if he survives that?"

"The main castle gate will fall on him."

"And, if someone prevents that too?"

"Then, the last peril is to strike at night. The royal couple will be in the lap of their sweet slumber around midnight when a black female snake will emerge from the roof above them. A drop of its venom will fall on the sleeping queen's cheek. The king will awaken and kiss the queen's cheek and ingest the poisonous drop. He will die an instant death.

"And, there's this one thing, my eagle queen! If anyone hears our talk and reveals it to another human, that teller of this secret will turn to stone!"

And then, the eagles themselves go to sleep.

Manasāgaro hears all this. He understands bird-talk. His first thought is, *"No way! I have not come this far to let my master die now!"*

The entourage leaves in the morning. Manasāgaro catches a parrot and takes it along. Then, he steers the king's carriage away from the branch that was to fall and makes a longer detour.

The king asks, "Why this way?"

Manasāgaro says, "Because I want to." The king is not happy about that answer.

Soon, they arrive at the pass between two mountains. When close, Manasāgaro releases the parrot towards the mountains. The two mountains rush in to crush the parrot, meet head on and then start to return. Manasāgaro rapidly runs the king's carriage through the pass before the mountains can come back.

The king asks the reason for this strange maneuver. Manasāgaro remains silent. The king is even more irked now. *He is definitely plotting something against me. Upon my soul! How deep do these waters run?*

The king is now giving Manasāgaro the silent treatment. Manasāgaro is not offended by this. He quietly rides his horse ahead of the king's carriage.

Then they see the sun's rays bouncing off the ring on the path ahead. It shines brightly – *jhaḷaḷak! Jhaḷaḷak! Jhaḷaḷak!* Manasāgaro realizes that this is the ring the eagle had spoken of and immediately goes on full alert. He tries to use his horse to shield the ring from the king's eye by putting his horse between the two. But how could a ring shining with those brilliant colors remain hidden, when it is studded with blue sapphires, red rubies and other gems?

"That ring!" The king shouts from the carriage, "Looks like it dropped from the finger of a beautiful *padmini*!" He jumps out of the carriage and runs to pick the ring up. Manasāgaro thinks the king is about to lose his life. Before the king reaches the ring, Manasāgaro sticks the tip of his spear inside the ring and flings it far away. The ring-turned-*tamboḷiyo* hisses away but the king is too angry to notice it. Every cell in his body is on fire! Angrily, he asks, "Manasāgaro! Why did you throw my ring away?"

"Because I felt like it!"

Manasāgaro is not able to give the king the real reason. If he did, he would turn to stone. And . . . there were still three more deathly perils to avert. Manasāgaro keeps quiet. The frustrated king grinds his teeth in anger.

The entourage moves on and eventually arrives at the capital's edge. The seven score feudal chiefs have come to offer the ritual welcome to the royal couple. Town's young women are conveying their good wishes to the king and his queen with *kanku chāndalo* and cracking of knuckles on their temples. Sweet mellow notes from *sharaṇāis* [17] are filling the air. Big *naubat* drums are being struck in every temple. *Ghee*[18] lamps are lined up on the fort's battlement. In that celebratory atmosphere, what is Manasāgaro doing?

He does not join in with the festivities. A black cloud of concern looms over him. He stands and waits for the king's favorite horse to arrive as a part of *sāmaiyun* – the receiving ceremony. The steed – decorated in the silk-thread embroidered equipment, the bottom of his glittering covering flowing in the air, swinging the silk tassels, dancing on his silver anklet sporting legs – is walking towards them looking like one of the seven horses hitched to the Sun-god's chariot. A tuft of hair on his forehead blows in the wind.

---

[17] *Sharaṇāi*: *Shehnai*, an oboe-like wind instrument played on auspicious occasions.

[18] *Ghee*: Clarified butter.

"There he comes! My heartthrob, my soul buddy!" An overjoyed king expresses his happiness. Seeing his master after months of separation, the happy horse neighs back. The king runs to meet his steed. But, before he can reach the horse, one powerful swing of Manasāgaro's sword on the horse's neck, the head flies off, and *tarafaḍ, tarafaḍ*, the horse's carcass stands for a while stamping its hooves!

The king is beside himself with rage. His nostrils flare up, lips quiver, body shakes and every hair on his body springs up, his face turns the color of red hot copper! This is it! *Either he dies or I die! I die or he dies!*

The king draws his sword. He is about to strike Manasāgaro down!

But Manasāgaro? He stands with his head bowed, his hands folded in supplication. He says not a word. His eyes are dripping affection.

The seven score feudal chiefs run to the king and hold him back. The sword is snatched out of his hand. *Calm down, Sire! Forgive him. Any hasty action now may result in much regret later!*

The *sāmaiyuṅ* ceremony is still getting under way. The king cools off and gets busy mingling with people, and catching up with the royal family's news. Manasāgaro slips away unnoticed.

He gets to the main gate and orders, "Gatekeeper, demolish the gate."

The gatekeeper is taken aback, "What are you saying, *Mahārāj*! That will be a really bad omen for the newly-wed king!"

"Bring it down now, or I'll take your head!" Manasāgaro roars. What is the poor gatekeeper to do? He is bound to follow orders! The minister's order, at that! He puts 50 people to work and the whole gate comes down.

Call the gardener! A platoon of gardeners arrives. "Weave

together a floral arch over the gate – and hurry! There is no time to waste!"

A new floral arch quickly takes the place of the old stone arch. With great fanfare the *sāmaiyuṅ* procession arrives. The king does not fail to notice that not even a pebble remains of the original stone gate and arch!

Says, "Who did this?"

Says, "Sire, the minister Manasāgaro ordered it."

What? He dares make such inauspicious change! I can hardly wait for the morning to put Manasāgaro in black clothes, put him on a black horse and exile him.

While the king is contemplating revenge, his carriage passes through the gate. And, *kha ra ra ra*! the floral arch collapses. There are flowers all over the king's carriage, and the king and queen are buried under the flowers.

The king thinks, *Surely the rogue is trying to please my queen!*

The new queen cooks thirty-two varieties of dishes and thirty-three different vegetables. The king sits down to dine. He takes three dainty morsels like a swan from the Lake Mānasarovar. Trading morsels with each other, the king and queen enjoy their dinner. They play *chopāṭ*[19] with gold *sogaṭhis*[20] and diamond-inlaid dice well into the night. Tired from their travel, they slip into a sweet sleep in their petal-sprinkled bed.

Light from translucent glass lamps burning high quality fragrant oil keeps the room gently lit. The lamps seem to be looking at the pink faces of the royal couple and smiling.

The gatehouse gong strikes twelve at midnight, and the guard makes the "All well!" call. That is when Manasāgaro appears at the

---

[19] *Chopāṭ*: A game of strategy played on a cross-shaped cloth "board" , wooden *sogaṭhis* and seven cowry shells as dice.

[20] *Sogaṭhi*: Wooden game piece used in *chopāṭ*. Each player gets four of these at start.

rear wall of the royal palace. He holds a *chandan-gho*[21] in his hand. He throws the lizard up to the palace wall. The *chandan-gho* sticks to the wall as if it has been nailed to it. Manasāgaro then climbs up the rope tied to the tail of the lizard. He enters the king's bedroom from a window. He carries a naked sword and an *andhārapachhedo* (a dark cloak) is wrapped around him. He hides in a corner of the room. His eyes are glued to the ceiling of the room.

Suddenly, he hears hissing sounds. *Fooṅ . . . fooṅ . . . fooṅ*! A black female cobra slithers out from the roof support beam: *drip*! *drip*! *drip*! Three drops of venom come out of her mouth. The green venom drops land smack on the queen's upturned cheek.

The dark-cloaked Manasāgaro lightly walks to the four-poster bed. He goes to the head of the bed and bends down. Down . . . down . . . down until his lips touch the queen's cheek. He slurps the green venom drops, and immediately rinses his mouth out with water from a flask. At that instant, the queen wakes up, "No!"

"What happened?" The king wakes up.

"A thief! Someone kissed me on my cheek!" The queen says in a quivering, scared voice.

"Stop right there, you sneaking thief!" The king springs out of bed . . . and sees a meek-as-cow Manasāgaro standing there with folded hands.

"You low life!" The king roars. "Is this why you were playing all those games? You had you lustful eyes on my queen!"

The king draws his sword. The queen is stunned.

Manasāgaro lowers his head and says, "Sire! Please think before doing something you may regret later."

"Then explain your *shenanigans*!"

"No good can come out of my explanations."

"Tell me, or I strike!"

---

21 *Chandan-gho*: Bengal monitor lizard.

"Fine, I will tell you. It's better to die revealing the mystery than with a blot on my character."

With that thought, Manasāgaro recounts the eagles' conversation he had heard. The king and the queen keep listening. By the time Manasāgaro covers the banyan branch threat, his legs below the knees have turned to stone.

"Please leave the rest alone, Sire! Look at my legs of stone!"

"No! You are a trickster. Speak!"

Manasāgaro tells of the crashing mountains, and his body below the waist is now stone.

"My king! Please let me stop!" But, the king is unmoved.

By the end of the ring peril, Manasāgaro's stomach is all stone.

The horse episode turns everything below the neck into stone. Manasāgaro's head is all that remains alive now. His voice goes hoarse and low, like coming out of a deep cavern.

"My king, are you going to force me to go on?"

But, the king's illusions are not gone yet. He still considers Manasāgaro to be a scheming sorcerer. He says, "Yes! Go on!"

Manasāgaro explains the reason for breaking the gate's arch down, and the stone is up to his chin. His tongue has difficulty working.

"Speak, tell me the last secret!"

"My king! I have but a few moments left. You will not accept my goodwill today. Later, if you ever think fondly of me, sprinkle your first born son's blood on this stone."

"I don't want to hear any of that. Tell me of your last act of ill-will."

Manasāgaro tells about the female cobra. Tears run down his face. He cannot lift his arms to fold his hands. He just looks at the queen. "Sister! My s . . . i . . . s . . . t . . . e . . . r!"

The rest of his head turns to stone as he says that.

Morning has broken. Sun's rays are trying to emerge. The human being that was moving and talking just a few moments ago is now a statue of stone. Even his last teardrop has petrified into stone. The king and the queen stand motionless in front of it.

Oh no! Is this what we did to the man that saved us from six deadly perils? I refused to believe his word to the very end!

"Manasāgaro, my brother! Please say something!" The king clings to the neck of stone!

The king has moved his bed from that room and made it into a small chapel for Manasāgaro. Morning and evening, lamps are lit, incense burns, red vermillion is applied, flowers and food are offered to the statue. At times, the king is so depressed that he just hugs the statue and cries his heart out.

Nine months go by, and Queen Padmāvanti gives birth to a son as perfect as a full moon. The parents take him to the statue room to get Manasāgaro's blessings. Neither parent has the courage to follow Manasāgaro's advice and sprinkle the son's blood on the statue. With passage of time, that matter is completely forgotten.

The prince grows up. He does not like to go out and play. He prefers going to Manasāgaro's room and play there.

One day, the little prince is chewing on sugar cane stem. A sharp splinter of the tough outer skin cuts the prince's little finger and it starts bleeding. The prince tries to wipe the blood on Manasāgaro's statue and . . . what is this? The stone has come alive! Manasāgaro presses the prince to his bosom and starts kissing him. They start talking.

What! Whose voices are these? The queen comes running and sees them.

"O my God! Ghost! A ghost!"

"No sister! Please don't be alarmed, I am not a ghost. I am Manasāgaro . . . a touch of the prince's blood has brought me back to life."

The king comes running. "My Manasāgaro! My brother! My all!" The two take each other in hard embrace and cry tears of joy and remorse.

The town goes crazy with celebrations. Every home cooks *lāpasi* for good omen.

Simhāsan : The Throne

PARA-DUKH-BHANJAN (the destroyer of others' sorrows) King Bhoj[1] reigns over the city of Dhārā.[2] A mammoth castle that can tame even a fierce Bhairav[3] girdles the city. The city boasts four castle gates opening into four directions, eighty-four markets, fifty-four neighborhoods and the countless millionaire mansions with sky-reaching urns at their tops. *Choghaḍiyā* drums play at regular intervals all through the day. Oil torches light up at dusk. There is not an unhappy soul to be found in Ujeṇi.

One day, King Bhoj summons his minister and says, "Badhsāgaro, I have traveled around here, but now I want to see Otarākhand – the northern lands."

"Certainly, Lord of Ujeṇi! Your wish is my command."

Badhsāgaro saddles up two fast horses with brass-studded saddles.The king and his minister tie their weapons on and ride away. They are about to cross the Ujeṇi town limits when a woodcutter calls out to them, "Hey there, brothers! Can someone give me a hand lifting this bundle of kindling on to my head?"

"Badhsāgaro! Looks like some old man too weak to pick up his bundle by himself. Let's go help."

The king goes closer. He sees a *brāhmaṇ*, no more than a heap of bones with scarcely a drop of blood in him; a running nose; flies buzzing around his mouth; a mere strand-thin *janoi* (sacred thread) is strung

---

1 Bhoj: Bhoj I, the eleventh-century king of Mālwā (a part of the present-day state of Madhya Pradesh).

2 Dhārā: Dhārā and Ujeṇi are used synonymously by the storyteller, but are different cities. Dhārā was Bhoj's capital.

3 Bhairav: A fierce manifestation of Lord Shiva.

across his chest.

The king sees this wreckage of a brāhmaṇ and said, "O venerable priest! How can you be in this poor state?"

"May you be well, Lord of nine million Māḷwā! I am born a brāhmaṇ, but, in this Ujeṇi of yours:

Bow down low to this city of elite,
Roam along it, street after street;
Nobody cares to offer us a treat

is the prevailing situation. My *gorāṇi*, the lady of the house, used to hand me a collection bowl at daybreak and to push me out to go seeking flour from door to door. I would return at dusk with a litter of screaming children waiting to maul me. I collected not even enough flour to make two *roṭlā*."[4]

"Shame! Shame! Shame on us! A brāhmaṇ's son – wearer of a sacred thread – and he is forced to cut wood to make ends meet! When would he find time to study *Veda-Bhāgavat* – the holy scriptures? Take this, O respected priest! Here is my note for one-and-a-quarter lakh rupees. Collect the money from my treasury. Now say *svasti*,[5] give me your blessings, O holy man!"

"*Svasam*, O king! *Svasam*!"

"*Svasam*? Why did you leave the blessing incomplete?"

"My king, any bully can beat me up and take the money away. Where am I going to find you if that happens? Give me a piece of land, and then we can fill our bellies with hard work."

They get a sheet of copper and the king writes up the permanent ownership deed of a farm there and then. He decrees the sin of four killings on whoever decides not to honor that grant. With that, he sends the brāhmaṇ's poverty into oblivion. *Kaḍaḍaḍa*! *dhoob*! The brāhmaṇ drops his bundle of kindling on the ground and leaves

---

4 *Roṭlā*: Coarse flat bread made of maize flour.

5 *Svasti*: "May all be well with you" benediction.

proclaiming "*Svasti*, O king! *Svasti* seven times over!"

Ḍaṇaṇaṇa . . . ṇa, the king and Badhsāgaro ride off. They visit territories and see all kinds of wonders. Lands where there are vultures big enough to swallow whole elephants; where if you hold a pot out to the sun, the food in it gets cooked instantly; where human beings have hair all over their bodies like bears; where people are born with male and female bodies joined together; where water level in wells is so deep that the man pulling the team of oxen needs to be informed with strikes on a drum that the water has reached the top. After a whole year of traveling through lands of all kinds, the king and his minister turn back and are homeward bound.

It is the lunar month of Āso at the end of the monsoon season. They are going past this farm on one side of their path. The lush millet sways in the wind, with stalks tall enough to swallow up a rider on horseback. The heads of millet are ripe and heavy enough to bend the stalk tops. A raised platform stands in the middle of the farm, the man standing on it makes loud *ho*! *ho*! noises and hurls small rocks from a sling to scare the foraging *vaiyuṅ* birds away.

The king asks, "Whose farm could this be? Last year there was nothing but thorny wild brush here!"

"Sire, this is the farm you donated to that brāhmaṇ."

That instant, they hear cries of "Wait up, o king! Wait up! The sin of killing a brāhmaṇ, of killing a cow on you, if you leave!" The man signals for them to come over to the platform. Reaching the platform, they see the brāhmaṇ with that threadbare *janoi* on his shoulder; he holds a container at his waist with one hand, the other hand holds the sling's strings and he is shouting *ho*! *ho*! (to shoo the birds away). The brāhmaṇ runs to meet them and says, "Sire, please take five heads of my green millet".

The king says, "*Gor*![6] Once we donate something, it is like blood

[6] *Gor*: The term for a brāhmaṇ priest who conducts religious ceremonies. By extension, any brāhmaṇ man.

to us! I cannot take it back."

"If you don't, I will break my head on Shiva's *ling*[7]!"

Badhsāgaro advises, "Sire, we will give it away to some lowly soldier. I suggest you make him happy."

The brāhmaṇ gets down from the platform and steps among the stalks. He holds a sickle in one hand, grabs a head of millet with the other. . . and shakes his head. He thinks, *This head is the cream of the crop. I can't raise my sickle on it!*

He moves to another stalk and touches the head and says to himself, "*This is a brother of the other one! No way I can bring myself to chop it off.*"

The brāhmaṇ goes back to the king, scratches his head and says, "Sire! On this side, the vagrants struck, cattle invaded and cranes ate up the rest. There's not one head of millet worthy of you."

The king and Badhsāgaro smile and walk away. The brāhmaṇ climbs back on the platform. As soon as he is up there, he starts yelling, "Come back, Sire! Come back . . . or the sin of four lives on you! Take some heads of millet!"

The king goes back to the platform and the brāhmaṇ says, "Sire, please wait. Let me grab some heads from the western side of the farm!"

The brāhmaṇ picks up the sickle and gets down to the western side. One after another he looks at the millet heads and sighs, "Oh no! This one is the best in the whole farm. And this one here is as good! How can I chop it off?"

He returns and meekly apologizes. "Sire, the vagrants and the cows got this side too. There's not one head left that is good enough to give to you, my king!"

King Bhoj smiles and starts out again. But, the brāhmaṇ is back on the platform and shouts again, "Come back! You must take some millet heads, or the sin of four lives be on you!"

---

[7] *Ling*: Shiva's phallus-shaped black stone idol.

The king asks, "Badhsāgaro! Something doesn't make sense here! The brāhmaṇ gets up on the platform and turns magnanimous. When he comes down from there, the state of his mind also takes a nose dive and he turns as uncharitable as the lowest of men! Any idea why that would be?"

"Sire, change of location would do that." Badhsāgaro smiles and replies.

"What does that mean?"

"Sire, it means every place has its own influence on people. I am pretty sure that either a big treasure or a great philanthropic king's abode is buried in the ground below that platform. That's why, when he climbs onto that platform, the brāhmaṇ's mind assumes the characteristics of a philanthropist. When he comes down from that platform, he reverts to being the poor brāhmaṇ he has always been."

"What if your prediction is proven wrong?"

"Then it's your sword and my neck."

The king has the ground under the brāhmaṇ's platform dug. The first strike from a pickax, and *ṭhaṇing* . . . the pickax strikes something metallic and rings out. On the second strike, the pointed end of the pickax is stuck in a ring of some sort. Careful excavation all around it unearths one-two-three-four . . . seven cauldrons filled with gold. Digging further down reveals a huge throne!

The king orders the wealth from the cauldrons distributed among the poor and needy. Cattle throughout the kingdom are fed. The throne is cleaned up and placed in the king's royal court where its radiance lights up the entire chamber. The four walls of the court are filled with shades of rubies and pearls. The thirty-two beautiful female statuettes encircling the throne's base twinkle and seem to be alive.

"None other than I deserves to sit on this divine throne!" Says the king and tries to set his foot on the first step, when . . .

Unearthly voices seem to come from nowhere: "No! King Bhoj! No!" and *jhaṇaṇaṇa* the 32 statuettes tinkle as they all raise their right hands.

"What? We dug this throne out, we got it cleaned up and decorated. After all that, who is inside there that is making these 'No!' sounds?"

Jhaṇaṇaṇa . . . the thirty-two statuettes start dancing. The lips of all thirty-two move as they break out with laughter . . . *khaḍ! khaḍ! khaḍ!*

"O statuettes, who are you? And, why do you laugh? What is the mystery here? Speak!" King Bhoj is so startled with the entire goings on, he stands motionless in front of the throne. And then. . . .

The first statuette folds her hands and finds her voice. In human tongue, she replies, "O King Bhoj! The thirty-two of us were the queens of your ancestor *veer*[8] Vikram[9]. This throne belonged to our husband. Sit on this throne only if you have performed feats such as he performed; otherwise, you will not look good and no good will come out of it."

"In that case, mother, please tell me about Vikram the Valiant's feats! I know nothing of them."

"Then listen, my son! This is how Veer Vikram managed to alter the fortunes written by Vidhātā – the divine Scribe of Destiny herself!"

And the first statuette begins her story . . .

[8] *Veer*: Valiant.

[9] Vikram: Vikramāditya, the legendary first century BCE king of Ujjain. His exploits are the subject of many legends.

Vikram and Vidhātā, the Destiny Writer

KING Vikram is traveling incognito around his realm to get a firsthand feel of the welfare and gripes of his people. After a long day of roaming around, he is spending the night at a brāhmaṇ's home. The brāhmaṇ's wife has recently given birth to a boy. Tonight is the sixth night in the boy's life.

An exhausted Vikram has laid his weapons by his head and is fast asleep. The brāhmaṇ has eaten up the *sheero*[1] made for the nutrition starved new mother, and is out cold with his hands on his stomach. The sound of his snoring fills the air like a blacksmith's bellows. His starving wife's eyes have also finally closed.

Vidhātā – the writer of destinies – arrives exactly at midnight. She carries a small pot of red vermillion in one hand, a dipping pen made of pearl stuck behind an ear, and an abacus to make her calculations at her waist.

The goddess steps ever so lightly into the room. She goes and sits down by the little cot where the boy is asleep. A little *ghee*-lamp burns nearby. The goddess adjusts its wick to raise the illumination. She commences drawing lines on the infant boy's palms and forehead.

What fortunes did she scribe?

She wrote an ample daily alms-collection of five pounds of flour; wrote charitable gifts of money; wrote generous fees for performing wedding ceremonies; wrote *dhoti* awards for priestly services; wrote a bride of sixteen; but, when she was drawing the lifeline. . . .

. . . *Oh no!* The pen falls out of Vidhātā's hand. Disappointed, the

---

1 *Sheero*: A sweet dish traditionally made by roasting wheat flour, ghee and *goḷ* – unrefined whole cane sugar.

goddess quickly rises to her feet. The lamp dims. She strikes her forehead in disgust and walks out of the room.

Out on the verandah, she stumbles on the body of a sleeping man. The man wakes up and quickly gets a firm grasp on Vidhātā's feet. He asks, "Who are you? A witch? A demon?"

Vidhātā says, "Let go of me, King Vikram! I am Vidhātā, the writer of destinies for all three worlds[2]!"

"Vidhātā, the goddess! What are you here for?"

"To write the brāhmaṇ child's fortunes on the sixth night after his birth!"

"Mother, tell me what you wrote."

"Don't ask, my son!"

"I cannot let you take another step until you tell me, Mother! Not when I am on watch here!"

"Vikram, everything I wrote is good as gold . . . except, he will live only eighteen years. In full bloom at eighteen, when he is on his fourth and final *fero* (wedding circuit around the sacred fire), a lion will pounce on him and rip him apart."

Vikram is aghast at hearing that. "Oh no, Vidhātri! You would leave a young brāhmaṇ girl widowed right at her wedding? Is there no way to change that?"

"Not possible. No way, no how!" With those words, Vidhātā starts walking away.

Vikram issues a challenge to her back, "Then hear my words, Vidhātri! Tonight you have sneaked past me and sentenced my host's son to death. But, the day I prove your writings wrong, you will know that Vikram always pays for someone's hospitality!"

Vidhātā is gone. The morning comes and Vikram gets ready to leave too; he leaves a gift for the brāhmaṇ and tells him, "When the

---

2 Three worlds [in Hindu mythology]: *svargalok* (the heaven), *mrityulok* (the mortal world) and *pātāḷ* (the nether world).

boy is to be married, send my invitation to Ujeṇi, *gor*! I will come with my wedding gift for him!"

Eighteen years pass like a blink of the eyes. The brāhmaṇ shows up at Vikram's door.

"Sire, here is your wedding invitation!"

"I am ready, *gor*! I will not miss it!" He issues orders, "Let the drums roll. Get our warriors ready. We are going to join my nephew's wedding entourage!"

The army moves out like waves after waves in the ocean.

"Everyone be on full alert! Surround the wedding *maṇḍap*,[3] stand shoulder to shoulder with naked swords at the ready. Others load up the matchlock muskets with gunpowder and shots, and keep the match[4] cords lit. Stand at the town's boundary. If you see a lion, shoot it dead!"

The town streets are completely deserted. The king of Ujeṇi is here to alter the fortune written by Vidhātā, to save a brāhmaṇ's son from death! Really!

The king himself stands inside the *maṇḍap* with his sword drawn and ready. The officiating priest announces, *samo varte sāvadhān! Last warning before you* commit *yourself*!

The bride and groom go around the sacred fire once! Twice! Thrice!

Who would dare! Just one more circuit to go before I disprove Vidhātā's writing!

Just as the pair start their fourth circuit, *hu . . . hu . . . hu . . . hu* comes a lion, leaping and flying its tail like a flag! It clamps its jaws on the bridegroom's neck and sucks blood out from him. Where did

---

[3] *Maṇḍap*: A canopy supported by four pillars under which the Hindu wedding rites are performed.

[4] Match: A piece of rope or cord soaked in saltpeter, which the shooter applied to a touch hole to fire.

it come from? How was this terrible thing possible? Did the ground split and let the lion out?

No, not from the ground, nor from the sky; the lion painted on one of the earthen urns stacked at four corners of the *maṇḍap* has come alive. Vidhātā has sprinkled life into it from above. Those oversized head and neck! Teeth the size of knives! Overall appearance fearsome enough to kill just by sight!

Before anyone can react, the lion sucks blood from the young bridegroom's neck and returns to the painting on the earthen urn.

Vikram has lost all his luster, all his bravado. If you cut him, not a drop of blood would come out. He has lost his face, and wants the ground under him to split and swallow him!

But, he snaps out of it in no time. "Do not get disheartened. Please don't cry anyone. Shed not a drop of tear, groom's father! Please think of your son being alive for the next six months. And, please do not consider your daughter to be widowed, O bride's father! I ask for six months of your indulgence. I will return with a jar of *amee*[5] to bring him back. If I don't, I will give up the reigns of Ujeṇi. Embalm the body with preservative herbs and burn eternal lamps and incense near him. After six months, if I come back empty handed, I will cremate myself with your son."

And then, Vikram mounts his horse and rides away. He goes farther and farther from home and eventually gets to a forest 70 miles across. He enters the forest and finds a fierce wildfire burning. He hears a horrible cry coming from within the conflagration. "I'm burning! I'm burning! Alas, if king Vikram were here, he would do anything to save me!"

Oh, oh! Some troubled soul seems to be calling out for my help!

He goes closer and sees a *nāg*, almost steamed by the intense heat. Vikram reaches into the hellish fire to pull the cobra out. The

---

[5] *Amee*: *Amrit*, akin to ambrosia in Greek and Roman mythology. Can bring the dead back to life.

nāg asks, "Who are you, O compassionate person?"

"The very same King Vikram you were thinking of!"

"*Āhā*! O king Vikram! Reliever of others' sufferings! My body is burning up. Let me sit in your cool stomach for a while. I will come out as soon as my burning subsides."

Vikram opens his mouth and the *sinduriyo nāg* quickly enters and settles inside the king's stomach.

After some time, the king says, "Hey, it is now time you came out, my friend!"

The *nāg* in his stomach says, "What do you take me for? I would be crazy to leave a cozy place like this and come out!"

Vikram thinks to himself, "No matter. I cannot violate my duty to protect those in my house. Let him stay in my stomach. I need my daily intake of opium as kasumbo, but that would kill the *nāg* in there. So, I renounce consumption of *kasumbo* as well."

He gives up opium. As a result, his feet drag when he walks. His belly grows into a big ball. His arms and legs become thin like rope. His eyes sink into their sockets. He changes so much that nobody would recognize him as Vikram. The pain in his stomach is unbearable.

The listless and miserable Vikram drags himself into an alien town.

What happens there?

The local king has two daughters. One day, the king lovingly asks his daughters, "Tell me, girls! Do you believe you are what you are because of me, or do you think you are self-made?"

The older daughter says, "I would be nothing without you, father!"

The younger daughter says, "Father, I believe that each of us in this world gets only what our deeds dictate. Nobody can erase the smallest bit from anyone's destiny, nor can add to it. Therefore, I believe it is my destiny that controls me and not you."

"Is that so, girl? So full of yourself, aren't you? Anybody here?" He summons servants.

"Not one but twenty-one of us, Sire!"

"Someone will drive my younger princess to the market in a carriage the first thing in the morning. Find some blind, dumb, handicapped or diseased man and marry her to that man. Let us see where her self-made destiny takes her!"

They go to the market, and find the unconscious Vikram lying on a shop's front porch. His eyeballs have risen up in their sockets. He seems barely alive. A hasty wedding ceremony later the younger princess is Vikram's wife.

They are given an old-and-dilapidated covered wagon and two oxen that can barely go 5 miles before needing rest. A female attendant is also sent along with them. The princess gets into the wagon with Vikram, and they are sent on their way.

In the afternoon, they stop in the shade of a banyan tree and the oxen are unhitched to rest up. The princess sits with a still unconscious Vikram's head in her lap. The attendant is fast asleep. The princess gently caresses her diseased husband's body. After a while she lays the husband's head on the ground, and goes to a nearby step well to fetch some water.

What happens in her absence?

Vikram the valiant is still sleeping unconscious with his mouth open. The *sinduriyo nāg* inside him slowly slithers up to get some fresh air. His head comes out of Vikram's mouth, and with his tongue flicking in and out, the *nāg* gets his bearings. Suddenly he hears a voice:

"For shame, you ungrateful, low-born snake!"

The surprised *nāg* looks in the direction of the sound. Another snake lays coiled up atop a snake-hole and chides, "You half-breed! You must not be from the nine divine families of *nāgs*!"

The *sinduriyo* snorts and hisses back, "Hey you! Why are you calling me names?"

"Why wouldn't I call you names? You did not find anyone else that you had to go into the stomach of Vikram – the reliever of others' sufferings? Shame on you, you miserable thief! All this is probably because you had nobody to teach you [right from wrong]!"

"Don't preach to me, you scoundrel!" *Sinduriyo* retorted, "Why are you sitting on someone else's money?"

"I am sitting on booty, not on someone's body, am I? You evil-doer, you'd get your dues if someone gets the juice of a pound and a quarter of *jher-kochalu*[6] and pours that into Vikram's mouth. Your pieces will fall out of him then!"

"And you think you are never going to die? You have called me a thief, but remember one thing. If someone pours twenty pounds of hot oil down your snake hole, you will freeze into solid gold! The seven urns of gold coins you are sitting on will also be found!"

And, the two snakes rock their hoods at each other, hiss and slink back, one into his snake-hole and the other into Vikram's stomach.

The princess has returned from the well and heard every word of the recipes for the two snakes' undoing. She wakes her attendant.

"Girl, run to the market and get me a pound and a quarter of *jher-kochalu*, *adhamaṇ* cooking oil and an iron cauldron. Hurry!"

The ordered materials arrive. The princess is faced with a dilemma! "If what I overheard were all lies, oh no, that would be a catastrophe! If I give *jher-kochalu* and it kills my husband, I would have committed the most unforgivable sin! So let me work on the snake-hole dweller first."

A fire is lit and the oil is heated to a boil in the cauldron. The two women pick the cauldron up and pour the hot oil into the snake

---

[6] *Jher-kochalu*: A poisonous herb. Its seeds and bark are used for medicinal purposes.

hole, and . . . *fooṅ*! *fooṅ*! The cobra rushes out of the hole, turns into gold and lies still.

They start digging into the hole. By the time they get knee deep, one urn, then two, three, four . . . all seven brass urns are uncovered! Each is filled with gold coins!

They cover the snake hole up with dirt. The pound and quarter of *jher-kochalu* is ground into its juice. The princess pours it slowly into Vikram's mouth. Not even a quarter pound of is in when a heavy breathing *sinduriyo nāg* slithers out quickly, only to fall on the ground in three pieces!

The princess takes a bowl of milk and starts to drip that into Vikram's mouth: *ghaṭak*! *ghaṭak*! As the milk gets into his stomach, Vikram's limbs get stronger. All thirty-two segments of the king's body light up like lamps. Vikram stretches his arms and sits up. He is aghast at what he sees.

"Oh no! What have you done, princess? Why is this *sinduriyo* in three pieces? Who killed it?"

The princess tells him the whole story.

"No, princess! Now you have saddled me with the grave sin of killing someone who had taken refuge in me!"

Vikram puts away the three pieces of the *nāg* in the hollow of his shield. He hasn't bathed in days, his golden body has turned ashy dark. His normal royal glow has dimmed.

"Princess, I would like to cleanse myself in that *vāv*."

"Certainly, my Lord! I will rub and cleanse you with my own hands."

They descend into the step well . . . and hear sound of a woman crying her heart out. Her silky smooth ankle-length hair is hanging loose, pretty-as-roses eyes are swollen from crying, ornaments appear to be plucked off and scattered on the floor, and her tears are flowing like a torrent. "O my husband! My Lord and Master!"

Vikram asks, "Who are you, gentle lady? Why are you standing in the water and crying?"

"King, I am a *nāg-padamaṇi*[7] from *pātāḷ lok* (the netherworld). Our palace is inside this *vāv. Sinduriya nāg* is my husband, and someone has killed him."

"Alas, beautiful lady! We are the people that killed your husband. Look, here is his body in three pieces."

"Wonderful! That solves my problem! I can bring my husband back to life from those pieces!"

The *padamaṇi* dives into the well and returns in a flash. She has a carafe full of life-restoring *amee* in her hands.

She assembles the three pieces of *nāg*'s body together and sprinkles some *amee* on it. One, two and three sprinklings, and . . . *jhadāp*! The *nāg* comes alive and sways its fearsome hood back and forth.

The *nāg then* speaks in human tongue, "Wife mine! I have done wrong. This king saved me from the inferno. He agreed to let me enter his stomach for a while. And, what a cool place that was! The ungrateful me refused to come out. And he would not consume opium because it would kill me!

"O Vikram! Ask for anything, and I shall grant it! Ask!"

"This is all I ask for, O divine *nāg*! A brāhmaṇ's son has died in the middle of his wedding ceremony. I carry the burden of allowing his death. Will you give me two drops of that *amee* to bring him back to life?

"Only two drops? Take the whole carafe!"

Vikram and his queen take the carafe of *amee* and hit the road to return home.

It is the last night of the six month term. Everyone is waiting for the king's return. The preservative-covered body lies there with

---

[7] *Padamaṇi*: Padmini, a beautiful woman.

three *ghee* lamps burning constantly. Incense smoke rises in gusts. Vikram's voice rings through that atmosphere –

"Hello . . . Anybody awake here?"

"We are all awake, O *rājā*! Nobody here has slept a wink in six months!"

One, two and three sprinkles of *amee* . . . and the boy sits up and stretches to shake off his sleep!

Vidhātā's voice comes from the heavens, "Vikram wins! I lose!"

The rest of the wedding ceremony is completed and the royal couple proceeds to Ujeṇi.

* * *

"So, Rājā Bhoj! Sit on this throne only if you have performed good deeds of that caliber. Otherwise, you will not look good and no good can come out of it."

The first statuette completes her story and goes quiet.

But, the second statuette starts dancing and speaks out with a smile:

"Listen, Rājā Bhoj! Listen to another tale of the great Rājā Vikram that occupied this throne."

Veeroji

RĀJĀ Vikram is holding court one day. The chamber is packed to its capacity, shoulder rubbing against shoulder. From two sides, elephants are swinging fans[1] to cool the king. Nimble-tongued poets are belting out verses. *Sharanāis*[2] play every hour and a half to announce the time of the day. Wrestlers are trading punches. Buffalo bulls are locking their curved horns. The king's feudal chiefs and warriors – who would not yield an inch to one another, thick necked and recklessly stubborn – were seated in their *veerāsan* stance, ready for a quick sword draw. Gold-hilted swords honed by [the famed sword maker] Māniyā Wāḍhāḷā and gold-studded rhinoceros-hide shields are arrayed in front of each of them. Gold laced sashes adorn the shoulders of all these warriors.

Suddenly, *viyāu*! *viyāu*! *viyāu*! fox cries sound from the west.

Kāḷidās[3] Paṇḍit, the scholar, is seated at the king's right. Vikram turns to him, "Kāḷidās Paṇḍit! You are supposed to know the past, the presence and what is yet to be. So tell me; what is the mystery behind that animal's call?"

Kāḷidās Paṇḍit pulls a roll of parchment from a fold of his turban. He rolls that open into the court, its end reaching all the way to the door. The king sees three things fall out of it: a pickaxe, a ladder and a fishing net!

---

[1] Elephants swinging fans: Many old paintings show elephants with huge fans held in their trunks.

[2] *Sharanāi*: *Shehnāi*, an oboe-like double reed wind instrument, played on auspicious occasions.

[3] Kāḷidās: Legend goes that Kālidāsa, the poet-playwright, was one of the fabled "nine gems" in Vikram's court.

A disgusted king blurts out, "I am shocked, Kāḷidās Paṇḍit! You, a brāhmaṇ's son, carrying a fishing net! What do you catch with it?"

"No, Sire!" Kāḷidās Paṇḍit says, "The matter goes a lot deeper than that. I am supposed to be Rājā Vikram's astrologer! If he asks and I say "This is not an auspicious time", I have to lower my head in shame. If that *moorat*[4] (auspicious time) is hiding underground, I would use my pickaxe to dig it out; If it flies off, I would climb the ladder to bring it down from the nine-hundred-thousand moons; and if it goes into the water, I would cast this net to snare it. Does that explain it, Sire?"

Says, "Well said, Kāḷidās Paṇḍit! Well said!"

With his forehead wrinkled, Kāḷidās Paṇḍit makes calculations, counting with his thumb on his knuckles. Calculations done, he shakes his head.

"What is the matter, Paṇḍit? Why did you shake your head? Whatever it is, spit it out!"

"*Khamā*! *Khamā* to the lord of all nine million Māḷwā! Bless Vikram the reliever-of-others'-hardships! Sire, the animals have forecast very bad things. How can I even speak what they said? The words would hurt my tongue!"

"Not to worry, Kāḷidās Paṇḍit! Let your words tell it exactly like you see it."

"My king! The animals' words predict that three and a half days from now Rājā Vikram's life will end!"

"Are you sure?"

"If my predictions don't come true, I will sear myself with a red hot iron bar."

"I see. But, I am ready and welcome that death! How much more can I ask than going to my Goddess' abode? I have no further desires left. I have conquered all the lands I wanted to. I courted

---

[4] *Moorat*: From Sanskrit *muhoort* (time slot).

52 *veers* and 64 *jogaṇis*. Now I can die happily."

He calls out, "Is anyone there?"

"Not one, but 21, Sire! *Khamā*!" The attendants stand with their heads bowed.

"Go, announce from the tallest balcony, spread the word with drumrolls in every neighborhood that Rājā Vikram's treasury is open for plunder. Come and grab what you want, fill your vats and coffers now. This chance will not come again!"

The drumroll sounded in every street. The king threw open all seven vaults of his treasury.

Crowds! Masses of people! Even at the palace's main gate, people have gathered like the ocean's water. The crowd is so thick that if you throw a platter at it, it will not hit the ground but just glide over the gathered heads. Vikram watches all this from a balcony high above. Bravo! bravo! bravo! His chest swells with pride to the point where the strings of his tunic are ready to snap.

The royal court meets three days later. Rājā Vikram arrives to bid his final farewell to everyone. And then, *viyāu*! *viyāu*! *viyāu*! come the fox cries again!

Says, "Kāḷidās Paṇḍit! What are the animals telling us now?"

Kāḷidās Paṇḍit rolls the parchment out again and charts the numbers to decipher the future, and blurts out, *khamā*! *khamā* to the Lord of Ujeṇi! The nine million Māḷwā is saved from being masterless today. Sire, the animals say King Vikram has fourteen more months to live."

"Paṇḍit, are you inventing a new fib every day? How did three-and-a-half-days beget fourteen months all of a sudden?"

"Sire! Sin runs away from good deeds!"

"Meaning?"

"The three days of treasure give away built layers upon layers of good *karma*!"

"Really!"

"Yes, Sire, really. If my forecast proves wrong, I, a brāhmaṇ's son, will burn myself alive."

A wedding-like celebration breaks out in every courtyard of Ujeṇi city. Temples reverberate with sweet sounds of *jhālar* gongs.

* * *

The midnight hour is approaching. Sleep eludes Rājā Vikram. He sits on his platform swing and smokes, his *hoko* gurgling *guḍuḍuḍu*! *Guḍuḍuḍu*!. His queen sits across from him and pulls the silk rope tied to the swing. The swing goes *keechaḍook*! . . . *keechaḍook*! . . . . The entire city of Ujeṇi is in deep slumber.

Suddenly, he hears the sound of someone's wailing:

Come, O Rājā Vikram!
Come, Lord of all Māḷwā!
Come, O reliever of misfortunes!

Jolted, the king jumps to his feet. "Who could be crying like that and calling for me at this time of the night? Who in Ujeṇi could be in such despair as to be so restless even at midnight?"

Again come the heart-wrenching sounds of anguish and pierce the king's heart. He puts on his darkness cloak, ties a quiver with 360 arrows on his shoulder and a shield made of rhino's hide on his back, picks up his metal *hoko* and *kaṭ*! *Kaṭ*! *Kaṭ*! descends the steps of his palace. He follows the sound of that wailing down the bazaar street.

He reaches Māṇek Chawk – the central square – and finds not a soul there; not even a dog is awake. Pitch black darkness! A dome of thick clouds is overhead. The night is so devoid of light that one cannot see one's own hand. *Tram*! *tram*! *tram*! go the night crickets.

There's nobody here! My obsessed mind must have conjured up echoes of calls of despair! Time to go back!

But, as soon as Vikram turns around to return home, the wailing is heard again.

Come, O Vikram, my son!
Come, O Lord of all Māḷwā!
Come, O reliever of misfortunes!

"Sounds like someone is crying at the town's gate." The king walks through the now desolate bazaar. He reaches the fort's gate to find no one there, not a black-haired human nor a stray dog.

"*Me and my restless soul! So much ado about absolutely nothing!*" With that thought the king decides to start back when he hears the wailing again. The king listens intently and decides, *Yes! Someone is crying across the River Safrā, on the far side of the Gandhrapiyu cremation grounds, inside Goddess Kāḷkā's*[5] *temple.*[6]

The Safrā River flows full reaching both banks. The king traverses its chest deep waters to reach the opposite bank. When he gets inside [the Kāli Temple], he sees the 50 pound ghee powered flame burning bright. The Mother Kāḷkā stands there with an empty *khappar*[7] in hand. Tears stream from both her eyes.

Vikram folds his hands with reverence and asks, "Mother! Who was wailing my name out from the temple?"

"*Khamā*, my son! It was I, Kāḷkā."

"You! Why would the goddess of four ages need to weep calling my name, Mother?"

"Look at my *khappar*, my son! It has gone empty, and who can fill it but you?"

"Say the word, Mother! What can I offer to fill it?"

---

[5] Kāḷkā: Kāli, Kālikā or Harasidhdhi; goddess of time and change; sometimes depicted in a dark, violent form; consort of Shiva.

[6] Harasidhdhi Temple built by Vikramāditya – Rājā Vikram.

[7] *Khappar*: A large oblong bowl sometimes made from coco de mer, used to receive food into and to eat from.

"Son, I need the blood of a *batris-lakshaṇo* – someone perfect in all thirty-two human attributes!"

"You must be joking, Mother! Such people are not sold in the market!"

"You are one yourself!"

"Really? That is wonderful. I am ready, Mother! If you want, I will give you my head right now!"

"What? Perish the thought! The nine million Māḷwā will be orphaned if you die. The entire world will say that Kāḷkā was not a goddess but a man-eating she-demon! Listen, son! In the Gohilwāḍ province, King Shāḷavāhan rules over the kingdom of Mungipur. All four of his sons are *batris-lakshaṇo*. Their hands and feet have lotus outlines on them. All are as good as *gaṇas* – Lord Shiva's attendants. Veeroji, the youngest, will sacrifice his head for you."

Khaḍ! *Khaḍ*! *Khaḍ*! Vikram laughs and says, "Mother! You want to spare me and devour someone else's hale and hearty son in my place? Did you think about how beloved Veeroji must be to his parents? You want me to stand here and watch him give his blood to sate your thirst? Shame on that! Shame on my very existence if I let that happen!"

"Vikram, my son! Go home. You are the Lord of this land. Hundreds of thousands depend on you for their daily meals. Too many daughters will be widowed if you are gone. And, I will get the blame. You go home, son! I will go and ask Veeroji myself."

Assuming the form of a kite, the goddess takes to the skies flapping her wings in the dark night . . . *kha ra ra ra ra*. Her flapping wings slap the mass of dark clouds and scatter them. The wind blows in gusts when so punished by those powerful wings.

Veeroji, the prince of Mungipur, sits in his opulent palace with cross beams made of sandalwood, roof tiles of crystal glass and walls of gold! The clock has just struck the midnight chimes *ṭananana*! *Ṭananana*!, but he is not sleepy. His princess wife pulls the string to rock his platform swing. *Keechuḍ*! *Keechuḍ*! The two are in the prime of their youth and their love simply radiates from both pairs of smiling eyes.

Gha ra ra ra! Mother Kāḷkā – the kite – lands on the roof . . . and *kaḍaḍaḍa* the whole mansion shakes.

"What was that? Did a piece of the sky fall or what?" Grabbing his bow and arrows, Prince Veeroji springs like a saffron-maned lion from his room onto the balcony. He looks at the roof and beholds the fearsome being there!

"Who are you? Speak! Speak NOW! Are you a witch? A she-demon? Answer, or I will shoot you down with my arrow!"

"*Khamā*, my Gohil prince! *Khamā*, Veeroji, my son! *Khamā*! I am not a witch or a demon! I am Goddess Kāḷkā!"

O ho ho ho! Veeroji takes the arrow off his bow, wraps the tail of his *pāghaḍi*[8] around his neck in worshipful respect and says, "Blessed is this moment, great is my fortune that Mother Kāḷkā herself comes to my door to honor me with her glimpse! And, so fortunate is Rājā Vikram that you are there to answer to his call all hours of the day! How great must that feel! Mother, is Veer Vikram in good health and spirits?"

"Vikram's situation is very uncertain right now, my son!"

"How so, Mother?"

"He is to die in fourteen months!"

"Why so suddenly?"

"What can I do? My *khappar* is dry! I need the blood of a *batris-lakshaṇo*!"

"O Mother! Is there a dearth of *batris-lakshaṇo*s in this world that you want to bring down Vikram – the pillar that props the sky up?"

"Veeroji, my son! You are a *batris-lakshaṇo* yourself. The same lotus outlines are etched in your hands and feet as well. If you

---

[8] *Pāghaḍi*: turban.

sacrifice your head instead, Rājā Vikram will live for 1,100 years!"

"Consider it done, Mother! I commit this head to Vikram right now. My only regret is I have but one head. If I had ten like Rāvaṇ[9] did, I would gladly take them off one at a time to put in your *khappar* and give Vikram near immortality on this earth. But, Mother! If all you want is my onion-bulb-sized head, why are you begging me for it?"

"Because, son, Ujeṇi is too far from here! You will not get there in time [for a ritual sacrifice]!"

"Then tell me what to do."

"Here, take this pinch of incense. In the morning, take your horse to the lake and cleanse him thoroughly. Then light this incense and give him a whiff. If the horse sprouts wings, know that it indeed was Goddess Kāḷkā that visited you. If not, consider it to be a ghost's haunting!"

With those parting words, *faḍ*! *faḍ*! *faḍ*! the goddess flapped her wings and took off for Ujeṇi. Her fly off boomed in the midnight sky. The nine-hundred-thousand stars watched this *jhaḷaḷaḷa* dazzling orb in the dark sky with awe.

Veeroji returned to his quarters with a beaming face.

His heart is bursting with pride. The joyful thought of sacrificing his head so that Vikram may live makes his chest swell so much that the strings of his tunic are snapping. Then he sees big tears roll off his wife's eyes *ḍaḷak ḍaḷak*! Veeroji says, "What is the matter, *rājpootāṇi*![10]"

"*Ṭhākor*, my husband! Who did you promise your head to? How could you agree to have your wedded wife's bracelets snapped, to make her a widow? If this is what you wanted, why did you marry me?"

---

[9] Rāvaṇ: The demon king of the epic *Rāmāyaṇ*. It is believed that he had ten heads.

[10] *Rājpootāṇi*: female Rajpoot, wife.

"Shame on you, *rājpootāṇi*! Surely a drop of some low-born wet nurse's milk stayed in your stomach. How else can such words come out of a true *rājpootāṇi*'s mouth? Wife mine! When a pillar of this world like Vikram is to be saved, how can you hold your conjugal bracelet and your passion dearer? I had thought that when I cut my head off, you would catch it in your *sāṛi*'s end with a smile. Woman! Woman! When the chance has come to do something that the nine continents will remember us for, you are going to sit there and shed tears?"

The *rājpootāṇi* wipes her tears, runs and hugs her husband. She folds her hands and says, "*Ṭhākor*! I erred. Go with joy. All I care about is, how will I know what has happened? I don't want to be left too far behind![11]"

"O princess! Take these two seeds. Sow these, water them regularly and nurse them into plants. As long as the plants remain lush green, know that not even a hot gust of wind has touched Veeroji; if they wilt, you will know that Veeroji's life is over. Then do what your faith tells you to do."

Morning comes. He bathes and gets ready: a *pāghaḍi* with a crest on his head, a snug-fitting tunic on top, *ṭhoḷiya* studs at mid-ear, heavy gold anklets: a four-foot Mānāsāee stout sword caressing his shoulders, a curved dagger shaped like a lion's claw stuffed into his waistband, a shield strapped to his back, a quiver with 700 arrows, a nine-colored bow on his neck, a waxed and braided twin-tailed whip in one hand and a sky-reaching lance in the other.

He is decked out and armed thus. His *rājpootāṇi* has prepared the ceremonial red *kanku* paste and places a dot of it on Veeroji's forehead. Then she applies a pinch of rice to it. She bows, touches her husband's feet . . . and peapod-shaped fingers of her hands drip sweat, two pearl-like teardrops form in her eyes.

---

[11] An expression of the desire to immolate herself and join her husband in heaven.

"So long, *rājpootāṇi*! I will see you in the next life!"

* * *

After bidding that final farewell, the prince gets on his swan-graced horse and sets out on his path to a certain death. He gets to the lake, bathes and cleanses his horse. And then, when he lights the incense the Mother Goddess gave him and directs the smoke towards the horse, *khararara*! Two golden-hued wings sprout from the underbelly of the horse!

"Hail the Mother of the Universe!" The Rajpoot prince jumps on the horse's back. The horse takes to the skies, resounding like a flying craft of the gods. The little bells attached to the horse's ankle bracelets and the saddle cover tinkle *raṇaṇa jhaṇaṇa*! *raṇaṇa jhaṇaṇa*! in the sky. Cities and towns, big and small, pass below them. The horse neighs repeatedly and the cosmic dome of the skies echoes them back.

In the early afternoon, they see a mammoth fort stretch below. Inside the fort, there are mansions seven stories tall. Thinking this may well be the Ujeni city, Veeroji decides to land the horse here. The horse folds its wings as it nears the ground and lands on the bank of a lake.

Some young women from the city have come to fetch water from the lake. They see the rider and freeze like characters in a painting.

"Oh oh! Look at that horse! No, look at its rider! Is he handsome or what? Look at his style! Look at the glow on his face! Girls, can you imagine how beautiful his wife must be?" The star-struck women talk among themselves, and just plain gawk!

The rider says, "Ladies! Sisters! This is the city of Ujeṇi, right?"

"*Ho . . . ho . . . ho . . . ho . . .*!" The women slap each other's palms and burst out laughing. "He looks so good while he has his trap shut! One word comes out of his mouth, and he gives it all away! The maker gave him all those looks, but must have forgotten to add even a pinch of salt![12] *Ho . . . ho . . . ho . . . ho . . .!*"

"Sisters! I am from a distant land, a stranger. Please stop your ridicule, and tell me what I asked."

The water-fetching women said, "Brother! You are about 500 miles from Ujeṇi! This is the ninth fort of Avaḷachand Rāṭhoḍ's. *Khamā*, my brother! Look behind you. That over there is the court of the Rāṭhoḍs!"

The assembly is 12,000 strong and in full swing. Warriors, the bravest of brave, thrice-armed headmen, of a contrary disposition, unwilling to yield to anyone – are seated in their *veerāsan* stance to be ready for a quick draw of their sword. So heroic are they in appearance that you see one and forget the other. The aura of bravery appears to surround them.

Veeroji thinks, "If I come this far and go away without showing my face, the Rāṭhoḍs will say that the prince of Gohilwāḍ hid his face and sneaked away to save a drop or two of *kasumbo*. Let me stay here for a day and treat them to a bit of *kasumbo* and then be on my way."

He walks close to the court where the Rāṭhoḍs are assembled and men come running and take the horse's reins from him. Cries of "Welcome! Welcome!" greet him and he is led to the front of the assembly. When they learn his identity, everyone breaks into words like "How wonderful! The Prince of Mungipur rides into our home all by himself! Our lucky day! We feel honored!"

Veeroji says, "I am the one honored to share food and drink with you". He pulls out five kinds of opium from his shoulder sack – *māḷavi, koṅṭāi, bilesari, āgrāi* and *misari* – and offers it to the hosts. *Khasarak bhuṭāk*! *Khasarak bhuṭāk*! The opium is ground in a mortar into a *kasumbo* paste thick enough to flow in a finger-sized drip when poured. Mixed with some water, the liquid concoction is poured through a strainer.

---

12 Pinch of salt: A grain of sense.

Offered to each other in palms of hands, sprinkling some on friends, the whole assembly partakes of the *kasumbo.*

The hosts ask, "When did you leave home?"

"This morning."

The Rāṭhoḍs look at one another and trade smiles. "*Mungipur is hundreds of miles away. That was some yarn our buddy spun*!"

The perceptive Veeroji says, "That was no lie, brothers! Look at my horse; the Mother of the Universe has given it wings. I am on my way to offer my head in place of Rājā Vikram's."

After the early evening meal, Veeroji takes his Rāṭhoḍ hosts' leave and rides out. He gets to the town border and sees an *ekdaṇḍiyo mahel* – a palace built atop a single tall pillar. It is surrounded by a moat seven fathoms deep and filled with fine grass from mustard plants. The interior of the palace is ablaze with a single flame. Someone with a sweet voice inside the palace seems to be chanting the name of the Mother Goddess.

Veeroji stops his horse and asks the guard, "Hey brother! What is this palace in the middle of nowhere? And why does it need this grass-filled moat?"

"*Ṭhākor*! Avaḷachand Raṭhoḍ's princess lives here and worships the Mother Goddess. She doesn't even eat any food cooked from a masculine-named grain. She has vowed to marry only the man that can cross this mustard moat, and to consider all other men as brothers or father figures.

"Does that mean no Rajpoot man has made it here yet?"

"*Ṭhākor*, many did come! All of them disappeared as soon as they set foot in the moat; gone . . . never to be seen again. You can swim across water; burning fire can be covered with living bodies and walked across. But how do you go across deep *seeṇo* – real fine grass!"

"Hail the Mother Goddess!" Veeroji dismounts from his horse. He tells the guard, "Brother! I have no desire to wed the princess.

I have a wife back home. Actually, I am on my way to a certain death. But, not answering this challenge would mean insulting my mother's womb that bore me!"

He steps out into the grass-filled moat, and it seems like he is stepping onto the palm of the twenty-armed Goddess. Two, three, four . . . and the Mother seems to support him at every step. *Kaṭ! kaṭ! kaṭ!* Veeroji crosses the moat [and back].

"So long, brother!" says Veeroji and gallops away.

"There he goes! There goes the rider! There goes the one that crossed the moat!" The guard is joined by others in those cries.

The princess learns that some Rajpoot has met her conditions and is now riding away. She catches a glimpse of the rider from her balcony. A warrior in armor, a mountainous horse and its long flying tail appearing like three separate riders!

"Quick, girls! Get a palanquin."

The palanquin appears immediately. The princess climbs in. Four woman attendants pick the palanquin upon their shoulders and start off on their chase of the rider.

But, a hot sun burns overhead. The earth boils. Hot embers seem to rain down from the sky. The attendants can't run to keep up, and the horse is galloping away leaving a cloud of dust in its trail. *There he goes! There he goes! He is getting out of sight!*

Watching the rider disappear into the horizon, the princess' heart is breaking. She shouts, "Girls! hurry up and catch him, or I will be widowed for life!"

Dhab! The four attendants drop the palanquin from their shoulders and blurt out, "Lady, it is you that want to marry that king, not us! We have our own young men – may they remain well – sitting back home! If you want to chase your man down, you better start running by yourself!"

And, getting that off their chest, the attendants turn around and run off like a storm of locusts. *Ghararara*!

The princess is left to fend for herself in the desolate surroundings. But, she is obsessed with the thought that she would marry that rider and every other man in this world was like a brother to her.

She starts running. The bottoms of her delicate-as-roses feet get cut and bruised. Throat goes dry and hiccups set in.

"Stop, you runaway rider! Stop, you Rajpoot thief!" She screams as she goes deeper into the desolate jungle.

Veeroji hears the faint shouts coming from behind. He stops the horse and looks back to see a seemingly helpless woman running and crying out to him.

The princess gets to him breathing heavily and vents her anger, "O Rajpoot! You fulfill my vows and then sneak away like a thief! Did you not feel a grain of pity for me? If such was your intention, then who forced you to cross the moat?"

The corners of the *rājpootāṇi*'s eyes have traces of blood in them signaling her wrath. A deeply embarrassed Veeroji says, "O *rājpootāṇi*! I am like a guest in this world; I am on borrowed time. I crossed the moat only because the entire Rajpoot community was losing face. But, princess, you have no reason to follow me to my death. You are young, and the tide of your youthful desires will take a long time to abate. I implore you to go back, find a good young man to marry, and experience the joys of your youth."

The young woman's face turns deep red to the tip of her earlobes. Her whole body shakes with anger as she says, "That is enough, Rajpoot! Nice words indeed! See this?" A dagger suddenly glitters in her hands, "Say no more, unless you want my intestines around your neck!"

Veeroji is flabbergasted. "O princess! How am I going to take you with me? We are not married, haven't gone around the sacred fire four times. Even touching the end of your *sāṛi* will be a terrible sin for me!"

"What you say is true, Rajpoot! But, our ancestors have provided rules for behavior under such conditions: *share a bed with a sword in the middle, and hold a dagger in between when sharing a horse ride*."

Without any further words, the princess springs like a doe and is on the horseback behind Veeroji and holds her dagger between them. The pedigreed horse carries the two with ease and sets off *jhakāk! bakāk! gham! khararara!*

After stopping for two nights along the way, they see the trees on the outskirts of Ujeṇi on the third day's mid-morning. They see a flower garden as they get closer. A banyan tree has spread like a vast tent of orange-red figs. A *ḍāyaro* (a good-sized assembly of people) is seated under the canopy of the mammoth tree.

Veeroji thinks this is Vikram's *ḍāyaro* for sure.

He says, "Princess! Please get off the horse. I cannot approach that *ḍāyaro* with you riding behind me."

"O prince, where can I go?"

"Why don't you sit here in this ditch? I will be back to get you after making proper arrangements for you."

"Rajpoot! You will not forget I'm here, will you? Please remember that I am but a helpless woman. Even brightly moonlit, a night is still a night!"

Veeroji is too preoccupied to really absorb those words and steers the horse towards the *ḍāyaro*. He does not notice a man get up and leave the *ḍāyaro* after seeing Veeroji.

"O *ho ho ho*! Veeroji-bhāi[13] is here! Our dear cousin is here!" Almost the whole *ḍāyaro* gets up and embraces Veeroji one at a time.

"Veeroji-bhāi! Rājā Vikram waited for you and just left here. We will take you to him. Is anyone else with you?"

Veeroji looks down and says, "Yes, my wife is along. In that ditch . . .."

[13] Bhāi: Brother.

"Sure, sure. Gor! Hitch a covered wagon and fetch our sister. Keep her in our guest house. We will send for her after settling Veeroji-bhāi down."

Two men escort Veeroji into town. There is a crush of people in the main bazaar of Ujeṇi. Hearts grind against heart in the madding crowd. In the midst of all that bustle, the escorts simply drop away from Veeroji.

"Where are you, brother?" Veeroji makes a frantic search in the crowd. But, the "cousins" have disappeared without a trace!

Veeroji manages to somehow pierce through the crowds of people and reaches Rājā Vikram's court. He is too embarrassed to mention that he is not alone, and by that night the princess has completely slipped from his mind.

Meanwhile, what has happened to the princess? A man disguised as a *gor* (brāhmaṇ) shows up with a covered wagon. He takes the princess to an adjoining mansion, escorts her to a room on the seventh floor, padlocks the door and leaves.

The princess peeps through the tiny barred window but sees nobody. She tries to open the door to get out, but the door is locked from the outside! *What is going on here?*

The evening comes. She hears wedding songs being sung down below. Someone is getting married.

Darkness falls, and the first *pahor* of the night passes. Then the door opens. A man in a bridegroom's attire steps into the room with a sword on his shoulder. The Creator probably had much time on hand, and must have put this man together from black coal dust . . . that's how dark and ugly this man is.

The princess leaps to her feet like a spring-loaded wooden doll released by a catch.

The man says, "Are you going to talk to me, or should I call my uncle?"

"Who are you?"

"I am your husband, who else? My uncle had made me a promise that the day I ruṇ a big swindle and bring home the big loot, he will get me married. Today was the day, and now I am married to you!"

"So you are not *gor*, a brāhmaṇ?"

"Sure we are *gors*, but rogue *gors*!"

The smart *rājpootāṇi* now has the whole game figured out. Her only recourse now is to use her feminine guile to get her out of this trap.

"Come in, please come, my husband and lord!" She invites the ebony body to sit next to her.

That sends the swindler into ecstasies!

"And what is this for?" The princess points at the sword.

"That's my sword! If you had said no, I would have cut your head off like this; do you understand?"

"O my mother! I am afraid to even come close to you! Please put that thing away."

"Sure! Now that you say so!" The swindler hangs the sword on a nail on the wall. The princess turns her charm on, talks to him non-stop. The rogue melts like a wax doll near fire. He loses all sense of security.

The princess springs like a lioness and grabs the sword from the wall. She swings it with the cry of "Hail Mother!". She takes the head off as cleanly as a potter taking a water-urn off his wheel with a string. *Dhakh! Dhakh! Dhakh!*, the blood gushes from the neck.

Thar! *Thar*! *Thar*! *Thar*! The *rājpootāṇi* trembles as if in the throes of a battle. But, there was a lot more role-playing to do yet. "If they get to me, I am dead meat!"

She dismembers the rogue's body and hangs the limbs and the head in the windows and the door. She stays up all night chanting the Mother's name.

In the morning, someone rattles the door chain and says, "Time to wake up, son! The roof tiles are shining like gold!"

The princess opens the door and throws the torso out. *Dhaḍbaḍ*! *Dhaḍbaḍ*! *Dhaḍbaḍ*!, it rolls down the stairs. "O my God!" Everyone runs out in fright.

When they look up from the outside, the head, arms and legs are hanging from the window!

"We have a complaint! Complaint, O Rājā Vikram! Complaint! Our son has been eaten up by a hag, a she-demon!"

"Hello! Anybody here?"

"Not one but twenty-one, Sire!" Responding to Vikram's call, Rajpoot warriors like Kasaḷo-bhi, Gumānsang-bhi and Merāmaṇ-bhi rush over with their swords and shields. One look [at the body pieces] and they scream "O my father! One dead body! No, two! Five! A hundred dead bodies!" and run back in terror. Their bodies are drenched with sweat.

"Hello, anyone else here?"

"Not one, twenty-one!" Miyaṅ Feṅfaṇe Feṅ, Falādeedaulat, Hānḍibooch and Malak-leriyā get going while caressing their beards. "Bah, those silly Rajpoots can't do a thing right!"

But, when confronted by the spectacle at the swindler's mansion – "Yā Allah! Yā Khudā! O my Prophet! The witch is throwing body after dead body! Run, let's get back to our wives!" – and, they run for their lives.

The king's court is in a state of shock. The king orders a platter with a challenge betel leaf sent around. The courtiers cast their eyes downward.

Veeroji gets up and accepts the challenge. He ties his weapons on him and leaves.

The princess sees Veeroji approaching from the mansion's seventh floor. Her heartbeats go up. She puts the sword down, covers her head and face with the end of her *sāṛi* and turns around.

Veeroji climbs the stairs *kaṭ*! *kaṭ*! *kaṭ*! He yells out, "Speak! Who are you?"

The princess taunts him from behind the head cover, "Bravo, you king of snakes, bravo! Even if a buffalo's calf is missing, the owner will go looking for it in the evening; he will not be able to eat or sleep. But you? Did you care where your woman was? Or your horse? Ever stop to think about it! Rajpoot, do you even understand what you heaped on my head?"

Zab! Out comes Veeroji's sword. "You man-eater! You came to devour me in the jungle. But, when I got away, you dare eat up someone's innocent son? Get in front of me, you witch, and start walking!"

An uncontrollably weeping princess in front and Veeroji with his naked sword behind her, the two walk through Ujeṇi's bazaar. The thick crowd has parted to let them pass. The otherwise buzzing city has gone dead quiet this evening.

Rājā Vikram sits on his throne to dispense justice. He says, "Woman, you are like my daughter. Uncover your face."

When the barrier is gone, Jhaḷaḷaḷa!, brightness emanates from the face of the princess. Her tears flow like the torrential rain in the monsoon months of Shrāvan and Bhādaravo. With heart-wrenching sobs, the princess relates her entire story.

Vikram looks at Veeroji. Veeroji looks down and says, "Sire! I am guilty of the gravest of crimes. I beg you to punish me."

Rājā Vikram marries them like he would his own son or daughter, and sets them up in a palace of their own.

* * *

It is the midnight hour. Strong gusts of wind typical of the lunar month of Posh are blowing outside. The king and his queen are talking in bed.

The queen chides Vikram and says, "My king, are all the men

that come to give their heads like this?"

"Why do you ask, my Rāṇee?"

"If the Mother Goddess calls asking for your head right at this moment, how is your Veeroji going to intercede? Will he be able to leave his new bride's bed?"

"Don't say that, Rāṇeeji! Not right to say such things about Veeroji. But, tell you what. Why don't you go to the window and try calling out for him?"

The queen calls out from the window, "Veeroji-bhāi!"

"At your service, mother!" Veeroji clears his throat and replies from the dark.

"How long have you been standing guard like this?"

"Since the day I arrived in Ujeṇi, mother!"

"You have not been home at all?"

"How can I do that?"

"Why not?"

"What will I do if the call comes for Rājāji without any warning?"

Vikram springs from his bed and goes to the window. "Bravo, Veeroji! Blessed is the mother you are born of! Go home, Veeroji!"

"No, Sire! I will have to break my head open [if something happens to you]. And, the seat of Mungipur will be humiliated."

"Go, my friend! I insist! In the name of the Mother Goddess! Go home for a night!"

Veeroji goes home. From the day of their wedding, the *rajpootāṇi* has waited up for her husband every night. She chants the Mother's name all through the night, sleeps not a wink. Tonight, finally he is home.

The rajpootāṇi
Massaged with herbs and fragrant oil,
Bathed in boiling hot water,

Hung a mirror on a pillar,
A pearl she stuffed in every hair,
And wore ornaments galore.
Left kanku *and saffron imprints*
With every step she took;
When she spoke,
Thirty-two petaled flowers rained down,
Love-captivated beetles buzzed about,
Such an eager, desire-filled beauty:
Eyes like those of a scared female deer,
Slim of waist like a hungry lioness.
Ripe like a growing mango tree, or
The branch of a succulent rāyaṇ *tree,*
The spear wielded by an outlaw,
The flame of a hoḷi *pyre,*
A full moon in bloom,
An old fence in flames, and
The hot sun of the month of Bhādaravo,
Folded she'll fit into a fingernail,
Shooed it flies and merges into skies;
When the east wind blows, it bends westwards,
To west wind, it yields eastwards,
If the wind blows from all four directions,
It breaks up and turns to dust.
Prettied up like that,
With a full platter in hand,
The beauty goes up three-sixty steps,
To hear the loving
"Come, come, please come!"
Such words of triple welcome.
Like the swan of Mānasarovar
Picking at its feed of pearls,
The husband takes three morsels,
And they spend a night of passion.

The *rajpootāṇi* now carries a child. Nine months later she gives birth to a handsome boy. Like the moon in its waxing phase, the child's brightness keeps rising. He grows more at night than during the day, and also more in daytime than at night!

The child is two months old and the twenty-armed Goddess shows up.

"Veeroji! Are you ready, my son?"

"I am ready, Mother."

"But, my son, I do not feel good taking the protector of Vikram!"

A visibly upset Veeroji says, "Mother, why are you playing such childish games?"

"Veeroji! Your son is a *batris-lakshaṇo* as well. Will you give him to me instead?"

"Mother, you will have to ask the one that carried him in the womb for nine months. I do not have that right."

The Goddess knocks on the door of Veeroji's house. The *rajpootāṇi* runs with a coconut to ritually greet her. The Goddess asks, "Daughter, what is dearer to you – your *chooḍalo*[14] or your son?"

"Mother! If Vikram's needs call for them, neither!"

"If I leave your *chāndalo*[15] intact, will you offer your son in sacrifice?"

"Mother, no bargaining is necessary! Take what you want. I don't want to live a second life without my husband!"

"Both of you bring your son to my temple tomorrow."

At midnight the next night, the husband and wife leave their house with the infant son. The mother dips her son into the Safrā River.

---

[14] *Chooḍalo*: Heavy metal bangles, worn only by a woman whose husband is alive; here a metaphor for husband's life.

[15] *Chāndalo*: The red *kanku* dot on the forehead worn by a Hindu woman only as long as the husband lives.

"What are you doing, *rajpootāṇi*? The air is cold enough to kill a grown man, and you dip this delicate *kesuḍāṅ*[16] flower in this ice cold water!"

"It would be sinful to offer a child's dirty body to the Goddess, my lord!"

The fearsome idol of the Goddess stands in the temple. Bright burning flames light up the interior. Veeroji pulls his sword. The *rajpootāṇi* holds the child. Light from the temple lamps playing on the shiny sword in his father's hand amuse the infant boy. He laughs and throws his hands and feet in the air.

Veeroji brings the sword down. The child's severed head rolls to the feet of the Goddess. The mother is left holding her son's body.

The mother cannot take this brutal spectacle. She hears the boy's calls to breastfeed him. She screams, "Ṭhākor, sacrifice me too! Perhaps the king will get a longer life!"

"Here, then!" Veeroji swings his sword one more time and the mother's head joins the son's.

"Wait, *rajpootāṇi*! I am joining you too! Mother, let this add to the king's life. Convey our farewell to him."

He takes a hard swipe at his own neck. His head now lies with the mother–son's heads.

"You man-eater! Killer-goddess! Shame on you!" A furious Vikram roars as he enters the temple wearing his darkness-cloak.

"Here, take this fourth sacrifice!" He aims his dagger at his chest. . . .

"Stop! Stop!" Somebody has the hold of his dagger-carrying hand.

"Get your hands off of me, you demoness! You kill three of my people, and now want to hold me back? How am I going to show my face to the world?"

---

[16] *Kesuḍāṅ*: *Butea frondosa*. It has bright orange-red flowers.

The Goddess appears in the form of a beautiful sixteen-year old woman. She covers the dead with the end of her *choondaḍi*[17] and moves her hand over them. The three wake up like rising after a full night's sleep.

Says, "Vikram, my son! Ask me and I will grant it!"

"I have no right to ask, Mother! Veeroji should be the one to ask. He sacrificed three lives to you."

"Veeroji, son! Go ahead, ask."

Veeroji says, "Mother, what do I ask for? I lack for nothing! I have Vikram's goodwill. I have the blessings of a twenty-armed Goddess like you. If you must give me something, then grant me this. Just like I walk in front of my master to protect him with my life, let my name always be placed in front of his name to continue serving him after my death."

"So shall it be, son!"

Since that day, whenever the world mentions the name of Vikram, it is always as VEER VIKRAM with Veeroji's name (Veer) preceding Vikram's.

[17] *Choondaḍi*: Shorter form of a *sāṛi*.

Phoolsaudāgar and Phoolvanti

The great city of Gendal bustles on the ocean's shore. Ocean traders from around the world come and moor their tall ships in the city's port.

A famous *saudāgar* (trader) lives in the city. He sails with his fleet of twelve ships and plies seven oceans of the world. He brings *kastoori* musk from Kashmir, horses and camels from Arabia, dry fruits and nuts from Kabul, ivory from Ceylon,[1] sugar from Java, spices from Sumatra and unloads them on his town's docks. Lakshmi – the goddess of wealth – has blessed him with all her four hands, and real pearls are swept up along with dust in his home.

As must be God's will, one day the *saudāgar* dies. His twenty-five-year old son Phoolsaudāgar is happily married and is princely in every way. The problem is, he has settled into a life of leisure and shows no interest in any kind of work. He spends his whole day sitting in a garden and playing his flute.

It is not long before the Goddess Lakshmi's *kanku*-red footprints start fading from the *saudāgar*'s house. The twelve heavenly ships miss their departed master so much that they decide to hide their faces deep in the ocean water.

One day, Phoolsaudāgar's mother goes looking for her son in the garden. In a tear-drenched *sāṛi*, she caresses the son's head and cajoles him, "My child, you are the son of a seafaring merchant. You belong on the bosom of the ocean. Your inaction dishonors your father's hard earned wealth and taints his good name."

Phoolsaudāgar sits up with a snap. He goes looking for the home of Jeevaṇ Khārvā – the family's longtime sailor chief – in Khārvā-

---

[1] Ceylon: Sri Lanka.

wāḍ, the sailors' enclave.

"Jeevaṇ Ḍosā! O Jeevaṇ Ḍosā!" *Hey there, old gentleman!*

"Phoolsaudāgar! What brings you here?" Jeevaṇ Khārvā emerges from his door.

"Get all twelve ships ready! We are going to take to the seas."

"Son, the twelve ships are all sulking at the bottom of the sea. We will have to appease Dariyāpeer, the Ocean God, with a sacrifice to get them back."

Lamps and incense are lit at the shore. Four pairs of coconuts are cracked into halves and offered up. Twenty pounds of rice and green gram are cooked and offered. Phoolsaudāgar slits his little finger and sprinkles blood towards the ocean.

"Accept these offerings, O Dariyāpeer! Please bring my twelve ships up from your bottom, Lord!"

Ha du du du du! The ocean waves roar. The unending waters part to form a wide swath. Dariyāpeer picks up the twelve heavenly ships and lets them loose to play on the water's surface.

The ships are painted, their damaged bottoms are repaired, brand new sails are raised and the ships are ready to sail for Java and Sumatra. The sailors' calls go, "*Shee . . . yo . . . rām*!"

"Mother! Sister! I am off, will not be back for twelve years. Look after my wife, please!"

At very last, Phoolsaudāgar goes to bid farewell to his wife. Her name is Phoolvanti.

The dam holding up the tears contained in Phoolvanti's heart is finally breached. She washes her husband's feet with tears. She wipes those feet dry with her yards long *veṇi* – the flower wreath for braided hair. She takes off her necklace made from tiny white conch shells, puts it around her husband's neck and sobs, "Lord and master! I have drenched these conch shells in my tears. Please preserve this memory of your helpless wife during your voyages!"

"Phoolvanti, my darling! I will be gone for twelve years and will return only after answering my mother's challenge. While I am gone, please do what is right, burn lamps and incense behind closed doors, chant the name of Mother Goddess; and, this sword will come handy in times of need."

With that, he picks up the conch necklace and leaves, boards his ship, the sailors raise anchors with chants of "*Shee . . . yo . . . rām! He . . . liyā Mā . . . lek!*" Flying pennants atop their masts, the twelve ships sail off cutting through the waves on an eastward course.

Phoolvanti stands at the shore and watches intently. Far in the distance when the water covers up the pennants at the tops of the twelve masts, Phoolvanti gives out a deep sigh and returns home. The empty shore seems to be gnawing at her.

* * *

The twelve ships move like ducks playing on the bosom of the ocean. The wind god's son Hanumān appears pleased and the ships' sails are filled with the westerly winds. Days stretch into months and six months elapse just like that. On the last evening of the sixth month, they see an island. A bright full moon is rising on the horizon. Wafts of fragrant smells come from the island. Happy chirping of birds is in the air.

"Drop the anchors!" Phoolsaudāgar's order rings out.

The anchors splash down, sails are furled and the twelve ships are secured with ropes to trees on the island.

Now it is almost midnight and all the sailors are asleep. Only Phoolsaudāgar lays awake, thinking of his wife in the moonlit night. Then he hears someone talking in the branches of a banyan tree.

"O swan queen!"

"Tell me, my swan king!"

"It's about this Saudāgar guest of ours."

"Yes!"

"Tonight is the full moon night of the month of Vaishākh. A really auspicious time of the night is approaching. If the *saudāgar* could be home with his wife, she would conceive Rājtej, a son with a kingly future."

"O husband mine! How can that happen? It is a six-month travel to reach home from here!"

"No, my dear! It can happen. If the *saudāgar* bathes himself in the ocean and gets on my back, I can get him home in three hours and back here in three more."

Phoolsaudāgar is taken completely aback by what he has just heard. *Surely sounded like a supernatural voice! Why not see if the bird told the truth or not?*

Phoolsaudāgar takes a dip in the ocean water and calls out, "O heavenly bird! If you truly are the vehicle of Goddess Saraswati, keep your word now!"

The swan flies down from the tree flapping his wings. Phoolsaudāgar climbs on and the swan takes off like a flying machine. It drops Phoolsaudāgar in his courtyard in three hours. He warns, "Phoolsaudāgar! Come back early. Make sure you do not fall asleep."

Phoolsaudāgar tugs on his bedroom door's chain and says, "Open the door!"

"Who is calling me at this late hour? I am a devoted wife and my husband is away for a whole twelve years. I burn lamps and stay awake reciting the Mother's chants. My husband has asked me not to open the door to anyone. I have a sword in my hand. So be warned, whether you are a god or a demon! Turn around if you want to keep your reputation intact!"

"Open the door, virtuous lady! I am neither a god nor a demon. I am your husband. A heavenly swan has brought me here. You are destined to conceive a son, Rājtej, on this Vaishākhi full moon night. Open the door!"

"How do I know you are my husband? What was the last thing I gave you to keep?

"A necklace of conch shells."

The doors open. Phoolvanti's long hair gets combed after six long months, she puts some red vermillion powder into the part of her hair, applies lampblack to her eyes.

Three hours go by. The swan calls, "Phoolsaudāgar, the Moon is about to set. We need to leave now! Let us go!"

Phoolsaudāgar gets up. Phoolvanti tells him, "Swāmi! My lord! Please show your face to your mother and sister before you leave! Otherwise, my life will be worse than death!"

Those words go in one ear and out the other, and Phoolsaudāgar gets on the swan's back. *Ghararara!* The swan is on the course back to the island.

On the way, the swan says, "Phoolsaudāgar, I forgot to mention one thing to you earlier. Your Rājtej's mother is going to face unbearable sufferings! You will not be around for twelve years and will probably lose that conch necklace some place. That necklace has the ability to save her. Why don't you give that necklace to me for safekeeping?"

"O divine bird! I owe you a mountain of debt. I can cut my head off and give it to you, but how can I part with the only keepsake from my wife?"

The swan stays quiet. His wings cut through the gusting headwind like a sword, and get his rider back under the banyan tree on the island by daybreak.

The anchors are raised, sails go up, and amidst echoes of "*Shee . . . yo . . . rām*!" the ships take to the seas again.

* * *

The morning is announced by chirping of the birds and, back at home, Phoolsaudāgar's hunchback sister wakes up. She notices that the house has not been swept, utensils are still unwashed and the earthen water urns have not been filled yet.

"Oho! Looks like Her Highness is still sleeping!" The deformed sister-in-law peeps into the bedroom through a crack in the door. What does she see?

Damnation! The chandeliers are ablaze with oil lamps. Phoolvanti is asleep in bed. Her clothes and hair are in complete disarray. The lampblack has run from her eyes.

"Damn you! You sinner! You and your fake holier-than-thou pretense! You bring shame on my family! My brother is away and you are living it up?"

"Wake up, Mother, you unlucky soul! Come and look at your daughter-in-law's contemptible behavior! Neighbors, come and look at this girl born in a family of repute!"

The women from the neighborhood gather, put their fingers on their lips in disgust, blow their nostrils in contempt and start badmouthing the poor Phoolvanti. "Holy Mother! This girl has shamed her seven generations, ruined our lives, put the whole neighborhood's character in doubt!"

The sister-in-law picks up a broom. *Dhaḍ*! *dhaḍ*! *dhaḍ*! She starts beating up the sleeping Phoolvanti. Then she grabs a shoe.

Phoolvanti wakes up from the sweet dreams of her husband – only to be treated with swings from a broom, blows raining down from seven shoes, and a crowd of women neighbors. An unholy clamor fills the air sounding like a group of female crows taking a poor mynah apart.

"Naṇadeebā, my dear sister-in-law! Why this punishment? What is my offense?"

I have left my father and my mother behind,
And forsaken the company of my friends.
For the sake of your brother, O Naṇadeebā,
I have left my brother and my sister-in-law.

I have left the comforts of my father's house,
And considered this house to be the paradise.
I've treated mother-in-law like my own mother
Have thought of you like my older sister.
Why then have you turned against me today?
Are sins of prior births here to haunt me today?
While she was feeding me her sweet milk,
Did I bite my mother's breast in the previous life?

But, all her wailing falls on deaf ears. The sister-in-law rips Phoolvanti's clothes off, gives her a coarse cotton cloth to cover herself, grabs her by her braided hair, throws her out the door, and says, "Get out, you damned adulteress! Go to the jungle, light up the chandeliers there, decorate your braid with flowers and put lampblack in your eyes!

Now Phoolvanti understands. *Oh no! My husband forgot to stop by his mother and sister. Who can I call as a witness? How can I convince them of what really happened?*

There is nothing to say. Jostled by her sister-in-law, falling and rolling in the dust, crying her heart out, Phoolvanti makes her way towards the forest.

* * *

Feet as delicate as lotus flower are getting scratched and cut. Thorns are piercing fingers as soft as *champā* flower buds. Her braid – long, thick and dark like a king cobra – is getting entangled in the bushes and branches. *Jharaḍ*! *Jharaḍ*! *Jharaḍ*! Her silken smooth skin is getting scratched up. The tear-filled eyes barely see the path she is on. And Phoolvanti still keeps walking . . . and walking.

Her incessant tears turn soil into mud. Big rocks break from the continual knocking of her head on them. Seven months pass like that. Then the birds from trees speak to her, "Do you know what you are doing, O Saudāgar's lady? Think, lady, think! You carry a Rājtej in your womb."

"Yes, you are right! Absolutely right!"

Phoolvanti wises up, starts taking care of her body. She fashions her clothing from the bark of trees, lets her hair loose and appears like a *jogaṇ* (a female ascetic). Birds bring fruit in their beaks for her, and she sates her appetite with that. She walks around with a bamboo staff in her hand.

One night, the woods around her light up. She hears footsteps.

"Who is it?" The *jogaṇ* roars like a lioness, "Whether you are human or a demon, stay away! Come a step closer and I will suck all your blood out!"

Under a sprawling tree stands a man. He has a lit torch in one hand, and an axe in the other. It is a woodcutter out to gather honey at night.

"Mother! Goddess! I am but a poor woodcutter." Shaking like a leaf, the woodcutter folds his hands in reverence, "Hail the holy woman! One among the sixty-four *jogaṇis*![2] My life has served its purpose today. Mother, give the word and I will give my life for you!"

"Brother, I am only a woman in distress. I just want to beg one thing of you."

"Mother! Goddess! You seem to be here in the guise of a human to seek something from me. Ask and I will do anything for you."

"Will you build me a small hut, brother?"

In no time, the woodcutter puts a hut together from tree branches and leaves. He returns to the *jogaṇ* and folds his hands.

"Brother, how do you make a living?"

"Mother, I sell bundles of these sticks of wood."

The *jogaṇ* looks up and freezes. *Āhā*! This is a sandalwood tree.

She snaps one branch off the tree and says, "Here, my brother!

[2] *Jogaṇi*: *Yogini* – a female associate of Durgā, the fierce aspect of the Divine Feminine.

Take this and some more sandalwood from this tree. Sell it only to a real *saudāgar*. Don't haggle with the buyer about the price. Take whatever he gives and come back here."

Axe in hand, and a bundle of sandal branches on his head, the woodcutter leaves. He goes from town to town looking for a *saudāgar*, but where was he going to find a *saudāgar* that values the sandalwood?

* * *

Morning comes. Then, the sun rises up in the sky. Why isn't the woodcutter home yet? The donkeys start braying in the afternoon, but no woodcutter yet. The woodcutter's wife stows the food for safekeeping in a hanging tray, and goes looking in the woods for her husband.

"Woodcutter, O cursed woodcutter!" she shouts, but nobody answers her calls.

Suddenly, she sees a hut in the shade of a tree, and a *jogaṇ* standing in the door of the hut. Clothes made of tree bark, dazzlingly beautiful, the belly of a full-term pregnant woman. She looks like a female peacock about to lay eggs. The woods around her seem to be lit up with her aura.

Phoolvanti stands there looking towards the path to town and calling out, "O brother woodcutter! Please come back! Sell the sandalwood and come back now! I don't have much time left!"

"*Āhā*! Now I understand!" The woodcutter's wife assumes the woodcutter has found another woman and built a house for her in the woods.

Seeing her approach, Phoolvanti goes inside the hut and closes the door.

"Open, sister! Open the door! The woodcutter is here!"

The door opens. Phoolvanti sees the fearsome, hag-like appearance of the woodcutter's wife, faints with fear, and drops to the ground. The spasms of impending childbirth start shaking her.

"You brother-less co-wife of mine! If you give birth to a girl, I will drown her in milk; but, if it is a boy, I will raise him! Let me get at you!"

A woodpecker speaks to her from a tree, "Woodcutter's wife, hurry back to town and bring a midwife quickly!"

So, the woodcutter's wife leaves for town. Now, it so happens that the town's queen is also in full term and about to give birth. The big drums roll, astrologers are trying to predict what is to happen, *bhoovās*[3] are trying to read grains. But, the baby is not coming out. The woodcutter's wife runs into Gāṅgali Ghāṅchaṇ[4] at the royal palace's gate.

About four foot tall, ebony dark complexion, catlike gray eyes, clumpy short hair not even reaching her neck, real short legs, feet one-fourth the normal size, overall shape of a cotton ball! Wears her *sāṛi* on her shoulder not on head, knows magic spells, is able to bring the stars and moons down from the skies – that about sums up Gāṅgali Ghāṅchaṇ for you!

"Gāṅgali Māshi![5] O Gāṅgali Māshi! I have something to tell you." Māshi hears the woodcutter's wife out. The two immediately leave for the woods.

When they reach the hut . . . birds, birds, birds . . . birds are everywhere. Parrots, mynas and pigeons; peacocks, parakeets and cuckoos are gathered as if to sing songs of happy occasions. The entire herds of deer have stopped grazing and are standing around the hut.

It is exactly midnight. *Zaḷaḷaḷa*! : a bright glow radiates from

---

[3] *Bhoovā*: Worshippers of Mother Goddess; exorcists and fortune-tellers.

[4] *Gāṅgali Ghāṅchaṇ*: The evil sorceress character that shows up in many stories.

[5] *Māshi*: Aunt, mother's sister. Gāṅgali is generally addressed thus.

the hut. Birds and animals have assembled to get a glimpse of something.

The two evil women enter the hut to witness a handsome-as-a-god infant boy sucking his mother's breast. The aura of a royal birth emanates from his forehead.

A . . . choo! The boy sneezes, and genuine pearls rain from his nose. He yawns, and diamonds drop from his mouth.

"*A . . . hā . . . hā . . . hā*, Gāṅgali Māshi! Let us take the boy!"

But, neither of them has the heart to snatch the boy from his mother's bosom! As luck would have it, fourteen thieves are passing by, and come to rattle the chain on the door.

"Who is it?"

"It's us, Māshi!"

"Come in, nephews, come in!"

The thieves come into the hut and see the unconscious mother and the son sleeping next to her. What glorious dreams make the infant's eyes smile and give off bright rays that play in the night!

"Nephews! Grab that child!"

"Ugh, Māshi! How can we steal a child from its mother's bosom? If we do, would the Mother Earth bear the weight of our sins?" The thieves have no courage to commit such a heinous crime. They jostle one another to put some distance between them and the boy.

Gāṅgali sees that and barks. "Don't you move, you idiots! May the evil spirits devour you! Pick him up NOW or I'll turn you into crows!"

The poor thieves are left with no choice anymore, because Gāṅgali Māshi is a powerful witch. They close their eyes and take the boy from his mother's side. Then, the fourteen thieves, Gāṅgali Ghāṅchaṇ and the woodcutter's wife run from the hut.

The source of light is gone from the hut and the jungle is dark again. The birds and the animals scream. The trees shed their leaves.

* * *

The new mother Phoolvanti regains consciousness. Her stomach is burning up. She looks at her side, and . . . O my God! Where is my son?

At the loss of her child, the mother loses all sanity and starts running. She stops to look in the trees and runs again. The jungle echoes with her cries. She is moving so fast that animals and birds think it is the living flames of a wild fire that are going around. She laments her loss –

In which birth, dear mother mine
Did I commit such horrible sins?
Did I snatch their little calves away from suckling,
And the mothers' sighs return now to haunt me?
From their mothers' breasts did I pull
Innocent little infants and starve them?
I must have plucked fruits not quiteripe,
And tortured little trees into tears, O Mā!
Or, in the form of a black she-cobra,
Did I eat up itsy bitsy baby chicks?
Today those sins are asking for payback,
My own little jewel is stolen from me!

Phoolvanti runs with tears gushing from her eyes . . . and runs, and runs. She searches mountains, valleys, ravines and finally stops at the ocean's shore. Skies above, water below and wind all around . . . there is nothing else in sight. She runs and jumps into the water. The waves take her under in no time.

At that same moment, worlds away from there, as Phoolsaudāgar's twelve ships move under full sail on that faraway ocean, the conch necklace slips from his neck. The one-hundred-eight tiny conch shells sink into the ocean depths!

* * *

It is the final *pahor* of the night and even the guard at the palace gate is fast asleep. After sending the fourteen thieves away, Gāṅgali and the woodcutter's wife slip into the palace. During the night, the queen has delivered a stillborn child and in the process has died herself. Nobody else is aware of this.

An overjoyed Gāṅgali Ghāṅchaṇ cackles, "Woodcutter's wife, O woodcutter's wife! Quick, get ready! You are going to become the queen, and this boy is the newborn prince! What a stroke of luck for us!"

The two tie up the bodies of the dead queen and her stillborn prince and throw them into the river. The woodcutter's wife gets into the queen's clothing and lies in bed, with the "prince" sleeping next to her.

Gāṅgali tells the king, "Great news, Sire! Wonderful news! The queen has delivered a prince!"

And what a prince he is! So handsome! The royal aura already in evidence! The whole kingdom soon reverberates with drumrolls.

"But why has the queen's face changed so much? She looks very different!"

Gāṅgali says, "The delivery did that! The queen's beauty transferred over to the infant prince's body!"

"True! True!"

Everybody buys the story. The woodcutter woman has faked her way into becoming the queen. The prince is named Rājtej – the royal glow! Rājtej grows up. Genuine pearls drop from his nose when he sneezes. He goes to school, learns well and becomes a smart well-rounded person. He starts learning the ways of the royal court.

* * *

From the moment the conch necklace slipped from his neck and dropped into the sea, his wife has faded from Phoolsaudāgar's memory. Legs crossed, he sits on the upper deck of his ship and conducts his business with merchants from different countries. Thoughts of home no longer occupy him.

The conch necklace keeps sinking. Phoolvanti's tears had drenched its one-hundred-eight shells many years ago. Now the ocean's salty water adds to its weight. The necklace sinks all the way to the bottom of the ocean.

At the bottom lies a beautiful slab of sapphire. A female swan sits on the slab and broods her clutch of four eggs. When she sees the conches drop, she goes to peck at them and notices the whole necklace. She picks it up and arranges it around her four eggs.

After a full twelve years, the eggs hatch and four swanlings emerge. Rising to the surface and sticking her long neck out, the female makes the joyful cry, "Swan King! O my Swan King!"

The male swan comes down from the sky and lovingly greets his queen by joining beaks. The two descend to the bottom. There, while kissing his new swanlings, the swan notices the conch necklace.

"Oh no, my queen! This is Phoolsaudāgar's necklace! He must have lost it, and therefore must have forgotten his wife as well!"

The Swan-couple take the necklace and fly ashore with their young swanlings. They build a nest on a banyan tree on the bank of a river on the edge of Prince Rājtej's city.

One day, the male swan goes out to the sea. The swan mother is out to fetch food for the swanlings. In her absence, the young ones quarrel, the nest's grass strands are disturbed and the conch necklace slips out and falls to the ground.

Armed with his bow and arrows, Prince Rājtej is returning from a hunt. He spots the necklace lying under the banyan tree. Wow! That is a conch necklace! He puts it around his neck and returns home. *But, why did my chest turn ice cold as soon as I put it on?* thinks the prince.

* * *

With the bundle of sandalwood sticks on his head, the woodcutter roams from town to town but does not find a *saudāgar* that understands its value. Twelve years go by in scouring the country, and then he sees twelve ships unloading their cargo at a port, and the fleet's golden-clothed *saudāgar*.

The *saudāgar* asks him, "What are you selling, brother?"

"These are pieces of sandalwood from a branch that a goddess cut for me herself. If you are interested, tell me what it is worth to you."

The *saudāgar* looks closely and sees a *phool* (a flower) drawn on a stick.

Aah! Why am I suddenly reminded of my Phoolvanti?

He presses the sandal stick to his chest and . . . his heart starts beating wildly.

"What can I pay you for it, brother? Diamonds? Rubies? Pearls? Name your price."

"No, *Sheṭh*![6] What do I know about its worth? My revered Mother said to take whatever is offered."

"Who is this mother you speak of?"

"*Jogaṇ* with long braided hair; constantly chants the name 'Phoolsaudāgar'. Her weeping in the jungle makes the birds and animals cry. She is in her final days of pregnancy."

The *saudāgar* breaks into a sweat. His head is swimming. He asks, "Brother woodcutter, will you take me to her?"

"Yes, let's go!"

The twelve ships set sail. The woodcutter points the way.

The ships' bells ring *ṭanaṇaṅ*! *Ṭanaṇaṅ*! at the capital city's riverbank. The ships lay anchors there. At the head of the lead ship sits the golden-clothed *saudāgar*.

"Is anyone there?" The prince hears the bells and calls for attendants.

"Not one but twenty-one, Sire!"

---

[6] *Sheṭh*: Merchant; rich man.

"What were those bells? Who is the two-headed person with the nerve to ring bells in our city? Arrest him and bring him before me!"

The town's sheriff takes a squad and departs to carry out the order. He padlocks the twelve ships, ties Phoolsaudāgar's wrists with a rope, puts leg irons on his ankles and produces him at the court.

"*Aah*! The conch necklace on the prince's neck! The necklace my Phoolvanti gave me!" Love drips from the *saudāgar*'s eyes. Something tells him he is looking at his own son.

"Brother, what is the prince's name?"

"Rājtej."

"That's it! That is my son! My own flesh and blood! The heir to my twelve ships!"

"Just listen to his nerve!" The sheriff rams him with the butt of his musket. "He comes here and claims to be our prince's father! Put the scoundrel in the stockade!"

The *saudāgar* is jostled all the way to a jail cell.

But, why are there tears in the prince's eyes? Why is his heart hesitant in holding the court anymore?

"Sheriff! Dismiss the court for today!"

* * *

What is happening with Phoolvanti after she plunged herself into the ocean?

She sleeps for twelve whole years in *Pātāl* – the nether world at the bottom of the ocean. The daughters of Nāg Padamaṇi[7] surround her and fan her, apply fragrant sandalwood paste to her body and just sit with her sprinkling the life-giving *ami* water on her. Once a year, the virtuous Phoolvanti has been coming out of her slumber, calling out "Saudāgar! Saudāgar! Rājtej! Rājtej!" and slipping right back into slumber.

---

[7] *Nāg Padamaṇi*: *Nāg-kanyā* – the beautiful daughter of a *nāg*, a mythical serpent.

[Now that she is awake,] Nāg Padamaṇi caresses her and wipes her tears, "Daughter! You will get your husband back, and also your son!"

"When?"

"You must bathe yourself, eat and drink first. Then I will tell you."

They bathe her, feed her, dress her in a *sāṛi* made from Red coral and adorn her with a necklace of *pārasmaṇi*.[8] Then Nāg Padamaṇi takes her to the ocean's shore.

"Daughter, feel the wind from all four directions. Tell me where you feel the cool breeze coming from, and where hot winds blow from."

Phoolvanti removes the *sāṛi*'s end from her bosom and faces eastwards, then westwards and then southwards. But, when she orients her bare bosom northwards, her breasts seem to want to burst, milk bursts forth from them. It is like a stream of nectar has sprung.

"That settles it. You will find your son in the northern lands. Go there, daughter!"

"How do I go there, Mother?"

Padamaṇi calls out, "Pavan Devatā! Lord of the winds!". *Hoo*! *Hoo*! *Hoo*! They hear the gusts of wind blow.

"Take this daughter to her son, Lord!"

Phoolvanti takes to the waves with a blast of wind. Her *sāṛi* billows like a sail, and she goes like a fast sailboat. Wonder of wonders! A human being that walks on water!

By dark that evening, she has traversed six months of sailing distance. At midnight she reaches a place and her breasts overflow again. Fountains of milk come out of them. She sits under a tree on

---

[8] *Pārasmaṇi:* The mythical gem that can turn iron into gold by touch; philosophers' stone.

the bank of a lake. She is in Rājtej's city.

At dawn every day, the woodcutter's-wife-turned-queen goes to that lake for a bath. Today, she sees and recognizes Phoolvanti.

She orders her attendants, "Girls! Run over there, and kill that witch!"

The girls beat up Phoolvanti, dump her in a deep hole in the ground and cover it with a huge boulder.

Prince Rājtej goes to that same lake that day with some good friends.

"My, O my, did we bathe and swim today! My body has never felt this cool before. Why don't I sit down and rest on this boulder for a while!"

The prince's eyes turn groggy the moment he sits on the boulder. His eyelids get heavy. The prince slips into a deep sleep like never before.

But, who is crying under this boulder while the prince sleeps?

Meeting my son after a long twelve years,
My heart swells and my milk just gushes!
Let me sing you to sleep one last time, my son!
Your mother's soul has no more time to linger!

The minister's son, the *vajeer*'s son and the sheriff's son listen to it with amazement.

"Something curious is happening. Yesterday, that *saudāgar* comes and claims 'I am the prince's father!' Today, this rock laments 'I am his mother!' Let us wake the prince up."

The prince wakes up with a start, "*Mā*! *Mā*! Mother!"

"Who are you calling, my prince?"

"I can hear my mother's voice from under this boulder. Brothers, please move this boulder for me!"

But the boulder weighs a ton! The friends are not able to budge it.

Rājtej just touches it with his little finger and the boulder moves like a flower petal. They find the mother sleeping in the pit under it. Milk spurts from the mother's breast.

"Mother! My mother!" The prince clings to his mother. He carries her back to the court on his shoulder. Then he runs to his woodcutter-turned-queen mother.

"Mother, tell me the truth. Who is my real mother?"

"What are you saying, son? Surely a witch's evil eye has fallen on you!"

The prince loses all his appetite. He neither eats a morsel nor drinks a drop of water. Sleeping or awake, his mind is perpetually restless.

"Badhsāgaro! Minister's son! How do I find the truth? Who among those two is my real mother?"

"There is a way to tell. Make them both stand in the court. The one whose breast spurts milk into your mouth is your real mother; the other is a conniving fraud!"

[The test is announced for the following day.]

"Gāṅgali Māshi! O Gāṅgali Māshi! Hurry up and feed me spices, give me potions, twelve kinds of herbs. I must have milk in my breasts quickly. If I don't, they will put us both through the mill and get oil out of us."

So, the fraudulent queen mother eats twelve kinds of herbs and thirteen kinds of spices. She eats *dhoḷi* (white) *musaḷi* and *kāḷi* (black) *musaḷi*; she drinks vats of saffron-spiked milk. She stays up all night waiting to see if all this helps her produce the requisite spray of milk! But, not a drop of milk comes out of her breasts.

The next morning, the court is packed with people. The birds are sitting quiet with their wings folded. Leaves don't move on trees. The wind is at a standstill. Prince Rājtej is seated on the throne. His soul is thrashing like a tortured fish out of water for want of a confirmed mother.

The woodcutter queen arrives. Her appearance smacks of an overdressed puppy in excessive jewelry. But, after all, she is only a woodcutter's wife, not a queen. The hearts of the treacherous are always weak. Her whole body is trembling with fear.

And Phoolvanti! Her head is uncovered, and she wears no jewelry, not even a simple earring. And yet, her body emits an aura. Her eyes are steady and unblinking. She doesn't see anyone else. Her eyes are riveted on her son. His very sight produces incessant tears of affection in both her eyes.

The *vajeer*'s son comes forward and says, "Queen Mother, please listen. Stranger mother, you too please listen. Today, Prince Rājtej faces this dilemma of having two mothers. But, in this world of nine continents, if there is only one sun and one moon, why should there be two mothers? So, with the Almighty watching, the animals and the birds waiting, in presence of this God-sanctioned assembly, provide us the proof. Whichever of you is the mother that gave birth to the prince, milk from her breast will squirt straight into the prince's mouth."

The court is in shocked disbelief. The wind stops blowing. The silence is so total that a dropped needle would ring loudly enough to reverberate in the chamber!

"Queen Mother! Please come forward. You get the first chance to prove your motherhood."

The woodcutter queen stands waiting for a long time, but where is the milk going to come from?

"Queen Mother! That is quite enough time."

The woodcutter's wife turns ash black with embarrassment.

Then, Phoolvanti steps in. Her frail body seems not to have a drop of blood in it. There is no joy in her heart. But, as soon as she bares her bosom to her son sitting on the throne. . . .

. . . Milk spurts from her breasts in many strings. The prince's necklace gets wet, his mouth is drenched.

"Hail! Hail the virtuous mother! Let the treacherous bite the dust!" The chant goes up.

But, the woodcutter's wife is a real black she-snake! She uses her last drop of venom, "You idiots! Why doesn't someone ask that holier-than-thou pretender one question: who is the father of her son? When did the slut play host to the king?"

Those words spread a sad hush in the court. All heads hand down in shame as if their faces had lamp black spread on them.

Phoolvanti reels as if a huge boulder has dropped on her. She turns to stone, unable to move. But what was she going to say? How was she going to explain the truth? Her husband has instructed her not to reveal Rājtej's conception circumstances to anyone! Phoolvanti's mind is unable to cope with the happenings; she faints and drops to the ground.

From across the seven seas, Phoolsaudāgar's benefactor, the swan king, spreads his wings and, in a flash, their flapping is heard in the city's skies. The witness to Phoolvanti's immaculate character has arrived to defend her honor. Landing on the edge of the royal court's roof, the swan king recites a story in his song:

This is the story of Phoolsaudāgar's wife,
Phoolvanti is the woman's name, I say!
Her darling leaves her for distant lands,
And, she remains a pillar of virtue, I say!
He takes a conch necklace, as her gift,
He overhears a swan pair's talk, I say!
"Tonight is an auspicious full moon night, and
If he could be home to spend the night, I say!
She could conceive a Rājtej – the royal glow,
A boy whose sneeze would scatter pearls, I say!"
The male swan carries the husband on his back,
And flies straight to his virtuous wife's door, I say!
Their minds meet and melt that night,
The seeds of a king are sowed, I say!

He leaves in the night's fourth quadrant,
Forgetting his wife's instructions, I say!
Leaves without showing his face to his mother,
Leaves a big blot on the wife's character, I say!
The evil sister-in-law throws her out of their home, and
In jogaṇ's *disguise, exiled she lives in the woods, I say!*
In the ninth month, after the birth of a prince,
The mother lies unconscious by herself, I say!
Her infant son is stolen, the thief sneaks into the palace,
These are all the deeds of the woodcutter's evil wife, I say!
The real queen she consigns to the river's deep water,
The woodcutter's wife dresses up as the queen, I say!
Back in the jungle, the mother wakes up,
And finds her newborn son missing, I say!
She jumps into the ocean to end her life,
Is saved and kept in the Nāg palace, I say!
She travels afar, reaches her son's kingdom,
To be buried alive by the evil fake queen, I say!
Phoolsaudāgar, the father, loses that necklace,
It sinks straight to the bottom of the sea, I say!
The swan recognizes that sign from Phoolvanti,
Keeps it in his nest on the tree branch, I say!
The prince loses his heart to the necklace,
Gets a happy feeling wearing it, I say!
Phoolsaudāgar comes searching for Phoolvanti,
Sees the necklace around the prince's neck, I say!
His heart overflows at the sight of his son,
Nobody can understand the mystery, I say!
That father languishes in your jail,
Go, ask him to confirm this, I say!
But, I, the swan bird, am full witness to
The mother's virtue and innocence, I say!
The swan king finishes his story and flies away.

"God's word! God's word! God's word!" The town echoes with those cries. Prince Rājtej runs to the prison and falls at his father's feet. *Nobats* (the kettledrums) play on the raised platforms outside every house, palace and temple.

* * *

Even after finding his son, the *saudāgar* is still unhappy. *Where, O where, is my mistreated Phoolvanti? How am I going to spend the rest of my life without her?*

Nobody has informed the prince's father that Phoolvanti is right there in the palace. The unconscious Phoolvanti lies in bed in the Ocean Palace where the attendants fan her night and day with perfumed fans.

Phoolvanti finally regains consciousness. Rājtej goes and finds comfort in his mother's embrace. The son tells his mother about the father's presence. But nobody has still told the father about the now conscious mother.

The father is served thirty-two entrees and thirty-three vegetables every day. Rice as soft and white as a jasmine flower is served. "*Aaaah*, haven't had cooking this good in twelve whole years! O God of foods! who is the cook today? Why does my stomach feel so cool today? Why are these echoes of the past haunting me now?"

Usually, the *saudāgar* keeps his head down while eating. Today he looks up. His eyes meet those of the server's. The husband sees through the ravages of the past twelve years and recognizes the face of his wife. He grabs her hands and asks, "You?"

The good wife is too choked up to say a word. With tears of joy flooding her eyes, she touches her husband's feet. After twelve whole years, she washes his feet with her tears and wipes them with her braided long hair.

"Swāmi, my lord!" she finally says, "This happiness is not complete without your mother and sister! Please go and bring them here. Not doing so would be sinful!"

Yes! Yes! Phoolsaudāgar misses his mother too. The twelve

sets of sails go up. "Row, oarsmen, row! My mother must be pining away for me!"

One, two, three days and the twelve ships enter the port. At home, Phoolsaudāgar's mother hears the sound of ships' bells and she recognizes their tone.

"My boy is here! My flesh and blood is here! The savior of my seven generations is here!" Her joy spilling out of her, stumbling and tripping all over the wharf, the old mother runs to see her son. [She's changed so much.] Phoolsaudāgar can barely recognize her.

"Oh no, mother! You look terrible! What happened to you?"

Ḍaḷak! *Ḍaḷak*! *Ḍaḷak*! The mother's eyes flow profusely.

"My son, I am ashamed to even show you my face! We left the gem of a daughter-in-law out in the jungle . . . ." Her voice breaks. She chokes up.

"Don't be sad, mother! God has protected her."

Phoolsaudāgar sets up a boarding plank and brings his mother aboard the ship. All twelve ships turn around and set sail for the capital city.

That is when the evil hunch-backed sister shows up on the wharf. "Wait! Take me with you!" she screams, knocks her head on the wharf and jumps into the sea. A giant fish comes and swallows her up.

Back in Rājtej's city, the celebrations just go on and on and on.

All ate, drank and lived happily after that!

Raṅg Chhe, Bāroṭ!

(*Bravo, Storyteller!*)

Foreword To *Raṅg Chhe, Bāroṭ!* (A Treatise)

SOME people explain the term *bāroṭ* as derived from the Gujarati *bār haṭh* meaning "twelve unbending resolves"; in other words, a member of the Chāraṇ-bāroṭ community who conducts his life in strict observance of such resolves is a *bāroṭ*. Alternately, we find the term *dvārabhaṭṭa* in the Jain *prabandhas* – literary works of historical importance – to describe the warrior (*bhaṭṭa*) guarding the royal gate (*dvāra*). In conventional use, the term *bāroṭ* has become synonymous with Chāraṇ-bāroṭ, because the above *dvārabhaṭṭa* jibes with the connotation of *gaḍhavi* [*chāraṇ*] being the watcher-protector of a fort (*gaḍh*).

The Book's Title

The use of the word *bāroṭ* in the title of this book is a reference to the storyteller *bāroṭ*. What prompted that was the fact that I heard some of the stories in this collection from Jeṭhā Bāroṭ, who lived in the town Aṇiyāḷi in the feudal Kāṭhiawāḍi state of Jasadaṇ and was the genealogy recorder for a Kāṭhi royal family. Some of the stories he told me in our two or three meetings in the 1924-27 time-frame became parts of my book *Dādāji-ni Wāto* (1927). Many others remained buried in my notebook since then. All these years later, I went through the fragile pages of my notebook and attempted to reconstruct what I had tried to capture from his spoken words. I have put together the stories I could recreate completely, and they are included in this collection. The rest I have lost forever because my notes on those stories were brief and incomplete, making it impossible for me to erect their entire structure from memory.

Anyway, five out of the twelve stories in this book were obtained from Jeṭhā Bāroṭ. Also, when a *bāroṭ* is telling a story, the audience responds to him with calls like "Raṅg!", "Raṅg, Bāroṭ!", "Raṅg chhe Bāroṭ-ji!" roughly meaning "Bravo!" "Well said, Bāroṭ!". I chose *Raṅg Chhe, Bāroṭ!* as the book's title for both those reasons.

Sources of These Stories

The five stories I got from Jeṭhā Bāroṭ are "Vikram ane Khāparo", "Vikram ane Prabhāt Chavaḍo", "Chār Sār", "Parakāyāpravesh" and "Kāthikooḷ". (Earlier, *Dādāji-ni Wāto* included four of his stories: "Manasāgaro", "Siṁhāsan", "Vikram ane Vidhātā" and "Veeroji".)

The sources of the other seven stories in this collection are more diverse.

"Bāpu Bhālāḷo"[1]: Some young friends living in the city of Vadhavāṇ told me of a young brahmin farmer who they said "narrates this story in a long lyrical form". I went there in 1928 and spent almost five hours on a Vaisakh night listening to his narration while jotting it in my notebook. Those notes are still intact, although the narrator's name is missing.

"Dariyāpeer-ni Deekari": Way back in 1921-22, Darabār Shri Vajasoor Vālā, the ruler of Haḍāḷā, whom I consider my initiator and mentor in the field of folk literature, told me this story in his lucid, balanced and unassuming style at his mansion. I had written that up and he had read and corrected it. He sent all the verses and couplets later. He himself had heard the story from a storyteller as passed down through the oral tradition. (Most probably, it was a Chāraṇ gentleman named Sāmatbhāi Neelā in the court of the late Kalāpi, the king of the state of Lāṭhi, in the dawning years of the twentieth century.)

"Janamanā Jogi"[2]: This hymnal story was sung by a troupe of Nāthabāwā mendicants – Kānipānāth, Jhaveranāth and others – from the village of Pājawāḷi located near Choṭilā. Dr Bakke, a Western scholar, and his wife were touring India with a truck and

---

[1] Not included in this translated compilation.

[2] Also not included in this translated compilation.

a voice-recording machine researching folk songs, and had set up camp in Rāṇapur (in the late 1930s). The troupe sang for the recording session and I took notes. My notes were incomplete, but in the summer of 1941, another itinerant Nāthabāwā troupe camped on the outskirts of (my) Botād town; they sang it for us at a friend's farm and I completed my notes then.

"Nāg ne Bāmaṇ" and "Bheriyo ne Bhoojiyo"[3]: I heard both these stories from Balavantarāy Mahārāj, a story lover and worldly-wise friend, of my town Boṭād. He recollected these two from among many stories that he had heard from a Khojā (Ismaili Muslim) gentleman who was a storehouse of such lore.

"Chandaṇ-Meṇaṅgari": An itinerant troupe of 'Luhāriyā' – also known as 'Gāḍaliyā' – community has been spending the monsoon months in a plot of land, next door to me. Nathu Bhagat, the troupe's expert storyteller, and other members of his troupe recited this story to me. These Luhāriyās have a unique storytelling style where one man tells the prose parts of the story, but the entire troupe sings the verse segments.

"Khāniyo": My writer friend from Rajkot, poet Shri Tribhuvan Vyas, told me this story. He himself remembers hearing it years ago from a relative in the small village where he grew up.

The Purity of Form Preserved by Illiterate Ears and Tongues

One thing stands out when we analyze the sources of each of these stories: these are folk tales that are preserved intact in their oral detail even when passed from ear to ear among largely illiterate people who would not possibly have read them in the written form.

But, we cannot make the claim that these are original creations of folk minds. These stories come from a land where the ancient Vedic recitals have inspired epic poems, plays and story collections that were published in book form and widely

[3] Both are omitted from this translated compilation.

circulated; where the book-based stories from the *Panchatantra* and the *Jātakakathā* have roamed from one end to the other; where the stories written by extraordinary creators like Danḍee, Bāṇabhaṭṭ and Subandhu have circulated; where the triple tributaries from the *Brihatkathā* – the *Kathāsaritsāgar*, the *Brihatkathāmanjaree* and the *Brihatkathāshlokasāgar* – have flown; where the original Sanskrit works – the *Vetālapanchviṁshati*, the *Vikramacharit* and the *Shukasaptati* – and their translations by Shamalabhatt and others have continued to spread for centuries; and, where *charit*s and *prabandh*s (biographies and genealogical tomes) written by brahmins and Jains have reached the public as books. In such a land, it would be extremely difficult to separate pure and independent folk creations from the existing orally communicated stories. One way or another, the ocean of the published stories must have dripped into the stream of orally spread stories.

Drops from the Ocean

The story drops from that vast ocean have reached across provinces and spread to every nook and corner of the Indian subcontinent, to places where no published literature had ever reached. Those stories made inroads even to the remotest of the *ādivāsi*[4] habitats and got integrated into their scriptless dialects assuming native colloquial forms and shapes. Buried deep in nooks and crannies of every province, these amazing stories have become the subject of substantial research efforts over the last century. In fact, the last forty years have witnessed keen competition between Indian and Western scholars in collecting and compiling these stories that go by word of mouth. A very prominent name among the Western researchers collecting these Indian stories is [Maurice] Bloomfield.[5]

---

[4] *Ādivāsi*: an umbrella term for a heterogeneous set of ethnic and tribal groups claimed to be the aboriginal population of India.

[5] Maurice Bloomfield (1855–1928): an American Philologist and Sanskrit Scholar. His student W. N. Brown wrote his PhD dissertation "Modern Indian Folklore and Its Relation to Literature" under Bloomfield's →

He asserts:

> *"Quite certainly these books echo largely the old stories of the various Hindu classical literatures. Whether they contain material of independent sort, that is to say, old original stories which propagated themselves orally without ever having been written down in any Hindu language, is very doubtful."*[6]

The Use of Motifs

Either way, the principal elements that exist in the "[Hindu] classical literature" – the so-called "motifs" – show up in all their categories in these orally propagated folk tales being collected today. These motifs – the clever tricks or stratagems used to give the story momentum and keep it enchanting – (according to Dr Bloomfield) "*are distributed or rearranged anew in every time and clime of India. Everywhere each narrator and recorder takes up, as it were, the whole chain of these motifs, which we may liken to a chain of beads. He tears it apart, so that the beads scatter in every direction, and then he strings them up in a new arrangement. Thus any motif may turn up at any time, in any place, and practically in any connection in Hindu fiction and its tributaries.*"

Examples of Motifs

Let us try to understand what these motifs are in greater detail. They are the characteristics of a folk tale that open the way for the storyline to move forward when there seems no other way to do so.

One example: future being revealed through bird-talk. In the story "Manasāgaro" (in my collection *Dādāji-ni Wāto*), the minister Manasāgaro uses all his skills to get his king married to princess Padmāvanti, and then sets out to bring the newlyweds back home. At a stopover, the king and his queen are asleep, but the awake

---

← guidance in 1916.

6 Maurice Bloomfield, 1916, "On Recurring Psychic Motifs in Hindu Fiction, and the Laugh and Cry Motif", *Journal of the American Oriental Society*, 36: 54-89.

Manasāgaro hears a male–female pair of eagles talk about the six deadly perils awaiting the royal couple the next day. Manasāgaro understands the bird-talk and therefore knows what to expect and works out what to do. This is a point in the storyline where no message, letter or human warning can be of use to propel the story forward. And so, these birds are called in. They talk among themselves, some human hears them talk and takes steps to avert the impending doom. Warning by a pair of birds also figures in the story "Chār Sār" in this collection (*Raṅg Chhe, Bāroṭ!*). Be they a male–female pair of swans, sparrows, parrots or eagles, their talk never assumes a role in the principal theme, but provides otherwise unavailable important information key to averting the upcoming calamities.

The "Must-Not-Tell" Motif

The difficulty of keeping secrets, and the disasters that result from revealing them, is another powerful motif used in these tales. The earlier mentioned "Manasāgaro" uses this stratagem to provide momentum to the story and to create suspense. The night-time talk between two birds overheard by a person must not be conveyed to anyone, with the penalty of turning to stone if it is violated. If that restriction does not exist, Manasāgaro can tell his friend, the king, and they could jointly fight the six deadly perils. But the "turn to stone if you tell" restraint gets in the way, Manasāgaro acts alone to avert the perils and cannot tell why he does what he does. The king whose life Manasāgaro is trying to save gets more and more suspicious with each step. In the intense scene of the final peril, Manasāgaro goes into the royal bedroom, watches a female cobra sitting in the ceiling drip venom on the sleeping queen's cheek and tries to lap it up. The queen wakes up screaming in the process, but Manasāgaro is unable to explain his actions. In the end, to establish the purity of his motives, he is forced to reveal the forbidden secrets and turns to stone.

This motif freely appears in stories from our province [Gujarat],

Bengal, Mahākoshal[7] and numerous other Indian localities. The boon to understand the speeches of animals, birds and insects; the boon accompanied by the restriction against revealing to anyone content of the non-human talk so heard; the penalty of death for violating that restriction; the stubborn – frequently feminine – insistence to learn those secrets even at the risk of the revealer's life; and finding the encouragement to overcome such life-threatening feminine stubbornness actually coming from overheard conversations of some birds or beasts – this motif is used in the "Chār Sār"[8] story in this collection, but also appears in numerous folk tales from other parts of India as well. In "Chār Sār", a king receives the boon from a *nāg* (a cobra) which makes the king understand the language of any living being, and see the past, present and future. One day, his older queen's virtuous brother dies, and the spectacle of his soul clinging to the body and kissing it makes the king weep. Later, his new queen's evil brother passes away, but watching his soul emerge and try to beat the body with shoes makes the king laugh.

"Why did you laugh? You must tell me!" his queen insists and would not relent even when told that telling her would mean the king's death. The king decides to tell her and accept death in the holy city of Kāshi, and they set out on that journey. On the way, they pass a pair of goats grazing near a well. The female is pregnant. She demands that the male go down the well and fetch her the vine growing deep inside. The male goat tells her that he is not stupid like this king, and is not about to do anything his mate wants at his life's peril. The king heeds that rebuke, slaps his wife and takes her back home.

This motif of understanding the animal-talk and learning to follow their example seems to be born in the Jātaka tales[9] and is

---

7 Mahākoshal: A region in the state of Madhya Pradesh.

8 The story "Four Maxims" is included in this translated collection.

9 Jātaka tales are a voluminous body of literature native to India about →

widely plied in Indian folk tales in various forms. King Senak (in another example of its use) is sitting at dinner and a drop of honey, a granule of jaggery and a piece of *roṭli* (bread) fall out of his plate. Seeing that, an ant starts shouting "Hurry, everyone! The king's honey jar has broken, his jaggery cart has overturned and a whole cart-load of bread has scattered! Come, let's have a feast!" The king hears this and laughs out loud. His queen tries to draw the reason for his laughing out of him, and telling her means certain death. Unable to say no to her, he is ready to give in and tell her the secret when, again, it is (the utterance of) a male goat in love with a she-goat that brings him back from the brink.

This very motif is also present in tales from the Santhāl region,[10] Kashmir and Siṁhaladweep (present-day Sri Lanka). The tale from Laṅkā features ants' talk being overheard, and uses a taunt from jungle-dwelling monkeys (instead of goats) that makes the king see the light. He then gives his queen a good thrashing and shuts her up for life. Especially noteworthy is the fact that this stratagem is found in a tale from as far away as Italy. In the Italian tale, it is a rooster that saves the king. Thanks to a boon from Jesus, the king listens to a conversation between an ox and a donkey and laughs out. Subject to the same "must-not-tell" restriction, the king refuses to tell the queen [why he laughed]. Eventually, when he is about to tell her, he hears the rooster's arrogant words "unlike some, I do keep my twenty females in my total control".

The "So-and-So Regretted It, So Will You!" Motif

This trick has also been used to enhance the tale's attraction, give it momentum and keep its development going. In a Santhāl story, a cowherd pleases Lord Shiva and obtains a boon that enables him to understand the cows' speech. The cows' talk helps him find some

---

← the previous lives of the Buddha, in both human and animal forms. In whatever form, he exhibits some virtue that the tale thereby inculcates.

[10] Santhāl region: Home of the largest Indian tribal community spread across Assam, West Bengal, Bihar, Jharkhand and Odisha.

buried treasure. He reburies the treasure and goes home. His wife asks why is so quiet, but the cowherd cannot tell her the truth or he would die. So he makes up a story for his demanding wife: "the king went to the woods to relieve his bowels, and crows emerged from the king's feces". The wife fails to keep this to herself, and the king hears about it through a neighbor. The king summons the cowherd, interrogates him, the cowherd is compelled to tell the truth about the treasure and turns to stone. The king goes and brings the buried treasure home. His queen now insists on learning the whole matter. If the king tells her, he, too, would turn to stone.

So, the king says to the queen, "If you keep this up, you will regret it later – like the man that regretted killing his mongoose." The queen wants to know that story. The king tells her: This man had a pet mongoose in his house and an infant son. His wife went to fetch some water while the boy slept in a cradle. In her absence, a snake slithered up a cradle leg. The mongoose killed the snake and then went to get the *noḷavel*[11] herb to revive the snake-bitten boy. The man (or his wife) came home and saw the mongoose's blood-dripping mouth, assumed the animal had caused their son's death and killed the mongoose. When the truth was known, they both regretted the act.

The queen does not relent and repeats her demand to learn the truth. So, the king says she would regret this like the trader who killed his loyal dog. The queen asks what that was about. Again, the king starts on the story. Like that, stories emerge from stories and the tale's grip on the audience keeps getting firmer.

The very same trick is used in a folk tale from Bundelkhand[12] published there in the fortnightly *Madhukar*, and translated into Gujarati as "Dhutārāni Deekaree" (part of the collection *Sonā*

---

[11] *Noḷavel*: The mythical vine that is supposed to restore strength of a mongoose with one whiff.

[12] Bundelkhand: A central Indian region, mostly part of the state of Madhya Pradesh.

Padamaṇee). A rich man is trapped in the house of some conmen. The head conman's daughter, posing as the rich man's bride, sits on the man's chest brandishing a dagger and asks him for his jewels. The man tells her he doesn't have any jewels, and she may take his life and then regret it like the trader did after killing his dog. The woman is intrigued and wants to hear the story. "How can I talk with you sitting on my chest?" he says. So, the woman gets off him. The rich man tells her the story and then continues with stories of the "if you kill me, you will regret it like so-and-so-did" theme; among them is the story of the thirsty king whom a falcon prevented from drinking snake venom thinking it was water; the king kills the falcon in rage, and later regrets his hasty deed. With these stories, the man wins the conwoman's heart.

The "Sign Language" or "Symbols" Motif

This trick appears in our Gujarati folk tales frequently.

We have encountered this clever motif in the story "Manasāgaro" in [my] *Dādāji-ni Wāto* collection. The king lies [thirsty] in the jungle near a temple. A beautiful woman comes out of the temple, shows him some rice dipped in *kanku* and a coconut, raises six fingers, points a dagger at her stomach and leaves without saying a word. Manasāgaro decodes the message hidden in those gestures. Showing the coconut and rice meant in her mind she had already given herself in marriage to the king. Six fingers meant she would wait six months. The dagger on her stomach meant she would kill herself if the king did not arrive in that time. Manasāgaro finds and deciphers more clues inside the temple. She had offered *padma* (lotus) flowers in worship to Lord Shiva, meaning her name was Padmāvati. The lotus flowers were surrounded by *kanak* flowers, meaning her town's name was Kanakāvati. That information eventually leads them to Kanakāvati where they become guests at a florist's house. Every day, the florist woman delivers a flower blouse, a skirt and a short *sāṛi* for Princess Padmāvanti. One day, Manasāgaro offers to make those garments and hides a written message inside.

Padmāvanti acknowledges it by slapping the florist woman with a *kanku*-red hand leaving red fingermarks on her face.

Verrier Elwin[13] has given us a story named "Two Friends" that employs this symbols motif. He has written a paper entitled "Language of Silence" that traces the origin of these love riddles to the ancient *Kathāsaritsāgar*. (Actually, a Westerner named Crooke[14] had done earlier work on this topic and published in his book *Secret Messages and Symbols Used in India*.) In the original *Kathāsaritsāgar* story, a beautiful maiden makes these silent gestures to a prince: picks out an *utpal* (a lotus) from a garland and rolls it into her ear, picks up another lotus and puts it on top of her head; and last, she very pointedly puts her hand on her heart. The prince's friend figures out the meanings of these gestures. Placing an *utpal* in her ear (*karna*) meant she lived in King Karnotpal's city. Rolling the flower into the shape of a *dantapatra*[15] ornament meant she was the daughter of an ivory carver. By placing the second lotus (*padma*) on her head, she was saying her name as Padmāvati. Her hand on her heart meant she had given her heart to the prince. Now that he understands the message, the prince pays a visit to his beloved.

In that original tale (from the Sanskrit *Kathāsaritsāgar*), as in its numerous derivative stories from different provinces, the hero does not understand the gestures himself and has a third person crack the code for him. Thus, centuries after the original penning by Somadev [in the late eleventh century CE], this story has been circulating with minimal changes by word of mouth all over the country. Those symbol-laden gestures have become love's sign language, and, as Mr Elwin writes in his book *Folk Tales of Mahakoshal*,

---

[13] Verrier Elwin (1902-64): a self-trained English anthropologist and ethnologist who lived and worked among the Baigas and Gonds of central India.

[14] William Crooke (1848–1923): An English Orientalist and "the central figure in Anglo-Indian folklore" according to some scholars.

[15] *Dantapatra*: A bangle made of ivory (*danta* meaning elephant's tusk).

a variety of versions of these love riddles has been documented.

The "Indirect Warning" Motif

Similar to the sign-language motif, another very effective trick is to provide a warning to the principal character of a story to bring him back to the straight and narrow. A good example of that shows up in this collection's "Chār Sār" story. Before the hero's inherent nature gets him into trouble, a *fakir* or *sādhu* shows up just in time with some generic advice and, despite lacking any special powers or extraordinary wisdom in it, demands an exorbitant price for it. For example, a whole thousand rupees for each *sār* – each piece of advice! Impressed by that high price, the hero would buy the advice. And, only after getting paid, the *fakir* would provide these four gems:

Control your rage – rule one,
That's worth a thousand to you;
Stay awake – rule two,
Cost another thousand to you.
Welcome your enemy – rule three,
One more thousand from you.
Thrash your wife when she's guilty – rule four,
Cost another thousand to you.

Those four rules – maxims – are the pillars that support the whole story. Each of those maxims provides guidance for the immediate behavior of the story's lead character, and he survives the four calamities life throws at him.

A long story my father used to tell with much pleasure contained eight maxims that went something like:

Plenty provides a father;
Lack has a mother;
Wife is when with you;

***

[The story went:] A rich man's son buys eight maxims from a *sādhu* for a hundred thousand rupees, and right away the story picks up momentum. One by one the maxim's worth comes to light. The father throws the son out as soon as he hears about this foolish waste of money, thus proving the first maxim that says when you have nothing, you have no father. The mother struggles to keep the penniless son at home, making the second maxim come true that mother stands with you in times of need. The now poor son goes to his married sister's house and gets a cold shoulder. After his departure, his wife goes to her father's house and starts living it up – the third maxim saying one's wife is loyal only as long as she is with him. That is how the storyline shapes up and its flow continues.

The Riddles and Inscrutable Questions Motif

The reader will notice a variation of this same motif in the "Khāniyo" story in this collection. The entire story is woven around two things. One, identifying the genuine from the fake between two identical statuettes; two, providing answers to four questions:

Who is noble of birth, but of despicable conduct?
Who is low of birth, but noble of deed?
Who are the dogs of the royal court?
Who is the ass in the assembly?

The lead character in the story answers those questions by premeditated orchestration of circumstances to his chosen results. He slaughters a lamb and makes it appear like he has killed the son of the Shah of Persia. With that one climactic event, he demonstrates four things with visible proofs. One, the cruel and thoughtless behavior of his high-born wife. Two, the noble and intelligent behavior of a lowly courtesan whom he had offended badly. Three, how the very courtiers whom he had wined, dined and showered with gifts for months had now ungratefully turned and spat on him. Four, the actions of the Shah of Persia himself, who had known him closely for six months but foolishly ordered him beheaded without making the slightest verification of his guilt.

With all that clear evidence in support, Khāniyo – that lead character – answers the four questions. The person "noble of birth, but of despicable conduct" was his own wife. The "low of birth, but noble of deed" person was the courtesan with impeccable and thoughtful behavior. The "dogs of the royal court" were the courtiers who had wagged their tails to him while he fed them, and then bad-mouthed him no end without any cause when the feeding stopped. And, "the ass in the assembly" was the Shah of Persia who acted without thought and reason expected of him.

This same motif seems to ply in the oral tales of other provinces as well. In the previously mentioned Bundelkhandi tale "Dhutārāni Deekaree",[16] a *fakir* sells four "rules" to the rich man in the lead role:

Do not plant a berry tree in your courtyard.
Do not make friends with a policeman.
Pick up what you find in the street.
Pat your cot clean before sleeping on it.

These seemingly simple words bear incredible and miraculous fruits for the main character in this cleverly constructed tale.

The "No Father" Taunt Motif

I wonder if this trick is present in any of the *Kathāsaritsāgar* tales.

King Vikram marries this woman and then forgets all about her existence. Her young son, Vikramcharit, is playing in the street and inadvertently hits an old woman with his ball. For the first time in his life, he hears the taunt, "You fatherless imp!" He goes to his mother and gets the whole story, learns the identity of his father, goes to Ujeṇi, performs a variety of stunts to confound the father who had abandoned his mother and finally reveals himself as Vikram's son. I had heard Jeṭhā Bāroṭ tell this story, and heard it from other people as well.

---

[16] Dhutārāni Deekaree: Literally, the swindler's daughter.

Is there anything in the *Thirty-two Statuettes*[17] series that could have given rise to this story? In oral traditions, this "taunt" is frequently the spark that touches off the entire story. "Bāpu Bhālaḷo"[18] is a pure folk story [not based on any other work] that starts from this motif. Princes Bāpu and Buḍho are growing up at their maternal uncle's house when they get into some mischief. One shoots a lead ball from his sling to poke a hole through the metal urn carried by women fetching water, and the other shoots a wax ball to plug that hole. An old woman gets caught in this game, the boys make a mistake, and her clay urn is smashed into pieces. The woman cries out "You fatherless brats! Why don't you stop breaking poor women's water urns and go find your father's killers instead!" The taunt hits home, and the two brothers set out on a life of big adventures.

The "Do Not Go There" Motif

"Don't go in such-and-such direction", "don't spend a night at so-and-so place", "do not ever open the door to that room" are the warnings everywhere. And, it is not the following those subtle instructions but disobeying them that makes the story move forward, become colorful, gain the mystery element. This motif has found much use in our folk tales. The story "Chhaḍilakhaṇo and Manasāgaro" is one in which this trick has worked well.

Prince Chhaḍilakhaṇo and Manasāgaro – son of the king's minister – set out to roam the world. They get to a *vāv* (a stepped well) on their way. Manasāgaro goes down the steps to get a drink of water. While drinking, he reads something written on the wall of the *vāv*: "Nobody should enter this *vāv*; if you do, do not drink the water here; if you drink, do not stay here for the night."

---

17 *Thirty-two Statuettes*: a part of the Veer Vikram legend, originating from the Sanskrit work *Siṁhāsana-Dvātriṁshikā*, translated into English by Franklin Edgerton as *Vikrama's Adventures* or *The thirty-two Tales of the Throne*.

18 Bāpu Bhālaḷo: This story is omitted from this translation.

Manasāgaro thinks Chhaḍilakhaṇo must not read this message, because, given his obstinate nature, he is sure to do exactly what the message says not to. With that thought, Manasāgaro covered the wall-engraved message with mud. Chhaḍilakhaṇo arrives, drinks some and then playfully spits out a mouthful of water onto the wall, washing mud off the message. He reads it and then stubbornly decides to spend the night there.

Gains from Ignoring the Ban

In a different story form, doing what is forbidden would routinely result in a bad outcome. Instead, only through that forbidden act, a sequence of events is put in motion. The two young men climb a tree and spend the night there. Late at night, flames come out of the *vāv*. A fearsome *nāg* – a king cobra – comes out carrying a *maṇi* – a gem – on its head. The *nāg* drops its brightly sparkling *maṇi* under the tree, and, in the *maṇi*-brightened night, goes hunting for food in a two-mile radius. It comes back, picks up the *maṇi* and returns to the *vāv*.

The next day, Manasāgaro goes to a nearby town and buys a *bakaḍiyuṅ* (a shallow, round metal trough) with sharp spikes attached to its convex side. He ties a string to it, and climbs the tree at dark. The *nāg* comes out, leaves the *maṇi* under the tree and goes hunting. When safe, Manasāgaro lowers the string-attached spiked trough on top of the *maṇi*. The *nāg* returns to see the trough where the *mani* should be, attacks it with its hooded head, impales the hood on the metal spikes and dies. The two friends come down from their perch, pick up the bloodied *maṇi* and go into the *vāv* to wash it. But as they go down the steps with the enchanted *maṇi*, the water level keeps dropping and eventually they reach a palace where a *nāg-padamaṇi* (beautiful cobra-maiden) resides. The prince stays there to live with the *nāg-padamaṇi*. They come out of the *vāv* every day to take their walks. One day, a sudden noise causes them to return to the *vāv* in a hurry, and in that rush the *nāg-padamaṇi* leaves an anklet outside. Another prince shows up, finds the anklet and decides he will marry none other than the wearer of that anklet. [The evil sorceress] Gāṅgali Ghāṅchaṇ finds out that the anklet belongs to the *nāg-padamaṇi*. She sits at the top of the *vāv* and starts crying loudly. The *nāg-padamaṇi* hears her crying and comes out. Gāṅgali tells her "I am your *fui* (father's sister), and have come here to mourn your father the *nāg*'s death." The *nāg-padamaṇi* takes the *fui* to the palace inside the *vāv*, and lets her stay with them. Once, Gāṅgali manages to go out of the *vāv* with the *nāg-padamaṇi* and hides the *maṇi* without which the water will not make way back to the palace. Gāṅgali arranges for the *nāg-padamaṇi*'s abduction, etc. More in this chain of adventures and obstacles ensues, and the story ends with all calamities averted, the lovers reunited and the evil destroyed.

The "Stalling for Time" Motif

An abducted heroine does not reject her abductor's demand for marriage outright. Saying she has made a religious vow and needs six months, a year or twelve years to fulfil the conditions of that vow, and when that time is over, she would gladly marry him is the trick she uses to buy time. The story's events transpire and, in the end, the sundered hearts reunite. We are no strangers to this motif. Many a folk tale has benefitted from this stratagem.

Likewise, "How do I do that? Why don't you show me?" is another familiar trick. The lead character – man or woman – is in the clutches of an *aghoree bābā*, a black art practicing mendicant. The *bābā* has a big cauldron of oil boiling. He then tries to make his victim believe that circling the cauldron seven times will give the captive some definite powers. The real aim, of course, is to perform some requisite rites and then to push the victim into the boiling oil to turn him or her into a carcass of gold. This victim is wise to the *bābā*'s intentions but is unable to escape from captivity. He or she cleverly feigns ignorance and asks the *bābā*, "Would you please show me how to make the seven rounds first?" They would go around – the *bābā* in front and the victim behind him – and on the seventh round the victim would push the *bābā* into the cauldron. The victim not only saves own life but also gains a golden carcass . . . and the story moves ahead with a new momentum. This, too, is a very powerful motif.

Other Miscellaneous Motifs

An unequipped brave hero on his way to faraway adventure gets a divine gift – that of an enchanted mare or horse (as Bāpu Bhālaḷo, in the story of the same name, receives the black mare "Keshar"), Lāliyo Dhoko (an enchanted short but stout wooden staff), *ooḍaṇapāvaḍee* – the flying wooden sandals, or the flying tree. Or he may get a flask of elixir that can bring a dead man back to life even from a bone fragment. Or, it could be the grant of some magical chant. The hero, going in harm's way, would leave something that would tell his wife whether he is still alive (for example, a garland of flower which if wilted would indicate he is dead). A certain *rākshash* demon's life is secured in some cave, at some unreachable location, or in the body of a parrot and that secret can be learned only from the demon in a certain way. All these and other clever tricks that make a folk tale livelier are woven into diverse compilations all through India. Most of these tricks can be seen in written form in ancient story collections like the *Kathāsaritsāgar*, the *Thirty-two Statuettes*, the *Panchatantra* and the *Jātaka Tales*. These written publications were first translated into Arabic and Persian. From there, the stories crept into various European languages, assumed Western names and attire, and spread far and wide, with their Eastern themes and character remaining intact. The Western scholars recognize this, and accept the debt owed by Western folklore to Indian folk stories.

Went to Europe from Bengal?

Shri Dineshchandra Sen, an eminent scholar on Bengal's oral folk literature, makes this statement

> . . . the folk tales of Bengal, told by village women and mostly

> composed by them, in the quiet environment of shady *mālati* groves amidst which stood their straw-roofed mud-huts like the coy *mālati* flowers that bloomed in the evening there, did not venture to peep out and show themselves to strangers. What conveyances could carry these – our family treasures – to Europe in the remote past? These stories passed from mouth to mouth and were never written in Bengal itself, till the middle of the sixteenth century. . . .[19]

He answers (his own question about the conveyance to Europe), "This could only be possible by the humbler classes of Indian people coming in contact with European men." For example,

> . . . Sankhal, the king of Kanauj[20] "sent 10,000 men and female *Luris* recruited from different parts of northern India, who could play upon the lute" to the Persian king Behram Gor in CE 120 at his request. These *Luris* travelled to Europe and settled in various parts of it and came to be known as gypsies. Their language bears a close affinity to Hindi and other Aryan dialects of India. . . . It may be that these people brought their folk tales to Europe. Or, who knows, but that the hulls and ships which landed the cotton fabrics known as the Dacca muslin on the European shores also landed our folk stories there!

Similar Western–Eastern Tales

In support of that assertion, Shri Dineshchandra Sen compares stories "even now being narrated in the lower Gangetic valley" and their European versions. For instance, take the story of "Faithful John" from *Grimms' Popular Stories.*

The faithful servant John is bringing the king and his newlywed queen home on a ship when he overhears the talk of three ravens.

"Wow, look at these newlywed king and queen!"

---

[19] Dineshchandra Sen, 1920, *The Folk-Literature of Bengal,* Calcutta: University of Calcutta.

[20] Kanauj: Also Kannauj, a city in Uttar Pradesh; derived from Kānyakubja, the early seventh-century capital of Harshavardhana's empire.

"When they disembark from the ship, a fox-red horse will approach them, and if the king gets on him, the horse will fly away with him."

"Is there no help?"

"Yes, but the only way is for the rider to kill the horse with the dagger stuck in the saddle. The king will be saved but if his savior tells anyone about this, he will turn to stone from his feet to his knees. But, there are still more threats on their lives. The queen will attempt to put on a brocade-like wedding gown, the gown will catch fire and she will burn to the bone."

"Oh no! Is there any escape from that?"

"Yes, there is, if someone throws that garment into burning fire. But if that person reveals this, his body from knees to chest will turn to stone. Then, there is the third threat during the after-wedding dance. The dancing queen will suddenly turn deathly pale and fall down as if dead. If someone lifts her up and sucks the three drops of blood from her right breast, she will be saved. But if this person were to declare this, he will turn into stone from his chest to the crown of his head."

With that, the three ravens fly away. Faithful John follows all those instructions and saves the royal couple from all three threats. But, forced by the king to explain his reproachable behavior, John tells all and turns into a stone head-to-toe. Then, the king sacrifices his newborn son and sprinkles his blood to bring John back to life. With God's grace, the infant son is also restored to life.

The Bengali "Bihaṅgam–Bihaṅgami" Version

Shri Sen pits this European tale against the Bengali folk tale "Roopmālā". In the latter, a minister's son plays the role of faithful John.

The young prince and his newlywed princess have set camp for the night and are sleeping. Being in a desolate land, the minister's son is standing watch when he overhears the prophetic talk of two birds – Bihaṅgam and Bihaṅgami.

Bihaṅgam (the male bird): "The minister's son will find it difficult to save the prince in the end."

Bihaṅgami (the female bird): "Why so?"

Bihaṅgam: "Many dangers await the prince. The prince's father, when he hears of the approach of his son, will send for him an elephant, some horses and attendants. When the prince rides the elephant, he will be thrown to the ground and will die."

Bihaṅgami: "But suppose someone prevents the prince from getting on the elephant?"

Bihaṅgam: "He will, in that case, escape that particular danger, but a second danger awaits him. When the prince is in the act of passing through the lion gate of his father's palace, the gate will fall upon him and crush him to death."

Bihaṅgami: "But suppose someone destroys the lion gate before the prince gets to it?"

Bihaṅgam: "Yes, then he will survive, but a third danger awaits him. When the prince sits at a feast prepared for him, the head of a fish cooked for him will stick in his throat and choke him to death."

Bihaṅgami: "What if someone snatched the head of fish from the prince's hand?"

Bihaṅgam: "Yes, his life will be saved; but a fourth danger awaits him. When the prince and the princess are asleep in their bed, a poisonous cobra will come into the room and bite him."

Bihaṅgami: "But what if someone lying in wait there cuts the snake into pieces?"

> *Bihaṅgam:* "Yes, that can save the prince's life. But, if the man who kills the snake relates the conversation between you and me to the prince, that man will be turned into a stone."
>
> *Bihaṅgami:* "But, will there be a way to restore the stone statue to life?"
>
> *Bihaṅgam:* "Yes, there will be; by the prince washing it with the blood of his firstborn."

This Bengali folk tale ends pretty much like its European counterpart. The prince's [sacrificed] son is returned to life by the benevolence of Goddess Kāli. The similarities between the two stories are potently obvious. When the [first] English translation of Grimms' stories first appeared in 1823, a critical review [by Oxford University Press according to D.C. Sen] noted that "The tale is a singular one, and contains so much of Orientalism that the reader would almost suppose himself in the *Arabian Nights Entertainments.*"

The Future-telling Birds are Everywhere

Shri Sen writes:

> . . . a careful student of Oriental literature will see that this story is not of the nature of Arabian fables (which are) characterized by flights of unrestrained fancy, chiefly aiming at amusing the young. The Indian fables have, on the other hand, a deep ethical and moral lesson underlying all creations of fancy. The idea of *sakhya*, of dedicating oneself to the service of his friend, at all costs and sacrifices, to open the mouth knowing its consequence to be turning into a marble statue, this ideal friendship in a folk story marks it out as pre-eminently Indian.

Not stopping there, Shri Sen makes the claim,

> . . . I am inclined to trace the home of this story to Bengal, the land of Bihaṅgams and Bihaṅgamis, the birds of prophetic sayings in hundreds of our folk tales.

When mulling over such a claim, we must not forget the story "Manasāgaro" from Gujarat-Kaṭhiāwāḍ which is virtually identical to the stories compared above. Read that Soraṭhi-Gujarati story and you will be struck by its native colloquialism.

The illiterate storyteller Jeṭhā Rāvaḷ – who lives in the deep interior of the Saurashtra peninsula and could not possibly have heard even the name of [Bengali] *Roopmālā* – told me the story *Manasāgaro*[21] like this:

> The king's entourage stops to spend the night under a banyan tree. The king and his queen are sleeping in their tent, and Manasāgaro stands watch outside with his naked sword.
>
> It is now past midnight and Manasāgaro hears two birds talking in the banyan tree's canopy above.
>
> "Listen, my eagle queen!"
>
> "Yes, my king!"
>
> "This king and his queen are our guests tonight, but his kingdom will be without their master tomorrow!"
>
> Says, "Why so?"
>
> Says, "The king faces six lethal perils tomorrow."
>
> Says, "What perils?"
>
> "The first: when their carriage departs, a huge branch of this banyan tree will break and fall on the king and the queen and crush them."
>
> "Can someone not save them?"
>
> "Yes, if the carriage goes a different way, the couple can survive this. But, a short distance from here, they will have to pass two mountains. If any living beings try to pass between them, the two mountains converge on them and

[21] Manasāgaro: A story in the author's collection *Dādāji-ni Wāto*. Also included in this translation.

collide. There the king and the queen will be flattened."

"And if they survive that?"

"A diamond-studded gold ring lying in their path will tempt the *king*; when he tries to pick it up, the ring will turn into a *tamboḷiyo* snake and bite him."

"What if he somehow gets out of that peril?"

"His horse arriving with the receiving procession back home will throw the king and crush him to pulp."

"What if he survives that?"

"The main castle gate will fall on him."

"And, if someone prevents that too?"

"Then, the last peril is to strike at night. The royal couple will be in the lap of their sweet slumber around midnight when a black female snake will emerge from the roof above them. A drop of its venom will fall on the sleeping queen's cheek. The king will wake up and kiss the queen's cheek and ingest the poisonous drop. He will die an instant death.

"And, there's this one thing, my eagle queen! If anyone hears our talk and reveals it to another human, that teller of this secret will turn into stone!"

And then, the eagles themselves go to sleep.

Shri Sen says the prophetic birds Bihaṅgam and Bihaṅgami show up in many Bengali tales; but, we too can assert that the pair of male and female eagles are present in numerous of our [Gujarati] tales. And, the Bundelkhandis would respond, "Hey, we have them too!"

The Bengali Story "Sukhu ār Dukhu"

Shri Sen points out some more similarities: He calls the Grimm Brothers' story "The Devil with the Three Golden Hairs" as the European edition of our own story of "Chandrahās". He likens another tale [*Sheeta-Basanta*[22]] - featuring two brothers named Sheeta and Basaṅta who encounter two talking birds and each brother eating one bird from the pair, with the result that "when he laughs, *māṇiks* (red diamonds) will drop from his mouth" - to a Grimm brothers' story called "Salad". He establishes the Bengali story "Sukhu ār Dukhu" as the origin of the Grimms' story "Mother Holle". The conclusion Shri Sen draws from all these comparisons is that all these stories reached Europe ONLY from the shores of Bengal, because:

1. In India the highest culture and refinement were for ages represented by Magadha . . .
2. . . . from the ruins of which have now sprung up some of the cities and towns of Bengal.
3. . . . [with Bengal's] genteel society inheriting the traditions and ideas that floated in the metropolitan city [Magadha] of the old Indian world.
4. Magadha, Champa and Banga, the great political divisions of the province in those days were in touch with the rest of the world.

The Bengali tales Shri Sen presents as the progenitors of some European tales bear a remarkable resemblance to some Soraṭhi tales as earlier demonstrated with excerpts from the purely Soraṭhi tale "Manasāgaro". Also, how does "Chandrahās" (a story from the ancient Sanskrit epic *Mahābhārat*) become a Bengali tale? I do not know if the drama "Chandrahās" that used to be staged (in Gujarat) is really of Gujarati origin. However, the Bengali "Sukhu ār Dukhu" seems no more than a sketchy imitation of the purely Gujarati *vratakathā*[23] "Sheetaḷā Sātamani Wārtā".

---

[22] Rev. Lal Behari Day, *Folk-tales from Bengal*, London: Macmillan, 1912.

[23] *Vratakathā*: a story (*kathā*) revolving around (mostly) the women's observance of a socio-religious vow (*vrata*).

In the Bengali Sukhu ār Dukhu, the poor girl Dukhu is asked by her mother to put the cotton out to dry in the sun. A gust of wind carries the cotton away. The wind talks to a crying Dukhu: "Stop crying, follow me and I will return your cotton to you." The still crying Dukhu follows the wind and encounters a cow. The cow asks Dukhu to clear the dung from her shed. Dukhu, feeling sympathy for the animal, does the cleaning. Again following the wind, she heeds the call of a banana plant to pull out the weed that covers its trunk. Third, a *shawra* plant pleads with her to remove the dirt that has gathered around its roots. Next, a horse asks her to give it some fodder to eat. She does all that while trying to follow the wind. Finally, she meets an old woman who is very pleased (with Dukhu's selfless behavior) and showers Dukhu with fabulous clothing, jewelry and precious gems. On her way home, she gets gifts from the animals and the plants that she had helped on her way out.

Seeing all that, her greedy sister Sukhu starts out chasing the wind the next day. Instead of helping all those same elements (along the way), she haughtily ignores them, and badly mistreats the old woman at the spinning wheel. As a result, she returns home in quite the opposite shape.

The Grimms' "Mother Holle"

In this Western tale as well, the good sister among the two goes into the woods to find her spinning spindle that has fallen into a well. On the way, at an oven's request she pulls out a loaf of bread that was about to be burned. Farther down, an apple tree asks her to shake it so as to make the ripe apples fall and not to rot away on the tree. Finally, she meets an old woman who (being happy with her good behavior) showers gold and silver upon her. Subsequently, her wicked sister goes the same route, ignores all pleas for help, and heaps curses on everyone. At the end, the fairy in the guise of that old woman punishes her rather than rewarding her.

The Soraṭhi "Sheetaḷā Sātam" Tale

In this Soraṭhi tale, a poor woman, dead tired (after a long day of cooking), falls asleep and forgets to follow the traditional requirement of dousing the fire in her *choolo* (open wood stove) the night before the festive day of Sheetaḷā Sātam.[24] The Goddess Sheetaḷā Mā comes to play in the ashes of the stove and gets burnt. This results in the woman's young son being roasted alive. The woman takes her child's body and sets out in search of Sheetaḷā Mā. She encounters the following entities on the way: two ponds whose water nobody drinks; the mango tree laden with mangoes that nobody touches; the camel cow with a heavy grindstone tied to her neck from which nobody can free her; the huge fish that is thrashing about in the hot sands on the seashore but cannot reach the water; and two male buffaloes that keep fighting, unable to separate. All those beings stop the woman and ask her to convey the messages of their sufferings to Sheetaḷā Mā and to ask Mā how they can find relief. She finally meets an old woman whom she serves and soothes. As a result, the old woman – Sheetaḷā Mā – brings her son back to life and also provides explanations for the sufferings of those other beings. All of them were paying for their misdeeds in their previous human lives. The woman secures the boon granting relief for all those beings and returns home. Her evil elder sister-in-law tries to do the same (find Sheetaḷā Mā) with a purely selfish motive for personal gains, does not carry messages from anyone and bad things happen to her. (See the story "Sheetaḷā Sātam" in my collection *Kankāvaṭee*.)

The Same Story form Present in Different Provinces

Now, this particular story form is neither of Western origin, nor a purely Bengali or exclusively Soraṭhi product; it is found in all corners of India. That contention is corroborated in Verrier Elwin's

---

24 Sheetaḷā Sātam: the seventh day of the dark half of the month of Shrāvaṇ. On this day, no food is to be cooked, and cold food cooked the day before is eaten.

recently published *Folk-tales of Mahakoshal*, in a chapter entitled "The Hero on Pilgrimage".

A story from the Shimla region: A poor landowner goes in search of *kismet* (the fate). He meets a king who says, "I am building a palace, but anything I erect on one day falls down the next day. Will you ask *kismet* for the reason?" Then a turtle says, "Will you ask why I have this severe burning sensation all the time (even though I live in water)?" A plum tree asks, "Why are my plums bitter?" Finally, he finds a *fakir* that has been asleep for twelve years. He is *kismet* and provides the explanations: the king's palace will not stand because he has not given his daughter in marriage yet; the turtle burns up because he is selfish and does not share his ample knowledge with anyone; the bitterness of plums is due to the unclaimed wealth buried under the tree. The landlord follows the same path back. He digs the treasure urn out from under the plum tree and makes the plums turn sweet. The turtle gives half of his knowledge to the landlord and stops burning up. The landlord himself marries the king's daughter and the palace stops falling. (This story was collected by Mrs Dracott.[25])

Compare the mango tree and the fish from "Sheetaḷā Sātam" (with the fruit tree and the fish in the Shimla story); both find relief in exactly the same way in both the stories.

Verrier Elwin cites another story – "The Sleeping Naseeb" from western India: "The poor brother of a rich man goes to find his *naseeb* (luck) which lies sleeping beyond the seven seas. As he goes, he is asked by a mango tree, a fish, a rājā and a horse to discover the reason for the various trials that afflict them." Three of the reasons as provided by *naseeb* are the same as in the above (Mrs Dracott's) story, and the fourth – the horse – is waiting for a rider. And, the poor brother makes gains by helping solve all four of their problems. (This story was collected by a Mrs. Wādia.)

---

[25] Alice Elizabeth Dracott, 1906, *Simla Village Tales; Or Folk Tales from the Himalayas*, London: John Murray.

In a story from northern Bihar recorded by Sarat Chandra Mitra, the poor son of an old woman goes looking for Bhagavān (God) who had appeared to him disguised as a brahmin. The young man meets a king trying to build a bridge that falls down every evening. He then meets a *sādhu* and his wife who cannot find a disciple. He comes to two *pakur* trees one of which is withered. Then he encounters an elephant whose trunk is stuck in the branch of a tree. When he finally finds the disguised-as-brahmin Bhagavān, the deity explains: the elephant is being punished because it has not carried people on its back; the tree has withered because there are ten urns of gold hidden at its root; the *sādhu* is miserable because he has not shared his knowledge with a disciple; the king's bridge falls down because he has not given his daughter in marriage. The boy himself mounts the elephant, goes to the tree and digs up the treasure, learns all the wisdom the *sādhu possesses*, and weds the king's daughter. These characters (and the storyline) correspond closely with those in the Soraṭhi tale "Sheetaḷā Sātam".

Verrier Elwin then cites two *vratakathā*s from Bengal which portray the two remaining characters from the Soraṭhi tale that are virtually identical – the two ponds and the giant fish.

Muslim Tales

We find similar plots in Muslim stories as well. A Muslim tale of this type was related to D.L.R. Lorimer[26] by a Bakhtiar[27] named Mulla Ilahi. Again, the poor brother of a rich man goes to find his luck and sees a tree with no fruit, comes to a country with populace that does not obey the king (in reality he is a woman in man's disguise), meets a wolf that gets nothing to eat. He carries their questions to get answers for them. His luck is asleep when he finds him. The man kicks him awake, asks for explanations for those matters and gets his answers: there is, of course, a treasure buried under the tree;

---

[26] Lt. Col. David Lockhart Robertson Lorimer (1876–1962), a British political official in the Near East, a linguist.

[27] Bakhtiar: an inhabitant of south-western Iran.

the subjects of the king do not obey him because he is a woman disguised as a man; and the wolf must find a stupid person. So, in order to find relief from their maladies: the treasure needs to be moved out from under the tree, the fake king needs to marry a man and the wolf needs to gobble up the first stupid man it meets. The poor man turns back, but . . . he does not take the buried treasure; the disguised woman-king wants to marry him, but the fool refuses; and so, the wolf devours the idiot in the end.

It seems to me, in this Muslim variation of the theme, the first half of the story has been dropped. In most of the stories of this kind, in the first part a good man or woman behaves politely, does all the right things and is properly rewarded. In the second part, jealous of the "good" person's rewards, a "bad" character tries to follow the same steps, behaves with rudeness and arrogance, and suffers. Apparently, the researcher here lost a page or two of this Muslim tale.

Neatness of the Soraṭhi Version

When comparing all these variations, I have personally found the Soraṭhi "Sheetaḷā Sātam" tale to be neat, well put together and appropriately proportioned in terms of intellect, artistry and imagination. What is more, it contains nicely woven-in mentions of conduct in previous births:

The ponds: Sisters-in-law in another birth, distributed sour and watered down buttermilk to others.

The mango tree: Was rich, but stingy, did not spend a penny for the good of others.

The camel cow: Was a woman, owned a grindstone, would not let anyone else use it.

The giant fish: Was a scholarly brahmin, knew the sacred Vedas by heart, did not recite them to anyone.

Two male buffaloes: Were two rival community leaders; schemed and fought all the time.

The Bengali Claim Goes Too Far

The neatness with which the deeds of a prior birth and their corresponding paybacks in the current birth are presented in the Soraṭhi tale outshines any of the other tales mentioned above. Even so, my point is not to claim that the Soraṭhi (Sheetaḷā Sātam) tale is the origin from which all the other versions have sprung. My point is that a (currently) prevalent Bengali story form is not sufficient ground to claim that Bengali women living in the beautiful homes surrounded by lush groves are the origin of those stories. Nor is it proper to infer that it was only from the Bengal's coastline that these tales reached Arabia, Iran and Europe's shores; Gujarat-Kāṭhiāwāḍ's shoreline was no less bustling with trade-shipping activity than the Bengali ports. Their [Gujarati] ships moored at the Arabian and Persian shores, just as the Arab and Persian sailors came to ports in Soraṭh-Gujarat. Some of them even set up residence in Gujarat. Shri Sen correctly states that these tales are the products of the Buddhist era. That, however, does not preclude Soraṭh region from seeing the rise of these stories there. The shining sun of the Magadh Empire's Buddhist era shone as brightly on Soraṭh-Gujarat. Other regions of the Indian subcontinent were not left out from a healthy feeding of Buddhism's cultural and literary influence. That cultivation was nationwide, its seeds were scattered to all corners.

Indian Story Element vs. Arabian-Persian Story Element

Shri Sen makes a very good point. Western critics are mistaken in believing that the Eastern values shining brightly in Western folk tales are products of Arabia or Persia, and also in confusing the folk tales with the one-thousand-and-one stories of the *Arabian Nights*.

There are major differences between purely Persian-Arabic folk tales and the purely Indian folk tales. In the Persian-Arabic tales, there is comparatively lesser emphasis on morality. Most Indian folk tales have animals playing various roles, whereas the Persian-Arabian tales feature "spiritual creatures" like *jinn*, headless *khavis* and beautiful *houri* playing major roles. In those tales of the Muslim world, the divine elements perform miracles and the descriptions of love affairs are excessively sensuous. In contrast, the Indian tales place greater emphasis on rewarding virtue and chastity, and protection for the weak and polite. The role that is played by a *houri* in the former (the Persian–Arabic), is played by an *apsarā* in the latter. The *Arabian Nights* atmosphere – filled with magic, unbridled fantasy and titillating impossibilities is suffocating. In contrast, human aspirations and emotions get free rein in the Indian tales.

Individual Expression from Each Province

It is beyond dispute that the roots of all Indian folk tales draw their nutrition from the ancient storygrounds of *Brihatkathā*, *Kathāsaritsāgar*, *Jātaka Kathā* and others. However, equally incontestable is the fact that each province's tales display their own unique stamp on the tales.

That provincial uniqueness lies in its characteristic story structure which (in Gujarat–Soraṭh's case) is self-evident in the stories included in *Dādāji-ni Wāto* and *Raṅg Chhe, Bāroṭ!*. In the very first story – "Vikram ane Khāparo",[28] – the dialogues, the weaving of events, the story's development, the built-in spell chants and descriptions of the characters all bear unique imprint of the Soraṭhi style of storytelling. I have taken pains to preserve its oral presentation in this print version.

The prose seen in these stories follows two different patterns. One part deals with the story itself and is unique to each story. "Bāpu Bhālaḷo", "Janamanā Jogi" and "Chaṅdaṇ-Meṇāṅgari" are the examples of stories (in *Raṅg Chhe, Bāroṭ!*) that contain only this pattern. The second pattern, seen in other stories, manifests in prose segments that invoke strong emotions such as valor, separation, sorrow, merriment; or couplets describing the distress of the sleepless, lines of prose providing definitions of various

[28] This story is not a part of this compilation.

kinds of women (e.g. a *padmini*), the list of nine families of *nāgs*, verses that enumerate the fourteen *vidyās* (skills), etc. These are all [extraneous] elements that each storyteller uses in his own style to embellish the main storyline. These are the universally applicable oratorical gems from the vast ocean of folk language.

My objective has been to present these folk tales to the reader in the exact shape and language that I heard them in. However, stories such as "Dariyāpeerani Deekaree" and "Khāniyo" came to me not from the original folk storyteller but through intermediaries, thereby forcing me to write them in my own style. Even in those, the events and the emotions have stayed intact.

The folk tale "Chandaṇ-Meṇāṅgari" contains influences of the Mārwāḍi dialect, because the Luhāriyā tellers of that story were originally from Tharād (a town near the Rajasthan border). Settled in Gujarat for three generations, these people have still preserved their colloquial tongue along with their traditions.

The story "Kāṭhikuḷ" stands out from the others in this collection. It can easily go into the "history" category, but is included here as another sample from Jeṭhā Bāroṭ's story treasure.

"Janamanā Jogi" is a lyric poem depicting the well-known story of King Bhartrihari. The prevalent beliefs about Queen Piṅgaḷā's infidelity, about her reputed lover Ashvapāl and the episode of *amarfaḷ* that led Bhartrihari to forsake worldly pleasures are not even mentioned in this poem. It is unlikely that a folk poem would ignore such noteworthy events. Based on that, we can emphatically say that those events must have been added in modern times.

At the end of the story "Vikram ane Khāparo", the mention of King Vikram having Queen Bhāṇamati's head shaven and throwing out is incorrect. In all the Vikram tales, King Vikram consistently displays the high ideal of treating even his ill-wishers with benevolence. This lapse is strictly mine, not Jeṭhā Bāroṭ's.

I have found much valuable information on the subject of

"motif" from the recently published *The Folk-tales of Mahākoshal*[29] by Verrier Elwin.[30]

On my part, this is just an attempt to point the way to the vast land of the folk tales. Those interested in exploring this field will find much material in their own towns and surroundings. My only suggestion to them is to make sure and capture the original oral form (of the folk tales) intact.

[*1945*] **Jhaverchand Meghani**

---

[29] Verrier Elwin, 1944, *The Folk-tales of Mahākoshal,* London: Oxford University Press.

[30] Verrier Elwin (1902-64): Self-trained English anthropologist, ethnologist and tribal activist; lived in India most of his life.

The Four Maxims

THE KING and his chief minister Manasāgaro were such good friends that their hearts seemed to beat like one. Neither could do without the other's presence near him.

But, the king's attitude suddenly changed one day. As the saying goes, one can never predict how kings, musical instruments and monkeys would behave at any given time. Something must have gotten into the king's head and he just ostracized his minister friend, refused to even see his face.

King, my wise king . . .
He that your soul accepts,
Let your mind not push away;
Even if the body withers away,
Abandon him not, O Bāṅdarā![1]

Don't you know what happened when there was this falling out between the swans and the pond?

The swans spread their wings,
Got ready to take to the air;
There's pickings here no more,
'Tis time to look elsewhere.

The pond has gone dry; there is no food to be found here anymore. The swans cannot wait to go and look for new waters. Disappointed, the pond says:

O swan,
Shallow is the love of crows,
The slightest pain, and away they fly;

---

[1] Bāṅdarā: Poet's name!

The true love is only algae's,
She wilts when the pond goes dry.

If only the swan would listen, wise men would advise him thus:

O swan,
Go make peace with the pond,
Fold your hands, express regret;
What makes you look and feel good,
Such friendships must never end.

Further,

Stay only with the pond,
Where waters stay within the brink;
Serve not a worthless king,
Who's whimsical and does not think.

But, the swan did not listen. As he left, he said there were many other ponds out there, that there was nothing special about this one to hold him here.

The pond sighed and said:

Swans have many ponds,
A flower attracts many a bee.
Good men will make good friends,
Whether you stay or flee.

Manasāgaro, our ostracized minister, keeps his cool and waits patiently. He fervently hopes that the king will some day come to his senses.

God must have heard his pleas and so willed that, one day Manasāgaro heard a loud voice from the street: "Any taker for my four maxims to live by? A thousand rupees for each; worth a million if you get the meaning, worth nothing if you don't!"

"So who is this guy hawking his four maxims!" The minister wondered. He stuck his head out of the window and saw a *fakir* in the street. The *fakir*'s voice came again:

"Come get them! Four golden rules to live by: One thousand rupees for each; worth a million if you get the meaning, worth nothing if you don't!"

Passersby laugh at the words and make fun of the *fakir*. Some even say "The man has gone mad, pay him no heed!"

But Manasāgaro, the minister, called out to the *fakir*, "Hey Sāṅi! Will you step in here for a bit?"

He had the *fakir* brought upstairs to him, put four thousand rupees in front of the man, and said, "Here's your money, now let's see what you have."

The *fakir* handed over a piece of paper. Manasāgaro read it:

Control your rage - rule one, that's worth a thousand to you;
Stay awake - rule two, cost another thousand to you.
Welcome your enemy - rule three, one more thousand from you.
Thrash your wife when she's guilty - rule four, cost another thousand to you.
Each worth a million if you get it, worth nothing if you don't!

"Very good, *bābā-ji*! Now do me a favor. Take this paper and go to the king's palace. Don't hand it to the king, but nail it on his doorframe. Do it after dark, and then just leave quietly."

The *bāwā-fakirs* of the time were a trustworthy lot; they had unrestricted access even to the king's palace. Our *fakir* had no problem in getting into the palace and attaching the "four rules" paper to the doorframe as instructed by Manasāgaro.

* * *

Gods must have further willed and *bhawāyās* (a group of itinerant actors) were to perform in town that same night. The central square in town was trumpeted with the sounds of their *bhooṅgalā*;[2] their cymbals filled the air. The king himself came out to watch them perform.

[2] *Bhooṅgaḷā*: Wind instruments.

The king's young sister wants to see them too, so she disguises herself in a man's attire and also goes. Her attendants go along in similar disguises. The *bhawāyās* are set up to perform in a circle. The king is seated atop his *dholiyo* (decorated cot) on one side of the circle. His sister is on the opposite side, dressed and armed like a man. Nobody recognizes her and assumes her to be a visiting prince from out of town.

The *bhawāi* performance got under way. One after another, the various traditional acts appeared – the act of Ganesh, the trunked god; that of Dāgalo; and then the act of brāhmaṇ. *Nāyaks* (the leaders of the troupe) maintained the quick beat with their cymbals and tambourines, and sang:

Wāwadi khode re bhramyo, Rām-Rām-ji re,
Nāvan kare re bhramyo, Rām-Rām-ji re,
Bhojan kare re bhramyo, Rām-Rām-ji re.

[The brahmin digs a well, bathes himself and then sits down for a meal.]

And then, the refrain went:

Bhalā more Rāmā, bhalā more Rāmā,
Āj more Rāmā, bhalā more Rāmā!

A couple of male performers, disguised as *purabiyā* (men from the eastern part of India) and each flanked by two women, made their way into the circle . . . dancing, spinning umbrellas around them and filling the atmosphere with their singing.

They were followed by the act of Kerabo featuring some fabulous dancing.

savar pad ghoogharke bājat bajāy sindhu,
veeṅchhiyā aṇavaṭkee phoj asavāree hai;
ghooghar rav jhāṅjharke pākhar beechhāy ghoḍe,
bhoojan par bājanki ḍhāl baḍee bhāree hai;
seesan par cheeranke nejā jareen sohe,
dhajā patākā aroo kaṅchan jyuṅ dhāree hai.

> A well-decorated horse of the *sindhu* pedigree tinkles the anklet bells on its feet; a whole army of toe rings (worn by the rider) is astride the steed; it has a saddle pad with sweet sounding little bells hanging from it; the rider carries a heavy shield to make striking noises with; his head is adorned with silver-threaded silken *pāghaḍi*; flags and pennants fly from golden urns held high on a staff.

The king so enjoyed the act that he showered a gift of one hundred rupees on the performers. The principal *bhawāyās* immediately acknowledged it with cries of "Alright!"

"Girls, we can't let my brother steal the show here!" The royal sister whispered to her attendants, and announced her own two hundred rupee gift, doubling that of the king. This was greeted with much applause, and set every nerve in the king's body on fire. Afraid that her visibly angry brother might recognize her, the king's sister got up and quickly departed for the palace. Being extremely tired, she didn't even bother to change out of her male attire, fell in her mother's bed and was asleep immediately.

The king also returned to the palace, still smarting from his loss of face. The palace was ablaze with lights, and as he passed his mother's room, he saw a man in bed with her! All sixty-six thousand hairs on his body stood up straight. He drew his sword: "I'm going to cut them both to pieces!" As he was about to enter the room, his hand touched the paper affixed there by the *fakir*. The first line read:

Control your rage - rule one, that's worth a thousand to you.

When anger hits you, slow down, think, don't let it control you . . . was what the thousand-rupee rule was telling him!

'Wait, what is happening here? Who put this message here? Something deeply mysterious is definitely afoot!'

He swallowed his pride, backed off from the door and sat down. His eyes went back to the enigmatic message on the door. Its second line read:

Stay awake - rule two, cost another thousand to you.

'Ah, the mystery deepens. Surely that is meant for me, someone is trying to warn me of impending danger. I better not sleep, stay alert!' The king just sat and waited.

In the third *pahor* (quadrant) of the night, he heard a pair of swans talk from their perch on a tree.

One says, "O king of swans! How long do you think this king shall live?"

Says the male swan, "Three more days, my queen!"

"What? Only three days! How can that be when he has no sickness, not even in a follicle in his body?"

Says he, "True, my love, but he will die of snakebite three nights from now."

"Snakebite at night? How?"

"A young snake lost its tail when the king's horse had stepped on it. Now that full-grown snake will come seeking revenge."

With that, the swans flew away. The king was drenched in sweat after listening to that exchange. He went back to the message on the doorframe and read the third line:

Welcome your enemy – rule three, one more thousand from you.

Morning came and the king realized that following the first rule had truly paid off for him. The "man" in his mother's bed turned out to be his sister! Had he followed his impulse and killed the two . . . how much he would have regretted that now! If that was so, then the second rule for staying awake had also worked and warned him. The snake was sure to come to avenge its deformity. *What do I do now?*

He re-read the third rule of the message on the door – *Welcome your enemy . . .*

"I get it! The snake is my enemy. He is coming here to get revenge. If I welcome him into my household and treat him well, something good is bound to come from that. But, how does one go about welcoming a snake? What must I do?"

On the third day, the king ordered a huge amount of flowers to be brought to the palace. His bedroom floor was covered with flowers, a thick canopy woven solid with flowers hung from the four bedposts spanning the four corners of the bed. In the evening, a pot of thickened milk was placed under each bedleg. After that, the king climbed into the bed and sat in its middle. His body trembled uncontrollably with fear. But, it was his implicit belief in the four rules that gave him the resolve to sit and wait.

Just past the midnight hour, the awaited snake arrived. He is a *nāg* (hooded cobra), and hot steam came out of his huge hood as he hissed. *Fooṅ, fooṅ, fooṅ!* The entire bed-suite seemed to have turned red hot with his arrival. The king could barely hold himself from screaming in terror.

The *nāg* slithered across the flower-covered floor to the bed. He tried to go up the pot's wall to reach one leg and his mouth fell right into the thickened milk. He slurped up all the milk in that pot in no time at all. Then he stopped and mused: *I cannot go up this leg . . . after feeding myself here.*

Being of a divine pedig ree, the snake could not violate the hospitality he had received, and quickly turned back from that leg. Of the nine different varieties of *nāg*s, this was not a *tamboḷiyo, aḍadiyo, taliyo, gaḍagaḍiyo, dhāmaṇ, aiyar, shitaḷo* nor a *kanjunāg*. This one belonged to the ninth and the highest pedigree of snakes – *phoolnāg.*

So, the *nāg* turned around and rolled and frolicked its way through the soft flower-strewn floor, and reached the second leg of the bed. Again, trying to climb up the pot to reach that leg, his head landed in the pot of milk.

Again the *nāg* drank the milk and turned around. The same thing happened at the third and the fourth legs. The *nāg* knew that he could not go back and climb up any of the four legs and abuse the hospitality he received there. He knew he had to find another way to reach his intended victim.

"Does the king think he can get away from me like that! No, he is going to die tonight!" With those thoughts in his mind, the *nāg* crawled up the wall to the room's ceiling and then let his body drop to the bed. What he landed on was the flower-knit canopy above the bed.

"How can I bite someone that is so nice and hospitable to me?" The *nāg* had a code of conduct to follow, because this was no ordinary snake. He belonged to the noblest category of pedigreed *nāgs*. He was a descendant of Vāsuki, the divine king of *nāgs* (whom the gods used as a rope to churn Ksheerasāgar, the ocean of milk).

The *nāg* was pleased no end. He showed himself to the king in his divine form, and told him, "O king! Make a wish. You have my word that you will get anything you want."

The king said, "O Lord Vāsaṅgi, give me the ability to understand the language of everything alive, and eyes that can see into the past, the present and the future."

"O king, what good will all that do for you? Ask for something else!" The *nāg* saw no wisdom in the king's wish.

The king said, "Lord, if you really want to grant me a wish, that's my wish – to be able to understand the speech of all living creatures, and to gaze into the past, the present and what's yet to come."

The *nāg* said, "Alright, if you so insist. You shall understand and see as you ask, but I have one condition."

The king said, "Name it, Lord!"

"O king, you must not mention any of what you so hear or see to your wife. The day you do that will be your last." With that, the *nāg* left. And, from that moment on, the king's ears and eyes roamed the universe. He understood the parlance of every insect, animal and bird; space and time opened up to his eyes.

One day, God must have willed and the older queen's brother died. The man had lived a good and virtuous life, and his soul just clung to his body and kept kissing it, not wanting to part from it.

With the *nāg*'s boon, the king could see everything in the world. He saw what was happening and that vision made him cry.

A few days later, the younger queen's brother died. His soul hovered over the dead body and started beating it up on the head with a shoe! The king saw that and the spectacle made him laugh.

"My brother dies, and the king laughs like that! Surely he has a reason?" The queen had to know why, and she asked, "My king, tell me why you laugh."

Says, "No, I cannot tell you."

"You must tell me. If you don't, I will stab myself to death!"

The king was in a quandary. If he told her the reason, he would die, and if he didn't, the queen was threatening to kill herself!

"I am going to have to tell her. But, if I die here, my soul would never find peace. Best, let me go to the holy city of Kāshi and tell her there. If I die there, my soul will definitely go to heaven."

So, the king asked the queen to go to Kāshi with him and promised to give her the answer there. As they left the palace, he read the "Four Rules" message on the doorframe:

Control your rage – rule one . . .
Stay awake – rule two . . .
Welcome your enemy – rule three . . .
Thrash your wife when she's guilty – rule four . . .
Each worth a million if you get it, worth nothing if you don't!

They passed a well on their way. A pair of goats was grazing near the well. Just as the king and the queen walked by, the female goat said to the male goat:

"Listen, you bum! I am pregnant, and have this craving for that vine I see deep inside the well near the water. I want you to go down there and get it for me, or I won't talk to you."

The male replied, "You dimwit female! Do you think I am as stupid as this king that I would risk my life for you like that! Keep behaving like a brat and I'll have to ram you hard and teach you a lesson. I'm not a sissy like this king that I'd put up with idiotic demands from my wife. Is that clear?"

That shut the female goat up.

The *nāg* had granted the king the ability to understand all animals, and the goats' talk took him completely aback. On one hand, the male goat's words hit a nerve; on the other, he was reminded of the last rule: *Thrash your wife when she's guilty. . . .*

Wasting no time, he turned to his young queen and screamed at her: "Hold it right there! We are going nowhere, and I'm telling you nothing! Do you want to go back quietly or want my fist on your face? If you don't listen, I'll horsewhip you right here, woman!"

That scared the queen to death. She begged for mercy, "I will never ever make such demands again. Let us go home, please!"

After their return, the king realized that all the four maxims in the paper on his doorframe had come true for him. He investigated who had put the paper there.

When it turned out that chief minister Manasāgaro was responsible for it, the king sent for Manasāgaro and apologized for his mistreatment of the wise minister. The king was very careful after that in dealing with all his good friends.

And, it was time again to eat, drink and rule wisely.

Occupying Someone's Body

ONCE AGAIN, Vikram the Valiant, the king of Ujjain, mounts his horse and hits the road all by his lonesome. Vikram is so driven by his need to relieve other people's sufferings, he has difficulty sleeping at night when he is not actively so engaged.

Those who can't sleep at night,
Include the king and the peacock;
Sleeps not the night-roaming burglar,
Nor does the kāṅkaṇahār *bird.*
Sleep also eludes the lonely woman,
Who's pining away for her man.

A king worth his salt, a peacock, a *kāṅkaṇahār* bird and a woman missing her beloved – how can such beings sleep peacefully at night?

So, the king rides, and eventually finds himself at the gates of a fort city. There are guns, swords, spears, shields – all kinds of weapons – hanging on the walls, but there is not a man around. Within the walls, the shops and marts are fully stocked with wares, but the streets are completely deserted; there is not a soul to be found. The city seems to be overflowing with affluence . . . but without any human presence.

His horse finally reaches Māṇek Chawk – the central square – with a big palace on one side. The horse stops in the square and gives out a long neigh. A head looks out of a window of the palace. To the valiant Vikram's surprise, it is the head of a woman. And, what a beautiful woman! Surely of the *padamaṇi*[1] variety!

---

[1] *Kāmasutra* and other books define four categories of women based on their psycho-physical characteristics: *padmini, chitriṇi, shaṅkhiṇi* and *hastini*. This storyteller seems to have given them his own interpretations. These four categories – *padmini, chitriṇi, shaṅkhiṇi* and →

The padmini *woman's meal is but a quarter pound,*
A hastini *woman consumes a good half pound,*
A chitriṇi *woman puts away a whole pound of food,*
A shaṅkhiṇi *goes berserk with food.*

The padmini *sleeps just a snooze a day,*
The hastini *sleeps for an hour and a half,*
The chitriṇi *snores away half the day,*
The shaṅkhiṇi's *sleep knows no limit.*

The padmini's *hair drops down to her feet,*
The hastini *boasts waist-reaching hair,*
The chitriṇi *sports a whipcord-thin braid,*
The shaṅkhiṇi's *fuzz barely reaches her neck.*

Vikram realizes at the first glance that this woman is no *shaṅkhiṇi*, no *chitriṇi*, nor a *hastini*. She is surely of the *padmini* category. And yet – God forbid – could this *padmini* be the demon that devoured this whole city?

The woman's sweet voice calls out: "O brave gent, why have you come to this lifeless city?"

He says, "Woman! Would you be the she-demon that ate this poor city?"

She says, "No, brave sir! Not me. I am but a wretched prisoner in this home of Ḍhunḍhā Rākshas, the big bad demon. Turn around and leave if you value your life."

He says, "Woman, my life certainly is dear to me, but dearer to me is my mission to relieve people of their miseries. So tell me about yours. Who are you? Who brought you to this dead city? What makes you stay here? Tell me, because I am Veer Vikram, and I need to know about it."

"The Veer Vikram? Vikram the Valiant? Oh no, Sire, you must leave right away! I can hear the echoes of your death knell already!

← *hastini* – symbolize feminine characteristics in the order of the ideal to the least desired levels.

Can you not hear it?"

And, indeed, Vikram's ears pick up the terrifying noise . . . and he feels the ground shake under him. "*Thaḍak, oothaḍak dham! Thaḍak, oothaḍak dham! Thaḍak, oothaḍak dham!*"

He says, "What is that sound?"

"O great king! That is Ḍhunḍhā Rākshas returning from his hunt. He will be here in moments only. There is nothing you can do to him. No weapon can hurt him. He is immune to death. There is no time for you even to get away. Come inside here!"

Vikram goes inside the palace after setting his horse loose. The trained horse wanders out of the city.

The woman puts her hand on Vikram's head and recites an invocation to the goddesses:

Holy Mothers!
Eighty-four chāraṇ *goddesses,*
Nine fort-dwelling Mārwādi goddesses,
[Harasiddhi] From the Baraḍā retreat,
[Shakti] From the center of Pātaṇ city,
[Shikotar] From the nilgāi's[2] *forest refuge,*
[Chhinnamastakā] Of the ghastly well,
[Khoḍiyār] From the deep Tāṅtaṇiyo pool,
[Chāmuṇḍā] Of Kāṅchh Paṅchāḷ,
[Melaḍi] From the tamarind tree in Anjār,
[Ambikā] From the caves of Mt. Girnār,
[Bahucharā] From Chuṅvāḷ's courtyard,
[Āshāpurā] From the shrine's veranda,
[Momāi] From the holy hang out in Kaḍachh . . .

"Divine Mothers! Please protect this man from harm!"

With that, the woman puts Vikram inside a *paṭāro* (a sturdy top-lidded storage chest), closes the lid and places a honey pot directly

---

[2] *Nilgāi*: A large, long-legged antelope (*Boselaphus tragocamelus*) of India.

on top of it. Honey drips into the chest through a crack and provides sustenance to the locked in Vikram!

Outside, the giant Ḍhunḍhā arrives. He has a few dead bodies on one shoulder and a few more on the other. He breathes heavily and fills the surroundings with the panting sounds of "*Thaḍak, oothaḍak dham*! *Thaḍak, oothaḍak dham*! *Thaḍak, oothaḍak dham*!"

Ḍhunḍhā himself starts the chant:

I smell man! I eat man!
I smell man! I eat man!

So the woman says, "The only human around here is me. You will have to eat me if you want to eat 'man'!"

He says, "You? I cannot eat you! Without you, who will take care of me?" And he resumes his panting: "*Thaḍak, oothaḍak dham*! *Thaḍak, oothaḍak dham! Thaḍak, oothaḍak dham*!"

The woman feeds Ḍhunḍhā, and the exhausted Ḍhunḍhā stretches out in bed. The woman uses a steel mallet to massage his tired feet and legs, and pretty soon Ḍhunḍhā falls into a deep slumber.

Three days go by, and Ḍhunḍhā again sets out for hunting. The woman lets Vikram out of the *paṭāro* and tells him:

"Great king! Please leave this dead city and be on your way. I don't want your death on my conscience."

Every word from this woman sounds like the cooing of a cuckoo to Vikram's ears. "Such a delicate and beautiful woman, this glassy fragile physique, the floor-reaching braided hair, the fairest of complexions . . . all that in the clutches of this demon! Hell, no, I cannot let this continue."

He said, "Lady, I am going nowhere until I take you out of here."

"You cannot liberate me."

"And why not?"

She says, "Because this Ḍhunḍhā cannot die. He cannot be killed by a man or a god, with any weapon, by fire or water. Countless brave warriors have tried, but have themselves fallen prey to him."

But, Vikram the Valiant is not a mere warrior. He is proficient in fourteen *vidyās* – fields of knowledge and skills:

First skill is one's education, the second of tightrope walking,
Third is the knowledge of grammar, the fourth being archery,
Fifth is the use of make-up, the sixth is home decorating,
Seventh is the art of cheating, the eighth is snake-charming,
Ninth vidyā *is horsemanship, the tenth the knowledge of gems,*
Eleventh being the art of singing, the twelfth that of a harlot,
Thirteenth skill is of worship, the fourteenth being a thief.

Vikram, having mastered all fourteen of these *vidyās*, thinks long and hard on how to proceed.

He says, "Lady, allow me to stay here for another day. Feed Ḍhunḍhā when he is back; then while you are massaging his legs, I want you to ask him some questions. You do know how to shed fake tears, right?"

"Of course I do!"

"Then use some of your feminine guile on him. Ask him who would look after you if he dies. Soften him up with your crying, and then get him to tell you the secret of his death."

She says, "I'll do it."

In the late afternoon, the earth shakes again and Ḍhunḍhā's snorting is heard: "*Thaḍak, oothaḍak dham*! *Thaḍak, oothaḍak dham*! *Thaḍak, oothaḍak dham*!"

Again, he has a few dead bodies on one shoulder and a few more on the other. He dumps the carcasses in the courtyard, enters the palace chanting:

I smell man! I eat man!
I smell man! I eat man!

Vikram hears these ominous words and breaks into a sweat inside the *patāro*!

But, the woman just laughs and says: "There is no man around here. Eat me if you want to eat 'man'!"

"Come on, how can I eat you when you take such good care of me?"

So, the woman feeds him, and sits down to massage Ḍhunḍhā's feet and legs with the steel mallet. Her sobs soon fill the air and eyes start dripping big tears.

Ḍhunḍhā says, "What's the matter? Why are you crying?"

She says, "Why would I not cry?"

He says, "So tell me why."

"You are getting on in age. What happens to me when you die?" She breaks out crying uncontrollably.

"Me? Die? No way. Nobody can kill me. I have this body of steel!"

"But, doesn't anything that live eventually die? Somehow?"

"Listen. See this hard-as-steel body of mine? After I bathe in the well, and when I am chanting the Lord's name, it turns soft like wax at that time. If a first-born of one father and one mother comes, cuts my head off, makes two dirt piles between my head and the rest, and invokes the names of Lord Shiva and Goddess Pārvati . . . only that would keep my head and body apart. If all that doesn't happen, a new demon would rise from each hair in my body! Now are you happy?" The easily deceived Ḍhunḍhā blurts out his secret.

She says, "Very happy. Now I know I have nothing to worry about!"

In a couple of days, Ḍhunḍhā leaves for his hunt, and the woman gives Vikram the whole scoop.

Ḍhunḍhā comes back. Eventually, he bathes and sits down for his worship. Vikram springs out of hiding, beheads Ḍhunḍhā with his sword, makes two small dirt piles and invokes Shiva and Pārvati. Ḍhunḍhā's head and torso briefly writhe to come together, but finally go cold.

Vikram takes the woman out of the dead city, learns that she is the princess of a neighboring kingdom and takes her home to her parents.

And then, he rides on.

* * *

On and on he goes . . . and reaches a farm where a *rākshas* (demon) is tilling his land. He has elephants hitched to his plow – a steel plow with a steel ripper. Big chunks of soil go flying as the demon runs his plow.

Vikram calls out to him, "My, my! Aren't you the macho guy around here! But, hey, you must have done some big wrong to be stuck here!"

The demon says, "Sire, I can't even begin to tell you about my misfortunes."

The king says, "What's the problem?"

The demon goes, "It's this demon Ḍhunḍhā. Lives only three miles that way. He has taken my *rākshasaṇi* – my wife – from me."

The king says, "My friend, my name will not be Vikram if I do not rid you of your misery."

So, Vikram rides the three miles and finds Ḍhunḍhā stretched out on the ground and snoring loudly. He looks nine times as tall as a palm tree.

"It wouldn't be fair to strike him while he sleeps! I must wake him first."

So Vikram wakes him up.

"*Ho*! *Ho*! *Ho*!" Ḍhunḍhā stands up. Frightened birds fly out of their nests from the surrounding trees. "Go ahead, take your shot first!" he says.

"If you say so! Here comes!" And Vikram shoots off three arrows from his bow. The arrows bounce off Ḍhunḍhā's skin like pieces of straw.

"Is that all you've got? Listen, you are a guest here. My conscience will not let me attack you on my soil. You have three and half days before I come after you. Now start running!"

Vikram runs for Ujeṇi,[3] his city. Just as he reaches the city limits, a one-armed cowherd is grazing his cows in a pasture.

The crippled cowherd calls out, "Hey great king, are you hiding your face to save a mere opium grain?"

Says, "My man, I am in a hurry because this Ḍhunḍhā is after me."

Says, "Is that all? Stop running now, my king. Let us see what poor old Ḍhunḍhā can do to you."

He uses his blanket like a flag and calls out to his cows. Snorting, the entire herd of cows runs to them, surrounds Vikram in a seven-layered bovine fortification.

"Here we go, my king! Have no fear and sit tight in this cow fortress now."

With that, the cowherd from Ujeṇi lights his *chalam* pipe and takes a deep pull on it. And, BOOM! The exhilaration hits him like a bolt!

One toke is enough to make a kitten attack a tiger,
Or for an ass to rise up and challenge an elephant.

The cowherd then milks a cow, catches the milk in a bowl made from broadleaves of the *ākaḍo* shrub and drinks the frosty milk. He wraps his blanket on his bad arm, and stands outside the fortress of cows with an axe in his good hand.

Soon, snorting "*Thaḍak, oothaḍak dham! Thaḍak, oothaḍak dham! Thaḍak, oothaḍak dham!*" Ḍhunḍhā arrives. The cowherd rears back, swings his axe at the demon's shoulder and takes a 50-pound chunk out of it.

Ḍhunḍhā screams in pain, "Mercy! Please don't swing your axe

[3] Ujeṇi: Ujjain.

anymore! I'll be a bastard to set foot in your king's land ever again!" With that apology, he turns around and leaves.

Vikram is ecstatic at witnessing such courage and heroism in a cowherd. His own heart almost bursts with joy, "Bravo, my man, bravo! You are a credit to the milk you drink. I feel so good, *gokaḷi,*[4] I want you to ask for something, anything! Ask for my entire Māḷwā kingdom and if I as much as blink, I will forsake my Vikram name! Name your reward, my man!"

Says, "Great king, because of you, I have everything I want. I have 200 cows, I have 300 goats, I have a wife that is healthy enough to feed four lions, and I have two sons. What more do I need? All I ask is that you treat my family as your citizens, and be kind to our humble home."

Vikram is now even more embarrassed with the cowherd's generosity. He asks, "I am curious about something. What happened to that arm?"

Says, "Great king! I was arm-wrestling with your Ujeṇi's Boḷiyo Dhobi.[5] He is a real tough guy, and broke my arm."

That is the first that Vikram hears of a strong man named Boḷiyo Dhobi living in Ujeṇi. Vikram is really fond of strong and brave people. Soon, Boḷiyo and Vikram become good friends. They hunt together and travel together. They become inseparable, two bodies that breathe as one.

On the night of Kāḷi Chaturdashi[6] Vikram is out with Bāwā Bāḷnāth to receive a special *mantra* – a magical spell – from him. They are on their way to the Gandharapiyu Smashān – the cremation ground on the bank of the River Safrā.[7] They see someone wrapped

---

[4] *Gokaḷi*: Colloquial for cowherd, *bharavād*.

[5] Dhobi: Cloth washer.

[6] Kāḷi Chaturdashi/Kāḷi Chaudash: Forteenth day of the dark half of Ashwin month of the Hindu lunar calendar.

[7] Safrā: The River Kshiprā.

in a blanket stretched out at the *smashān* gate.

Asks, "Hey, who are you?"

Says, "Sire, it's me, Boḷiyo Dhobi."

"Boḷiyo, what are you doing here!"

"It's the Black Fourteenth – the big night the evil spirits go on the prowl. I am here to keep them away from Ujeṇi, my king!"

"That's nice of you, but you can go back now." The Bāwā told Boḷiyo.

Says, "No way! What I see out there are those witches cavorting, angels of death clashing their cymbals, the headless fiends waiting for God knows what . . . and I leave my king here to face them? Hell no, I am not going anywhere."

Boḷiyo is determined to stay. And, Bāwā Bāḷnāth is determined to give the *mantra* only to Vikram. It is supposed to be so special that only someone really worthy can be trusted with it.

So, when they arrive at the Bāwā's hut, the Bāwā takes Vikram inside, then draws seven lines on the ground forbidding entry to anyone else. He, however, tells Boḷiyo to wait, "Stay, Boḷiyo, because I'm going to give you a *mantra* too!"

And then,

Deep into the northern skies the Bāwā gazed,
A powerful chant to Vikram the Bāwā granted.

The Bāwā then proceeds to teach Vikram this *Aghor Gāyatree* incantation:

Nectar –
An urn floating in nectar
The eternal auṁ *reverberating in the urn*
Auṁ *representing the formless*
The formless is the Unstained Supreme
The Unstained contains the five elements
The flame from the elements

Love emanating from the flame
The love-flame burns bright
The holy Mother Gāyatree
She is inscrutable to others
Cutting through the mysteries of life
Protecting the virtuous
Destroying the wicked
The Mother with covered head
Devourer of the evil dead
She comes and She goes
Descended from the Moon
Eighteen varieties of vegetation
Instilling fear in the hearts of evildoers
Establishing Her own following
Chant now! Declare "I am that"!

This powerful chant gives Vikram the power of *PAR-KĀYĀ-PRAVESH*, the ability to occupy another body. Anyone with this ability can leave his or her own body and enter another lifeless body.

"I must warn you, king! You must not tell Boḷiyo a word about this."

Then the Bāwā summoned Boḷiyo inside the hut."Boḷiyo, this scorpion spell is for you:

The black cow, black all over,
Goes up the hill, makes a dung heap
The heap is home to the scorpion queen
The queen gives birth to eighteen sons.
Six are black, six are brown and
Six more are the color of turmeric
Bring you down I will, not if,
Beware, dirty green thief
The peacock's coming
Its plumage a-strutting
Let me invoke the Lord's bidding

Heed His words, or perish standing.

They have their *mantras* and the king and Boḷiyo return to Ujeṇi, but Boḷiyo is back the very next day and starts crying.

Says, "Boḷiyo, what is the big deal?"

Says, "Great king, my wife has gone on a hunger strike!"

Says, "But why?"

Says, "Because she thinks the Bāwā taught you a *mantra* to create incredible wealth, but shooed me away with a silly scorpion chant! Great king, what riches do you not have that you need to create more? I must have that *mantra*, or. . . ."

Now, Vikram is so fond of Boḷiyo that he cannot hold back on him. "Listen, Boḷiyo! What I got is not what you think, but a chant for *par-kāyā-pravesh* – entering and occupying another body. Here, I will teach it to you."

Vikram, in a rare act of indiscretion, reveals the secret chant to Boḷiyo.

The next night, Boḷiyo comes to fetch Vikram to go deer-hunting.

Says, "Boḷiyo! It's only the middle of the night!"

Says, "No, Sire, the slaughterhouse rooster has been crowing [signaling the daybreak] for a while now!"

They leave for the hunt and are a long way from Ujeṇi by daybreak. They see some deer in the dawn's light. An antlered musk deer catches their attention and they press their horses to corner it. The chase takes them far away from Ujeṇi, but an arrow finally brings the animal down. The two look in admiration at the handsome beast.

Says, "Boḷiyo! Isn't that a magnificent body! What fun must this *musky* have had with the females!"

Says, "Then, Sire, what better time to test the *mantra* you got from Bāwā Bāḷnāth! Why not see if you can really switch to another body?" Little does Vikram know of Boḷiyo's treacherous schemes!

So, Vikram recites the chant, leaves his own body and enters the lifeless body of the *musky*. The animal jumps to its feet, and Vikram – in the form of the musk deer – gazes at Boḷiyo.

The crafty Boḷiyo says, "Sire, while you have the chance, how about a little romp among those females there? I will stand watch over your body here."

Vikram – now a musky – bounds over to the deer herd and is soon lost among the waiting does. The herd soon drifts away and goes out of sight.

Here, Boḷiyo wastes no time in using the chant he had connived out of Vikram. He leaves his own body and moves into Vikram's.

He stands up as Vikram, proudly strokes his moustache and says, "Now! My name is not Boḷiyo if I don't tame the 9.2 million strong Māḷwā kingdom and the 32 queens!"

Just then, the musky returns. The body of a musk deer, and the soul of Vikram the Valiant make for a magnificently handsome combination. Its horns held high and resplendent in a spotted skin, the unsuspecting and playful musky is coming back from his stint among the herd of female deer.

As the distance closes, Boḷiyo shoots an arrow which hits the musky in its antler. It summersaults and thuds heavily to the ground. Boḷiyo thinks the arrow has hit between the eyes! He covers the deer's body with a cloth and makes tracks for Ujeṇi in Vikram's body.

Inside the royal palace, the royal maids drop off bowls of sandalwood and saffron pastes to massage the king's body with. They leave to fetch other supplies.

Boḷiyo laps up the pastes before the maids' return.

When the maids come back with silk body-wraps for his bath, they find the paste bowls emptied out! The fake Vikram screams at them: "Stupid wenches! You want to use this food to massage my body? I'll tear you limb from limb. And, you idiots want to get this silk wet?"

The king lapped up the bath paste bowls! Doesn't want the silk bath-wraps!

The maids are horrified. Something is not right! Why is the king behaving like that?

Then the maids arrive with the king's dinner in a platter with 32 separate compartments. There is also a bowl with water to wash up after the meal.

The 32 compartments hold as many items of food, and has enough to feed fifty people. Boḷiyo puts everything together, mixes it up and then proceeds to polish it off . . . all by himself! And then, he guzzles down the water from the wash bowl!

God almighty! What has happened to the king? The story quickly spreads through the palace. Queen Bhāṇamati arrives and observes all the strange behaviors. She has a good idea of what must have happened. But who can she tell? The state of her mind is:

If I laugh, my teeth will give me away,
Cry and the running kājaḷ[8] *will rat on me.*

The body is definitely Vikram's, but the soul is someone else's! However, the time is not ripe to do anything about it.

She manages to get Boḷiyo to the courtesan Gauḍ Piṅgaḷā's quarters. She orders the security tightened up to let not even a bird into the palace premises. Queen Bhāṇamati summons a brāhmaṇ woman to read the holy *Rāmāyaṇ* to her.

In a few days, the word reaches the queen that a musk deer with one broken antler is running around the forest all by itself. This male stays away from the herd and sheds tears all day long.

Animal trappers are summoned and ordered: "Whatever you do, catch that musky alive and unhurt. There will be a reward of a hundred and a twenty-five thousand for it."

---

[8] *Kājal*: Black eye-liner.

The trappers get busy quickly. The musky's foot gets caught in a loop. His heart virtually breaks. He converses with his heart:

O heart mine!
I have left my palace behind,
Taken is my golden bed,
Ujeṇi's throne is gone too,
But, don't you give up just yet!

Heart mine!
A huge fire burns within us,
There is no smoke to see,
Only my soul knows it's there,
Though, nobody else is even aware.

The enemy's at my kingdom's door,
My Ujeṇi is shaken to the core;
But, missing is Vikram – their protector,
The son of Gandharvasen is no more.

At midnight, he frees himself from the trap with one mighty pull and runs straight to the temple of the Mother Goddess Kāḷkā. He starts smashing his head against the Mother's idol.

The Mother asks, "Who is here at this hour?"

Says, "I am Vikram."

Says, "What's the matter, my son?"

Says, "Don't you see? I don't have a single day of peace. Boḷiyo has stolen my body from me. The trappers are on my trail. What good is the 50 pounds of *ghee*[9] you take from me every sunrise? Stop accepting it if you cannot solve my problem."

Says, "Alright, my son. You will get your body back in three and a half days' time. Until then, move into this thing." The Goddess points to a dead parrot.

Vikram uses the incantation and migrates into the young

[9] *Ghee*: Clarified butter to burn in the lamps.

parrot's body. He intends to fly out in the morning, but falls into the hands of a woodcutter who's arrived with an axe and a piece of rope in the predawn darkness.

"Am I lucky today!" the woodcutter thinks. "I'll roast this bird and feed it to my starving kids at home. But, I need to cut some firewood first." So, he covers the parrot under a basket and goes to work.

Dawn arrives, and the parrot's God-given ability to speak gives Vikram an outlet. He starts singing an early morning hymn:

Made whenever in the past,
The promises are bearing fruit,
To save the honor of the Pāṇḍavs,
The Lord Himself showed up uncalled.

This wakes the woodcutter's children up. When the woodcutter gets ready to cook the parrot, it speaks to him: "Listen, woodcutter! You don't recognize me but I used to be your Savo Bāroṭ in my previous life. I went on a pilgrimage to Hiṅgaḷāj, and died there. Instead of eating me, why don't you try selling me? You should be able to name your price!"

"Pa . . . rrot for sale! Anybody wants a parrot!" The woodcutter's calls ululate as he roams the streets. Then he gets to the street Badhsāgaro, the king's minister, lives on. His daughter says, "Father, buy me that parrot!"

Says, "You there! How much do you want?"

Says, "I will take whatever the parrot says."

The parrot opens up, "Badhsāgaro! Don't make us set our price. Pay whatever you can."

The parrot changes hands. A pearl threaded with gold wire now decorates his neck.

The parrot tells Badhsāgaro's daughter, "The next time you go to listen to the *Rāmāyaṇ* with Queen Bhāṇamati, please take me with you."

So the daughter takes him along. The parrot has a long chat with Queen Bhāṇamati. The queen asks some questions, the parrot answers them. The queen now knows that this parrot is Vikram, not the shadow of a doubt about it. She says not a word to anyone, but keeps the parrot with herself.

There is nothing to do but wait. Nothing can be done as long as Boḷiyo occupies Vikram's body. And, Boḷiyo is busy living it up at Gauḍ Piṅgaḷā's mansion. His only other interest is in playing with his *bheḍar* sheep – the horned rams.

It must be God's will that Boḷiyo's favorite four-horned ram dies. Boḷiyo loves the animal so much that he wants to bring it back to life, at least for a while.

So, he leaves Vikram's body and enters the sheep's. The sheep plays around for a while and wanders over to Queen Bhāṇamati's palace. Boḷiyo wants to show off how he has brought the dead sheep back to life! Blinded in that arrogance, he hears the parrot's encouraging words.

Says, "Hey, good looking *bheḍar*! How about visiting those vegetable gardens and tasting a few of those fresh greens!"

The excited Boḷiyo just takes off for the gardens swinging his ram's head at imagined adversaries!

Here, Vikram's body lies unoccupied and Vikram leaves the parrot's body and moves back into his original form. The true Vikram finally wakes up and his characteristic appearance and attributes become visible. Queen Bhāṇamati orders the royal drums to roll and the trumpets to blare.

The royal palace that has felt empty from the day of the king's disappearance has now come alive. The royal court is filled to its capacity. King Vikram, with his head seemingly reaching the clouds, is seated on the throne! Ujeṇi city is humming again!

The *bheḍar* returns from his frolicking garden visit, finds Vikram's body gone. Boḷiyo figures out what has happened, and hangs his head down. The legend goes that since that day, the *bheḍar* sheep stand with their heads down.

Vikram tells him: "Shame on you, Boḷiyo! But, even after you did that to me, I am not going to be like you. I want you to stay with me. I will take care of you, and perhaps will even find a way to help you."

One day, the young son of a rich merchant dies. The family is crying its hearts out. Vikram hears of this and sends word, "Folks, don't cremate the body yet."

He goes to the cremation grounds and takes the *bheḍar* with him. He says, "Boḷiyo, move into this merchant's body."

Boḷiyo is reluctant, but Vikram tries to reason with him. Boḷiyo's shame knows no bounds. His soul sits in the ram's body, hating himself for his past misdeeds. He has no courage even to look up. But, this ultimate show of Vikram's compassion makes his tears flow. He leaves the ram's body and takes up residence in the young merchant's body.

The older merchant gets his son back, and Boḷiyo regains his human existence. His soul has been cleansed and the newly alive young man lives a straight life.

Vikram the Valiant continues his friendship with Boḷiyo even in this new incarnation.

Daughter of the Sea God

ON THE bank of the Ratanāgar Ocean stands the palace of Queen Meeṇalade, the consort of the king of Singaḷadeep.[1] All eight *pahors*[2] a day, the ocean's waters pummel the walls of that castle.

The evening has come, and the freshly massaged and bathed Queen Meeṇalade dries her hair standing in her balcony.

Still dripping from her bath, she dries her long hair,
Like a snake swinging from the branch of a sandal tree.

Unbeknownst to the queen, someone is casting a wistful eye on her. A *jati* (monk) is intently ogling her beautiful form from his [Jain] sanctuary in the side street below the palace.

Long flower-strands in her hair,
Shy of nature, and of slender wrists,
In soft shade He must have sculpted her,
The Creator has made very few
That cast such an irresistible spell!

The *jati* is going weak-kneed just looking at the queen on her high perch. Just then, a royal maid is returning from the bazaar carrying a small bowl.

The *jati* asks her, "What have you got there, woman?"

Says, "Only hair oil for my Queen Meeṇalade."

Says, "Hair oil, but so little?"

Says, "I go and buy it fresh just once every week."

Says, "Why only once a week?"

---

1 Singaḷadeep: Most likely, today's Sri Lanka (Sinhal Dweep?).

2 *Pahor*: From the Sanskrit *prahar*, an eighth of a day or three hours.

"The king has seven queens. He spends one night a week with each of them. It is my queen's turn to have the king at her palace tonight!"

"So how much do you pay for this oil?"

"Fifty."

"May I look at that oil?"

The *jati* takes one look at the oil and shakes his head. "Woman, I have oils here that are far superior to this! Your queen's head will feel so cool, the oil will smell so good that she will feel like rewarding you for it. And then there will be no reason to get oil from anywhere else. Want to give my oil a try?"

The *jati*'s words carry irresistible temptation. His appearance and demeanor define a forceful aura that would floor practically anyone. The queen's maid is still trying to decide what to do when the *jati* takes the bowl from her and goes indoors. There, he chants something over the bowl, comes out and hands the bowl back to the maid.

At the palace, Meeṇalade has dried her hair and sits facing the mirror. The maid puts the bowl down near the queen. Says, "*Ba*, I have a new kind of oil for you today. Let's try it on your hair. It smells really good, doesn't it, *Ba*?"

The queen too has felt some strange vibrations since the bowl has come into the room.

She feels good, and excitedly sits down to apply the oil on her hair. She takes one look at the bowl . . . and sees something weird. The oil in the bowl is going round and round. Goodness gracious, what is going on here? Why is this oil swirling around like that?

Queen Meeṇalade is a smart woman and her guard goes up immediately. Surely someone has put a magic spell on this oil! She gets up without using even a drop of the oil, calls the maid and says, "Girl, you go ahead and use this new oil yourself. Now go, get me the same old oil you always buy. I am so used to it, that's the one I want."

The maid's joy knows no bound when told that. She was going to use the hair oil that cost fifty rupees! Surely her husband was going to go gaga over her!

But then, she has second thoughts. *No, wait! The oil came from that jati. He must have played some trick with it. Otherwise, why would the Queen get so generous with her and give her such an expensive bowl of oil?*

So, the maid goes to the palace courtyard, finds a heavy flat rock slab and dumps the whole bowl of oil on it. Then she goes out and gets the usual oil for the Queen's hair.

Meeṇalade asks, "What did you do with the other oil?"

"In my hair, where else, *Ba*?"

The Queen sniffs at the maid's head, and sternly says to her. "You are lying! Now tell me where you put it!"

The scared maid immediately admits pouring the oil on the rock slab.

"Now tell me where you got the oil from."

The maid hems and haws for a while. Then the queen turns the screws, "Stop beating around the bush. Tell me the truth and I will not hurt a hair on you; but, lie to me and I will strangle you myself and bury you right here!"

When the maid finally opens up and tells her about the *jati*, sixty-six thousand goose bumps stand up on the queen's body.

"Idiot, do you know what horrible death I'd have died? Anyway, we will see how this oil thing plays out. Girl, go stand watch over that rock slab, and see what happens to it during the night!"

After dark, the maid settles down a safe distance from the slab and waits. The night is dark. The crickets have established the cadence of their chirping that fills the air. Almost everyone is asleep. The watchman at the gate is staying awake by knocking his staff on the ground.

And then, the rock-slab half buried in ground, starts wriggling.

The fear-stricken and shivering maid watches the slab shake itself loose from the ground.

> Ga. ṇa. ṇa. ṇa *the rock moves, by the magic spell it is bidden,*
> *Goes and bangs on the door, wake up, enchanter, I'm risen!*

Humming *ga. ṇa. ṇa. ṇa*, the risen slab moves in the air. The royal maid has to run to keep up behind the slab. The slab passes through the palace gates – left open by the queens orders – and keeps going. The maid follows it, unwatched by anyone.

Ga. ṇa. ṇa. ṇa! ga. ṇa. ṇa. ṇa! ga. ṇa. ṇa. ṇa! The flying rock reaches the *jati*'s abode and starts banging against the door. Bang! Bang! Bang!

"Who, Meeṇalade!" The *jati*'s voice is soft and sweet. "Patience, my queen! Patience! Here, I'm opening the door."

The maid hears this from her hiding place outside, and freezes in the dark. *O my God! The* jati *did put a spell in the oil! He wanted to summon the queen to himself!*

But, the enchanted rock slab shows no such patience and its banging gets harder and noisier. Soon it breaks through the door and enters the sanctuary.

The *jati* is decked out in his best clothes, has used fragrant hair oil and perfume and has readied a flower-covered bed. One glimpse of the "visitor" and he cries out, "No! This is not Meeṇalade! What is this black monstrosity doing here?"

The rock rushes him, the *jati* jumps aside and runs. The rock slab follows after him, so he climbs on top of a *patāro* – a top-lidded wooden storage chest – and the rock goes there. The sanctuary becomes the scene of a chase, the *jati* ahead and the rock slab staying right on his heels. Bedlam reigns in the place. It is not the poor rock's fault. What was it to do? The *jati*'s spell dictated that even one drop of the enchanted oil falling on anything would require that thing to end up on the *jati*'s bosom. It could not stop until that was accomplished.

Pandemonium runs in the entire abode. The *jati* is on the run, the rock giving chase. It is a matter of time before the rock sates its obsession to crush the *jati*'s chest. What does the *jati* do now to cool that obsession?

But gods must have willed so, and the *jati* runs past and gets his hands on a jar of *urad*[3] lentil. He grabs a few grains, mumbles a new spell and sprinkles them on the slab:

Return to your abode, O black-hearted stone,
My one desire not met, leave me now alone!

The rock slab responds to the enchanted *urad* grains, turns around and returns to the palace courtyard. When the maid gets back to the palace, the rock is back in its original place as if it has never moved!

The maid cannot sleep a wink through the night; at the first crack of dawn, she goes and recounts to Meeṇalade every little detail about the night's happenings. At the end, she falls at the Queen's feet and breaks into tears: "God above, *Ba*! Wouldn't it have been the death of us if that oil had even touched you!"

"Girl, stop crying over it, because

God's words, destiny's writings, on the sixth day of one's birth,
Not a pinch less, not a grain more, they decide our lives' worth."

"But, we have work to do! That *jati* must not stay in one piece. If he lives, he will ruin many other lives. Figure out a way, and bring him over here."

The next morning, the maid goes to see the *jati*, smiles and says, "My queen sends her regards!"

What! Meeṇalade is calling for me! Seems at least one drop of my oil got to her. Touché! I knew my spell would not miss its mark.

"Wait for me. I only need a moment." And the *jati* brings out the hair oil and the perfume, combs his hair, dresses for the kill, and sets out for the palace. He struts as he goes up the stairs.

---

[3] *Urad*: Black lentil, scientific name: *Vigna mungo*.

He enters the room, and eight stout sticks descend on him. Queen Meeṇalade had eight maids waiting for him, four on each side of the door, their sticks raised to smash the *jati*'s head. But, the *jati*'s luck saved him from the onslaught and the blows just clash above his head. He falls down unhurt. As the sticks go up again, the *jati* folds his hands and begs for mercy.

"O Queen, spare me and I will tell you something!"

Says, "What is it?"

Says, "Please, from now on, you are my mother and I'm your son! If you let me live, I will put a spell together so that the king ignores his other wives and spends every night only in your palace."

The Queen is hooked. After all, she is a woman! A moonlit night is still a night! And, greed can have a negative influence on anyone. She agrees.

The *jati* asks for some *urad* flour. He makes a doll out of the *urad* dough, and chants something over it. Says, "Here, take this doll. The night the king is here and has fallen asleep, move this over his head in circles seven times."

The excited Queen locked the doll away in a box.

The king arrives on his next weekly turn at Meeṇalade's palace. When he is asleep, the queen gets the doll out and brings it to the king's bed. But, being a wise and fair person, she has second thoughts. *No, this is not right. Those other six wives are just like me, they must have the same desires and aspirations. Is snatching the king out of their lives going to bring me any joy? No. The proper thing to do is for me to be content with my share of happiness. I will be happy with the one night a week he spends with me.*

Having decided that, she hides the box with the doll away. Then a terrible thought comes to her: *What if the* jati's *spell here is as powerful as the one on the oil, and an unforeseen accident were to happen? That could lead to a real catastrophe. This doll was an invitation to disaster, but what do I do about it now?*

She sees no way out. Just then, a group of the city's seafaring merchants pay her a visit. They say, "*Ba*, we are leaving on a voyage to Java. Is there something we can bring for you from there?"

The queen gives them a list of things she wants. Then suddenly she thinks of the *urad* doll that she badly needed to dispose off. As a matter of fact, it must go as far out of the kingdom as possible. What a stroke of luck to have these merchants show up at the right time?

Says, "Brothers, I have another small request for you. There is this box here with my *poojā* paraphernalia. I have pledged to have it consigned to the bottom of Ratanāgar – the ocean. Please take it with you, and only when you get to the ocean proper, drop it overboard."

The merchant flotilla casts off. Mid-sea, the Queen's box is brought out to do the Queen's bidding. But, a young prankster is too curious to go by the rules, and suggests, "Guys, why don't we see what kind of *poojā* material this is before we dump it!"

As soon as the lid of the box is popped, a little pink child jumps out and leaps overboard. The flabbergasted merchants just watch as the child goes headlong into the water and disappears out of sight. The box is quickly dumped overboard, and the ships speed away on full sail. The episode is never mentioned again, and the whole matter gets deep-sixed.

The *urad* doll, now in the form of a live child, cuts through the water swiftly, and gets to the bottom of the ocean to reach the gates of a magnificent divine palace. The doll goes in. A supremely handsome man is seated on a platform swing. The doll makes its obeisance and addresses the man: "Lord! Ruler of the Seas! My mistress, Queen Meeṇalade of Singaḷadeep summons you."

Even the gods bow to powerful *mantras*! Resplendent in his ocean blue and purple clothes, sporting gem-studded earrings and swinging a pearl-coral necklace around his neck, the Sea Lord starts off towards Singaḷadeep. The doll child sits on his shoulder.

It is a beautiful evening in Singaḷadeep. Queen Meeṇalade is sitting on the veranda of her palace. She sees a man, a stranger, walking into the queen's abode where men are not permitted. This stranger shows no hesitation, no fear and seems like he is very much at home here. His clothes are aquatic blue in color and shine like the ocean water reflecting sun's rays. Water drips like pearls from his hair.

Who is this shameless person? How does he dare walk in like that? Not even a bird can get in here uninvited, so who let this man in? The queen gets up and is about to walk away when the stranger comes and confronts her. He says not a word but has a big smile on his face.

The queen says, "Who are you? What are you doing here?"

The stranger replies, "I am the Sea God, Queen Meeṇalade! And I'm only here because you invited me!"

The startled Meeṇalade says, "I invited you?"

The doll child comes down from the god's shoulder and says, "Respected queen! Did you forget sending me with the Java-bound merchants?"

Meeṇalade is completely dumbstruck, her heart starts thumping wildly.

Dariyāpeer, the Sea God, says, "Queen, I am a god; elite among the elite. And yet, I am more vulnerable than the lowliest because I am required to obey your enchanted summons. I cannot turn back. You cannot make me turn back!"

Meeṇalade has no strength to resist his divine authority combined with the potent spell. Dariyāpeer spends the night with her. But, one night is not enough. The god–human pair go on venting their passions night after night and the god returns to his realm in the morning.

A week goes by like that. Suddenly Meeṇalade realizes that it was to be the king's night with her. He would arrive in the evening. And so would the god. *What do I do?*

The evening comes and the king arrives. A short time later he sees a strange man entering the inner sanctum of the queen's palace. The surprised king asks, "My queen, who is this man?"

Says, "I don't know him."

Says, "How can you not know him, queen? This man walks in without any fear. His demeanor says he is not a stranger to this inner sanctum. Look at the way he smiles, and looks all around him!"

Says, "I don't know him."

The god arrives. He flashes a smile at Meeṇalade.

The king asks, "Who the hell are you?"

The god asks back, "And who might you be?"

The king says, "I am the owner of this place."

The god counters, "King, you have lost that privilege."

The king draws his sword. When he tries to swing it, the Sea God waves his hand and the sword drops from the king's hand. The next instant, the king's hands and arms are bound in some invisible bonds. The god steps towards Meeṇalade.

The trembling Meeṇalade walks around the poster bed. In a seething voice she says, "Stop right there, Dariyāpeer! In the name of the three hundred and thirty million deities, I forbid you. . . ."

That invocation stops Dariyāpeer right in his tracks.

The furious queen continues, "Lord of the Seas! Merciless god! You stoop so low as to ill-treat my husband in front of me! Shame on you, god!"

Dariyāpeer looks down in shame. Humbled, he says, "Meeṇalade! Had we been together for fifteen days, a *chakravarti* (a world conqueror) son would have been borne to you. But, it's been only six days. You will give birth to a girl. Name her Umā. Now, so long! I will not return to this palace now."

Realizing that this 'man' is none other than Dariyāpeer, the king bows to the god.

"Lord, I just found out that you have made this abode your home! I cede all my rights on this palace. I will be honored to have you stay."

"No, king, I am forbidden. I have two things to say before I leave. One, don't ever mistreat your queen on my account. If you do, I will wipe you out. Two, please make sure to invite me to daughter Umā's wedding."

With that, Dariyāpeer – the Sea God – melts into thin air.

* * *

In nine months, a daughter plays in Meeṇalade's lap. The gift from Dariyāpeer is named Umā. A god's offspring, one couldn't begin to describe her incredible beauty!

The king has a favorite *chāraṇ* bard in his court. The *chāraṇ* is also blessed with a daughter about the same time. She is named Jumā. Umā and Jumā become inseparable friends.

Umā turns fifteen. Her engagement to the prince of a neighboring kingdom is arranged. Prince Achaḷo Khichi is scheduled to arrive to wed her.

The wedding invitations go out to people near and far. Drums roll, *sharaṇāi*[4] notes pierce the air. The entire Singaḷadeep is immersed in merrymaking; the best artisans of the city are busy putting finishing touches on the princess's apparel and ornaments. Suddenly . . .

"*Hā ḍoo ḍoo ḍoo! Hā ḍoo ḍoo ḍoo! Hā ḍoo ḍoo ḍoo!*" The deafening roar seems to come from the depths of the cosmos. Men run in from the shore with the news that the ocean is boiling over with high waves and roaring. The sailors barely save their crafts from sinking and bring them ashore. There is no wind, no rain . . . so why is the ocean on this rampage? Why is the tide knocking on the fort's walls?

---

[4] *Sharaṇāi*: Oboe-like wind instrument, also *shehnai*, played on auspicious occasions.

And . . . it dawns on Queen Meeṇalade! She yelled, "Quick! Someone get the wedding invitation to Dariyāpeer now! I have given my word to the Sea God!"

No one else understood this, but Meeṇalade knows that what is happening is the sound of a parent's threshing, a father's heart breaking. The ocean's roars are Umāde's real father's expression of yearning for his own flesh and blood. His own daughter's wedding and he is the only one without an invitation! No wonder the mighty Sea God is knocking his head against the wall.

The Queen sends for Jumā's *chāraṇ* father. She gives him a *kaṅkotari* – the wedding invitation – and begs him to hurry, "Deliver this *kaṅkotari* to Dariyāpeer. Please go before it's too late!"

The *chāraṇ* is aghast. "You cannot be serious, *Mā*! A *kaṅkotari* for Dariyāpeer?"

"Yes, for Dariyāpeer, *gaḍhavi*![5] To keep a pledge I once made."

"But, where am I going to find him? I don't know where his palaces are or where he holds court!"

Says, "*Gaḍhavi*! You are a *chāraṇ*! Go find him. And make haste, because it won't be long before the whole city is under water!"

He does not know whether to laugh or to cry. The *chāraṇ* takes the invitation and starts walking along the ocean coast. *Hā ḍoo ḍoo ḍoo, hā ḍoo ḍoo ḍoo*! The sky-reaching waves seem to be quieting down as the *chāran* walks.

But, who does he hand the *kaṅkotari* to? This Ratanāgar is one elusive quarry, he thinks. He walks quite a distance and then sees a lake close to the ocean's shore. Beautiful nymphs are bathing in the lake, with their apparel scattered on its bank. He hears the humming of bumblebees in the air. Some unearthly pleasant smell seems to be drifting from the lake's direction.

Being of pious origins, the *chāraṇ* turns his back on the bathing women. *Mother of gods! How can this be? There never was a lake here!*

[5] *Gaḍhavi*: A common address for a *chāraṇ*.

Surely I have stumbled onto a divine retreat.

The *chāraṇ* holds the *kaṅkotari* towards the ocean and calls out, "O Dariyāpeer, accept this invitation!"

No sooner the words are spoken, a hand appears out of the ocean water. Its palm is open as if ready to catch something. The *chāraṇ* hurls the *kaṅkotari* towards it and the hand catches it. The ocean water immediately goes flat. A voice from the water reverberates in the air:

"*Gaḍhavi*, tell them I got the invitation. But, I am forbidden by the three hundred and thirty million gods, and cannot attend daughter Umā's wedding. My heart will be with her, but I myself can't be. Give me a moment, *gaḍhavi*! I must send a gift for my daughter, but what do I give her? Oh yes, I know! See those nymphs frolicking in the lake there? All their clothes and ornaments are lying right there on the bank. Pick out whatever you like, and just grab it. Hurry, *gaḍhavi*!"

God almighty! Is this some racket or what? Somebody else's daughter's wedding, and the Sea God makes a big deal of it. Isn't that Dariyāpeer a piece of work! Sends a wedding gift . . . of stolen jewels! And, this poor gaḍhavi *becomes the errand boy! He gets to take on other people's troubles! Gaḍhavi, deliver this* kaṅkotari! *Gaḍhavi, go find Dariyāpeer! Gaḍhavi, hurry up and steal someone's jewelry!*

The grumbling *chāraṇ* arrives at the lake. *What has the world come to? Messing with clothes of these bathing women? What a job! What a job for this poor* gaḍhavi! *There must be loads and loads of gems just lying around at the bottom of the ocean. Giving a handful from that wouldn't have stuck daggers in his heart, would it? These god-types are nothing but trouble! A pain when they are pleased, and worse when they are angry!*

Muttering complaints, the *chāraṇ* attacks those heaps of women's clothing and jewelry. But, he has no need to really look. Shining like a star-studded constellation, a necklace outglitters everything else there. One in a thousand! Just one of those could pulverize poverty of lifetimes. The *chāraṇ* snatches that up and runs in the direction of Dariyāpeer. The god has emerged from the ocean and is standing on the shore.

The nymphs – *apsarās* from heaven – see the *chāraṇ* lifting and running away with the necklace. Their frolicking stops immediately. The *apsarā* whose necklace that was, runs after the *chāraṇ*. Before she catches him, the *chāraṇ* has grabbed the feet of Dariyāpeer.

The *apsarā* stops short of Dariyāpeer and scolds him: "Mighty Lord! How can you stand there and make this man rob me? Is there any shortage of gems in your house that you deprive us poor women of our few ornaments?"

Now, the *apsarās* make the paradise shine and make the gods look good. What the courtesans are to a town on earth, the *apsarā* are in heaven.

The Sea God laughs at such an *apsarā* standing there unclothed and humbly appealing to him: "Lovely being! You don't know this, but my daughter – my own flesh and blood – is to wed today. Must I not give her my wedding present? True, I have a whole treasury filled with pearls, but they are all raw pearls. The wedding is today and I do not have the time to have them polished up and stranded for my girl. And, you my dear, only have to get back to the paradise and some god will come running with a new necklace for you. Now do you understand, my nymph?"

And then, the God of the Seas just laughs and laughs. This really puts a crack through the heart of the already snubbed *apsarā*. Brokenhearted, she says: "You have taken my necklace away from me. But beware! No happily married woman will be able to wear it; only a separated woman will."

The happy god is on such a high that the *apsarā*'s curse does not even register on his mind. The *apsarās* return to their abode in paradise, and the *chāraṇ* takes the path back to the Singaḷadeep city.

* * *

Prince Achaḷo Khichi has arrived to wed princess Umā. They have gone around the sacred fire four times. The ceremony under the *chawri* canopy is complete. It is past midnight. Princess Umā is decked out from head to toe in her conjugal regalia. The gem-studded necklace, stolen from that *apsarā* and gifted by Dariyāpeer, is around her neck. With her divine pedigree, how could she be anything but the ultimate in beauty? Carrying the bridegroom's dinner platter in her hands, Princess Umāde climbs the stairs . . . *kaṭ, kaṭ, kaṭ*!

Upstairs, Prince Achaḷo is seated on the *hindoḷa* swing. One foot tucked under him, he pushes the swing slowly with his other foot –

The pillars shake, the house smiles, as he pushes the swing,
Your beloved is here, girl mine, the one you've been awaiting.

And, their eyes meet –

As substance joins the form, when eyes look into eyes,
The love for a total stranger, springs from eyes to eyes.

The two have never met, but that first meeting of the eyes lights the flame of love!

And then –

My mind has taken to yours, as has yours to mine,
Salt in water, water on salt, inseparable once we unite.

No words are spoken. But when the minds melt together, what is the poor tongue going to say?

Finally, Umā's words come out, "My lord, your food awaits you."

Prince Achaḷo keeps smiling, but makes no response. Umā says again: "Lord, your food is getting cold."

"My lady, you are reputed to have mastered all of the fourteen arts. Aren't you forgetting one royal custom?"

Says, "Lord, would you please tell me what I have forgotten!"

The princess *sits on her perch and pleads,*
Show me the way, won't you please, my prince!
I am hopelessly lost, O please, my prince!

Says, "O Umāde!

So says the Khichi prince, *listen to what I stress,*
You must remove my shoes, O Umāde princess!"

Umāde thinks the prince speaks in jest.

Says, "Remove your *mojaḍee* shoes? Why would I do that?"

Says, "That is the custom."

Umāde's face darkens like an eclipsed moon.

Says, "Custom? Whose custom is that?"

"That is the long held tradition in our family. On the conjugal night, the bride removes the shoes from the groom's feet."

"Are you serious, Lord?"

Says, "I am dead serious. This is no laughing matter!"

Says, "Lord! If any one takes your shoes off, it will be either a maid, or a courtesan; it will most certainly not be your bride. Let me call the chief maid. This is our family's custom."

Says, "My lady! This is only a tradition. All you have to do is just touch my shoe."

Says, "Lord, I already told you. This is a maid's job, not mine, in our family."

Says, "My queen, please do not argue, because no good will come out of it."

Says, "No matter what, I will not touch your footwear."

"So be it."

And, Achaḷo gets up from the *hindoḷa* swing. The dinner platter remains untouched. The bridal night is spoiled. The city's air itself seems poisoned.

Achaḷo orders his party, "Get ready, we are leaving right now."

Umāde's best friend Jumā, the king, Queen Meeṇalade and others learn of the disastrous happenings. They all scold Umā,

"How could you commit such a blunder? There's still time to admit your mistake – no matter how strong, you are still a woman; even moonlit but a night is only a night. Who knows how long or short the life ahead might be! And, the passions of your awakened youth will take a long time to abate."

But Umāde refuses to listen to anyone. As soon as Achaḷo and party leave, Umāde starts on the job of getting her youthful desires under control. The fancy clothes and ornaments are put away, and Umāde sets out on the path of austerity and worship. She keeps the *chāraṇ* girl Jumā with her. Jumā strums on her *been* (a string instrument) and sings hymns and other songs. The white-clad Umā sits and just listens.

After some time, Umāde begins to feel that her youth is reined in, her desires are under control. She keeps Jumā around all the time; Jumā has put off her own wedding to be with her friend.

The days pass, turn into months and almost a whole year goes by.

One day, Jumā, with Umā's permission, is off to visit her father in their village. Umā is all by herself. The night happens to be a full moon night of the month of Vaishākh. She is thumbing her *māḷā* – the prayer beads, but feels really lonely. The protective wall of Jumā's songs and hymns is gone. The breeze carries with it the fragrance of night blossoms. The words of the songs being sung by women in the square outside drift in –

Please tell me Lord Krishna is in the garden outside;
So disturbed, I'm besides myself, here in Gokuḷ.
My necklace broken, clothes in tatters,
Tears flow from my eyes profusely.
Someone tell me He is in the garden outside.

The beads of her *māḷā* slow down; a late night bird's insistent call for its mate fills the night air: *piyu-uuu, piyu-uuu, piyu-uuu* (beloved) . . .!

This is not going over well!

You want to get killed, crazy bird! Don't mention my beloved
to me;
Stop this craziness at midnight; I want you to get away from me.

"Maids! Someone shoo this crazy bird away!" The rocks thrown at it drive the bird away. But, the bird that is singing away in her mind is not that easy to shoo off!

. . .

The mangos sway in the wind, the juices ready to burst;
Someone tell my Krishna, this month of Jeṭh[6] *is the worst.*

The dams inside her are showing cracks. I need my Jumā back here! My heart is going wild. My control was only skin deep. The inner being is still the same!

Umā writes a letter: Jumā, please hurry and come back!
Help me appease my man, and I'll forever be in your debt.

Jumā comes running. "Have had enough? So much ado for nothing?"

Says, "Sister mine, I cannot bear this anymore!"

Says, "Are you ready to swallow your pride and go to him?"

Says, "Yes, I am."

* * *

With loads of dowry and half the population in tow, Umāde arrives at Achaḷo Khichi's town. Jumā is along.

Prince Achaḷo, on his way back home from Singaḷadeep (after his wedding with Umāde), has taken the princess of Mewāḍ in marriage. Why? Because the proud Umāde wouldn't touch his shoes, and he had to have that! What is the way out of this dilemma? Nobody knows that it is the *apsarā*-cursed necklace that is locking Umāde out from her desired destiny. Getting rid of the necklace (even if the anyone knew of the curse) would not solve the problem. The only way out of this mess is for the necklace to go on another woman's neck.

---

[6] Jeṭh: Jyeshṭha, a month of the Hindu lunar year; corresponding to May-June in the Gregorian calendar.

So be it! Jumā counsels patience, and sets up a second Pāṭan town right across the river from Achaḷo Khichi's own Pāṭan. Just like Achaḷo does, Umāde holds court in her own Pāṭan. Citizens of Achaḷo's Pāṭan also come and visit here. Umāde's beauty and her impeccable character are the talk of the town.

But, Achaḷo has been completely blinded by his Mewāḍi queen. His kingdom is being ravaged like a sparrow's nest. The Mewāḍi queen is a devastating influence on his kingdom. Achaḷo, under her sway, is neglecting to pursue his kingdom's affairs. All that the Mewāḍi queen cares about is her clothing and jewelry. The kingdom's resources are being spent on nothing but her grooming. Umāde, Achaḷo's other wife, is living just across the river, but Achaḷo is kept from visiting her. He is virtually a prisoner in his own palace.

No matter. Patience appears to be the only recourse. But, the cure for the cursed necklace also seems to be shaping up.

Bit by bit, the talk of Umāde's necklace reaches across the river. Just the verbal praise of the other-worldly necklace is enough to drive the Mewāḍi queen crazy. *The necklace bequeaths divine beauty to its wearer! O god, what if the king sees my rival Umāde with that necklace on her? That will be my complete undoing!*

Rumors claim that the necklace is enchanted. *Surely, its wearer will seduce the king away from me!*

It is, of course, Jumā who has started that rumor! It has the intended effect. The Mewāḍi queen sends the word, "I will pay anything for that necklace. Money, jewels, land . . . name your price!"

Jumā counters with: "No, none of that! You can have the necklace . . . if you send the king to spend one night here with my queen."

Says, "With pleasure!"

The Mewāḍi queen cajoles Achaḷo into going over for a night, "Poor woman has been waiting for six months now! The gossip is giving us a bad name. Just go for show, but don't even look at her. Promise you will not!"

Achaḷo gives his word.

The Mewāḍi queen gets the necklace, her greed is satisfied and she sends Achaḷo over to spend the night across the river. Achaḷo keeps his promise and sleeps on his side, facing away from Umāde in her bedroom.

Hour after hour goes by... and Umāde gets really nervous. *If he looks at me once, just once, I can wring all that poison out of his system. But he lays there like a rock, and the night will soon be over! Someone run and get my Jumā here.*

Jumā arrives. Umāde shows her the evidence of her continuing run of bad luck ... Achaḷo spending the night with his face turned away!

Jumā sits down with her *been*, tunes its strings and starts strumming. Jumā starts singing poignant *duha* couplets and the strings echo the sentiments.

Made a bargain, gave our necklace,

....

O cheating fortune! We thought we had a bargain.
We gave the necklace away,
But the thing we were to get in return never came.
What more can we say about our bad luck?

A sweet instrument like the *been*, an equally skilled player and the enigmatic words of the couplets ... they all combine to rouse the curiosity of a fully awake Achaḷo. Oh no! Sounds like these people have lost all their money, and have had to put their necklace in hock to make ends meet. He sits up and asks:

Which shop is it pawned to, who has lent you food?
I'll ride out there post-haste, to get that necklace back.

I will help you with whatever money you need to secure its release!

Jumā sings her reply to the accompaniment of her *been:*

Hocked it is to no one, we have begged for no food;
It's traded to a wench, in exchange for her husband.

The continuing riddle finds its mark and pierces his heart. Achaḷo springs from the bed and wants to know, "What are you saying? Answer me! What wench? Who has given her husband away for that necklace?"

Jumā relates the entire matter of the Mewāḍi queen and the necklace. Achaḷo is stung in every follicle of his body. He goes back to his Pāṭan and makes inquiries. Jumā's every word is proven true.

"Oho, Mewāḍi queen! You gave your loving husband away in exchange for a necklace! All my illusions are gone now. You desired that necklace so much, so go and enjoy it."

Mewāḍi, go back to Mewāḍ, take camels loaded with lace,
Umāde will get her Achaḷo, you keep your precious necklace!

The Mewāḍi queen is packed off to her parent's home. *Achaḷo* begins his life with Umāde.

Umāde just worships her friend Jumā for all that she did for her.

Chandaṇ-Meṇaṅgari

THE HEAVENLY throne of Hari – Lord Vishnu – is shaken up. Hari asks, "Will someone please tell me what is going on? What man has arisen on earth so virtuous to make my throne rattle like this?"

The answer comes: *Lord, a king named Chandaṇ rules over the kingdom of Loyāṇāgaḍh among the mountains of Ābu. It is the strength of his virtue that is shaking your throne.*[1]

So, Hari orders his *kood-kāvadiyā*[2] sidekick Nārad: "*Kood-kāvadiyā*! Go down to the Mortal world that is the Earth, and make King Chandaṇ stray from his straight and narrow path of virtue. Heap as much adversity on him as you can. But, be warned, nobody must die from this. Or else, be prepared for my wrath!"

With a sack on his shoulder, a stout staff in his hand and in the guise of a *bāmaṇ* (a brahmin), *kood-kāvadiyā* lands on Earth. He gets to the edge of a forest and asks, "Friends, whom do this land and this territory belong to?"

"O *bāmaṇ*! You are at the edge of King Chandaṇ's Loyāṇāgaḍh kingdom, and on the land of our Mā Meṇaṅgari."

"My cowherd friend! Which is the way to the town of Loyāṇāgaḍh?"

"Go left here for Dwārakā. Tḥe right will take you to Loyāṇāgaḍh."

---

[1] A recurring theme in Hindu mythology. A high degree of asceticism, especially when combined with extreme acts of penance, qualifies one for a boon of his or her choosing. The resulting power in unworthy hands may threaten the supremacy of gods.

[2] *Kood-kāvadiyā*: The servant who means well but employs deception and extreme measures in doing his master's bidding.

Kood-kāvadiyā skips the left and takes the right towards Loyāṇāgaḍh. Just inside the town line, he sees a *vāv*[3] (a step well).

He asks the women carrying water out of the *vāv*, "Who had this step well dug, and who built that beautiful ledge around it?"

The women tell him, "King Chandaṇ had the well dug, and our Meṇaṅgari Mā built the pearl ledge!"

Kood-kāvadiyā goes and stands at the top of the steps blocking their way. The women fetching water out of the *vāv* are trapped within, the ones trying to go in are stopped outside. Not a single woman tries to push past him.

This goes on for a while. The women are really concerned – *We have hungry little babies at home. We fed them last night and left them sleeping at home to come here to get water. We are really late now and will be taunted by our fathers-in-law and cursed by our husbands. . . .*

Still, not one of them crosses past the *bāmaṇ*; the ones inside stay inside, and those outside stay outside!

And, *kood-kāvadiyā* thinks to himself – *Just look at this! If an ordinary water-fetching housewife is so well behaved in this kingdom, what is King Chandaṇ himself like?*

He leaves the *vāv* and enters the town. What is the first thing he notices? Row upon row of big mansions. And women with snug-fitting gold chokers around their necks standing in the doorways. Necklaces hang down to their bosoms.

"O ladies! Which king's court is this?"

"Please come no closer, respected *bāmaṇ*! You are a person of superior birth, sir! These are not any palaces, only the humble houses of us untouchable sweepers and human refuse carriers of the Loyāṇā town."

What! If the lowly street scavengers are so well off in Chandaṇ's kingdom, how rich is the king himself?

---

[3] *Vāv*: A well in which a flight or flights of steps take one all the way to the water.

"My scavenger sisters! Where does King Chandaṇ live? How would we recognize him?"

Says, "Respected sir, see that white pennant flying there? In the center of the town there, you will see a group of people having their midday meal. You will find King Chandaṇ there – barefooted and bare headed, with a simple *potaḍi* (a loincloth) around his middle. Our king himself will be serving the food and waiting on the diners."

Kood-kāvadiyā indeed finds the king under that white pennant – a barefooted, wearing a simple *potaḍi* and bareheaded man – serving food to mendicants and visitors.

"Welcome, O Bhrammā![4]" King Chandaṇ greets *kood-kāvadiyā* with respect, "I am honored by your visit to my humble abode. Please cook[5] your meal and enjoy it!"

Kood-kāvadiyā replies, "O king! No way I am going to cook until you give me what I ask for."

Says, "O brahmin! I will give you much gold, will give you even the entire Loyāṇāgaḍh kingdom. Take all that home with you, but please have a meal in my house."

Says, "Oh no, King Chandaṇ! I don't want any gold, I don't want your kingdom. If you do not give me what I want, I am not cooking a meal in your courtyard!"

Says, "Bhrammā! Take my rocking elephants, or a whole row of horses home, but please cook a meal in my house!"

Kood-kāvadiyā says, "No! And, no again! King Chandaṇ, I ask for all four of you – you, your queen Meṇaṅgari, and your two princes Sāyar and Neer!"

Says, "O brahmin! My own self I can give you. Sons Sāyar and Neer are my flesh and blood that I can give. Consider those three as already given to you. Queen Meṇaṅgari is someone else's daughter

---

[4] Bhrammā: colloquial for brahmin, Brahmā or *Brahman*.

[5] Brahmins would not eat anything cooked or touched by a non-brahmin.

and not mine to give away. How can I pledge her without asking her?"

Says, "Then go and ask her!"

King Chandaṇ proceeds to the *rāṇeewās* (the queen's quarters).

Kichooḍ! *Kichooḍ*! *Kichooḍ*! Queen Meṇaṅgari is seated on a platform swing and her maids pull the string to make it go back and forth. The swing's chains and rings make the metal to metal rubbing noise. *Kichooḍ*! *Kichooḍ*!

King Chandaṇ walks in and stops in front of the queen, but it is evident that the king is nowhere near his usual bright and cheerful self. He is as down in his morale as he can get.

"My lord and master, I have never seen you so low! Have I done anything to cause this?"

Says, "My queen, don't say such things. How can you be at fault? If anything is at fault, it is our providence. This Bhrammā has shown up, and he has demanded the four of us as his *dakshiṇā* (donation) to him. I have already given what I can – myself and our two sons. But, you are mine only to hold in safe keeping; I have no right to give you away. I am here to learn what you think."

Says, "Lord, how can you think of me as not your own? I belong only with you. Let us go!"

The four present themselves, and *kood-kāvadiyā* says, "I want all four of you to change into a single garment each, and then to leave the kingdom."

Says, "Surely, Bhrammā! No problem at all."

Queen Meṇaṅgari goes to Balu Ghānchā's home. Says, "O Balu! Please take this money, and weave a big basket for me."

The basket is made and infant princes Sāyar and Neer are placed in it. King Chandaṇ puts the basket on his head and starts walking in his single *potaḍi* as asked. Chandaṇ leads and Meṇaṅgari follows. The citizens of Loyāṇāgaḍh watch.

How do the times change! This is the same king Chandaṇ who used to carry a curved dagger at his waist and walked with the slow and impressive gait of an elephant. One jolt of time, and he is now reduced to rolling in dirt!

And, this queen! She used to wear a whole pound of gold on her, and was so delicate of body that she was weighed in real pearls and flowers. One jolt of time, and now she will be fetching water for others' households!

The family of four gets going, but *kood-kāvadiyā* gets ahead of them. He tells the Sun: "O Lord of light, rain your heat down so hard on these four that the ground below their feet is hot enough to roast chickpeas."

And, the Sun burns red hot. The couple walks on with barefeet, without head cover and wearing single pieces of cloth. A disguised *kood-kāvadiyā* sits on the roadside with a water stand. When the king gets to him, *kood-kāvadiyā* calls out to him, "O King Chandaṇ, you must be thirsty. Have some water."

Says, "No, my man! I cannot touch even water before I am across the border."

With that, king Chandaṇ keeps walking, but *kood-kāvadiyā* quickly spills some water in the king's footsteps. Queen Meṇaṅgari, who has fallen behind, soon goes past the water stand.

Kood-kāvadiyā says to her, "Queen Meṇaṅgari! Here, have some water!"

Says, "No, brother, not even a drop of water for me before I leave this kingdom."

Says, "But look, king Chandaṇ did drink some!" *Kood-kāvadiyā* points at the wet ground where he had spilled water.

Says, "Brother! The king has me to answer to him, so he may drink your water. There is no one to answer to me; I cannot have that drink."

Kood-kāvadiyā wraps up the fake water stand, runs around the king and the queen, and gets to the Gaṅgā-Jamnā River ahead. He tells the river, "O Gaṅgā-Jamnā! I want you to split these four people up three separate ways."

Gaṅgā-Jamnā must comply with his wish because Lord Hari has decreed so. And soon, the king, the queen and the two princes arrive at her bank.

Chandaṇ Says, "My queen, these waters look too deep for you to cross by yourself. Let me take this basket across first and then I will come back for you."

Says, "As you wish."

* * *

King Chandaṇ gets the basket across the river, leaves it on the opposite bank and then starts to come back for the queen. When he is midstream, a big wave mysteriously appears in the river and drags him away.

Far downstream lies a city named Trambāvaṭi. The city's cremation ground is on the river's bank where a group of mourners stand watching a funeral pyre burn. The king of Trambāvaṭi has just died and that is his cremation in progress.

Hey, look, someone is drifting in the river! Some of the mourners jump in and pull King Chandaṇ's unconscious body out of the river. With some treatment and medicine, Chandaṇ recovers consciousness. *Looks like someone really down on his luck, poor fellow!* Chandaṇ keeps his identity to himself.

The Trambāvaṭi kingdom's tradition requires that when a king dies, all of its feudal lords are invited to select a new king from among them. A drunk female elephant chooses the new king by dropping a garland around his neck.

The subordinate lords are assembled and seated. *Get the female elephant intoxicated; put some oil and red vermillion on her head; offer her some incense and a coconut; now put a garland in her trunk and turn her loose. Whoever she garlands is the new king!*

The oil-and-vermillion-adorned female elephant starts going around the assembly of the lords with the garland held in her trunk. Each of them sticks his hopeful neck out but the elephant ignores them all. She walks out of the assembled group, goes to the roadside trash-dump where the tattered Chandaṇ sits, and puts the garland in his neck.

What? How can this be? The elephant selects that beggar! She must have a reason!

"O beggar, who are you really? Where were you born, where did you grow up, what is your town?"

Says, "I am King Chandaṇ of Loyāṇāgaḍh. I have left Loyāṇāgaḍh in the cause of truth and duty."

He goes on to tell the whole story. Everyone is convinced. King Chandaṇ is crowned the king of Trambāvaṭi.

* * *

What has happened to the basket left on the opposite bank of Gaṅgā-Jamnā?

The king of Morgaḍh is out on a hunt. The Hari-sent *kood-kāvadiyā* has assumed the form of a wild boar and is running; brandishing a spear, the king of Morgaḍh is in its pursuit. The boar leads the king to the bank of the river where the basket lies and then vanishes into thin air.

The king alights from his horse and looks into the basket to find the twin infants sucking their thumbs.

So! I am of ripe old age, but without a son, a pound of flesh I can call my own! And now, Gaṅgā-Jamnā has given me two instead of one!

The king takes both boys back to Morgaḍh with him and presents them to his queen. Even though her own womb has not produced a child, the queen's breasts fill with milk. The boys start suckling, one at her left breast and the other at the right.

* * *

And what happens to queen Meṇaṅgari?

Alone, she spends the night hiding in the clay quarry at the river's edge. At daybreak, a potter arrives with his donkey to dig clay from the quarry. The donkey sees something shining under the quarry overhang and starts braying. The potter looks under the ledge and finds this barely covered woman sitting there. Something glints on her left shoulder. The sun's rays and a birthmark on her shoulder combine and emit a blinding ray of light.

Says, "Who are you, woman? Are you a witch? A hag?"

Says, "O brother potter! I am not a witch, nor a hag. I am just a poor woman down on her luck!"

One look at her tells the potter she is a woman of high birth. He says, "Think of me as your brother, sister! Come home with me. I will take care of you."

But, as soon as the potter walks in with Meṇaṅgari, his wife yells her displeasure, "You lowly potter! You dare bring a second wife home while I'm still here!"

Says, "Shut your mouth, potter woman! May you live to someday see what your dirty mind is thinking now! For now, this is my adopted sister I've brought with me!"

The wife is convinced that she is not being deceived. She accepts Meṇaṅgari and says, "Here, sister, have this *rotlo*."[6]

Meṇaṅgari breaks off a quarter of the *rotlo* each for a dog and a cow, and eats the remaining half.

Then says, "O potter, my brother, please assign some work to me. I cannot accept your food for nothing."

Says, "As you wish, sister! This is what you can do for me. Take these freshly made *naḷiyā* – roof tiles – and put them out to dry. Bring them back when they are dry."

* * *

---

[6] *Roṭlo*: Coarse bread made from millet flour.

So, Meṇaṅgari puts the freshly moulded damp *naḷiyā* out in the sun, and stacks them up in shade when they dry. Twelve whole years go by like that.

One day, Lākhā Vaṇajhārā – the biggest of the itinerant traders – sets his camp in town. His caravan is loaded with diamonds, pearls, other gems and silk – tens of thousands of sacks in all. He has his four Mewāḍi queens along – and what are they like? Beautiful and virtuous enough to tell even the Sun to rise only after they wake up in the morning!

The tents are pitched, and the maids go to the potter's place to get the earthenware they need. There, they notice Meṇaṅgari's exquisite beauty roiling in mud.

The maids go back and talk to Lākhā: "O Lākhā! We saw this beautiful thing:

Her calves – round like a velaṇ *(a rolling pin);*
Her thighs – like the majestic pillars of a temple;
Eyes – shaded like pink coral;
Nose – the shape of an oil lamp's flame;
Eyebrows – like a bumblebee's wings;
Forehead – fair and shiny like the full moon;
Fingers – soft like green groundnut tubers;
Arms – slender like the branches of a flowering champā *tree;*
Hair – long and black like the Vāsuki serpent; and
Her belly – unwrinkled and shiny like the leaf of a peepaḷo[7] *tree.*

Lākhā Vaṇajhārā bursts out laughing: "Hā, hā, hā! How beautiful can a mud-sifter be?"

Says, "O Lākhā! She can make your four queens look like horse-dung cleaners!"

Lākhā thinks for a while. Then he saddles up a she camel and fills a saddle bag with diamonds, pearls and other precious stones. He instructs his people, "Break camp and get the caravan on the

---

[7] *Peepaḷo*: Peepal tree, *Ficus religiosa.*

road. I will catch up with you."

The caravan is soon on its way. Lākhā mounts the camel and arrives at the potter's door. He makes the camel sit, himself remains in the saddle and asks the potter to bring a flowerpot. He empties the valuable contents of his saddlebag into the pot.

Says, "What is this, Lākhā Vaṇajhārā?"

Says, "Brother! My wife is about to give birth. She needs your sister's help and I have come to fetch her. My caravan is in the middle of nowhere, and the baby is due almost any time now! I will bring her back later."

The potter tells Meṇaṅgari, "Sister, please go."

What is poor Meṇaṅgari to do?

When at someone's mercy, must
Eat what they throw you,
Go where they tell you.

Meṇaṅgari climbs onto the camel and departs with Lākhā Vaṇajhārā. Two miles, four miles, ten miles . . . but the caravan is nowhere to be seen.

"O brother Vaṇajhārā! Where is your caravan? How far are you going to take me?"

It is now that Lākhā Vaṇajhārā comes clean, "O beautiful woman! What caravan and what childbirth! I have brought you because I am madly taken by you. I want you to be my fifth and the principal queen, over the four Mewāḍi queens I already have!"

"O brother, your tongue is betraying you. Please don't say such things. You are to me like a brother born of my own mother! Please take me back to my potter brother."

Lākhā Vaṇajhārā stuffs Queen Meṇaṅgari into a sack, ties the sack across the camel's back and lets the camel run like the wind.

Please loosen the ropes a bit, O Vaṇajhārā!
It is time for my prayers to my Lord!

Please relax the bonds a little, O Vaṇajhārā!
Why put me on camel like some load!
Barefoot I'd graze your camels, O Vaṇajhārā!
Loosen these bonds so I can breathe.

Finally, Lākhā Vaṇajhārā catches up with his caravan. It has set camp on the outskirts of the town of Morgaḍh. Lākhā orders Meṇaṅgari to cook a meal. He then takes the food to serve to Khākhu – his father. Khākhu is an old man, blind in both eyes. Khākhu, the father, eats Meṇaṅgari's cooking and calls out:

"Lākhuḍā, my boy! All this time, the food cooked for me by your wives always had little stones and pits that ground on my teeth when I ate. I even have spitted their eyelashes out from the morsels in my mouth! But, today's cooking is entirely different. This seems to be cooked by someone really cultured. The only other time I had such a good meal was at King Chandaṇ's home in Loyāṇāgaḍh and that meal was cooked by Queen Meṇaṅgari!"

Lākhā is taken completely aback. *This blind old man can spill the beans on me! Hey, someone shut my father up in a gunny sack!*

Poor Khākhu the blind is also locked up in a sack.

It's night time. Hundreds of tents have been pitched. Bells around the necks of nine hundred thousand oxen ring and fill the night. In the huge tent in the middle, the heavy *dholiyo* bed is laid out in its ten million rupee glory. It is strung with thick silk ribbons to form the sleeping surface, its four legs are studded with gems. Lākhā sits on the *dholiyo* with four bottles of booze within easy reach.

Lākhā calls Meṇaṅgari over and says, "Hey beautiful! Why don't you drink some and serve me some!"

When Meṇaṅgari turns him down, Lākhā cracks a whip across her back. *Faḍāk*! *Faḍāk*! *Faḍāk*! Meṇaṅgari is bent double under that onslaught and responds. What does she say?

"O Vaṇajhārā! There was a time when I wore a whole pound of gold on me and was so delicate of body that I used to be weighed in pearls and flowers. One jolt of time, and here I am sitting in your tent!

"I had a husband like King Chandaṇ. One jolt of time and the rushing waters of Gaṅgā-Jamnā carried him off!

"One jolt of time and my two sons Sāyar and Neer got stranded on the far bank of that same river!

"Today, your lashes land on me, and carve their painful message on my body! My teeth were seen by nobody except the *dātaṇ* stick that I brushed them with. Only my husband got to see my open face. One jolt of time, and now your lust-filled eyes are on me!

"And, all this would not have happened had we not given the Loyāṇāgaḍh throne away in the cause of truth and duty!"

* * *

Those midnight sounds of the lashes and every word of Meṇaṅgari's wailing emanating from somewhere in Lākhā Vaṇajhārā's camp are clearly heard by two persons. They are assigned the guard duty for that side of the town for the night. Lākhā Vaṇajhārā is to pay a levy of 1,25,000 rupees for the privilege of camping there and the state of Morgaḍh is providing these guards for the camp's security.

But, those two pairs of ears really perk up when they hear the part about "my two sons Sāyar and Neer" in the woman's wailing.

The two men look at each other. One says, "Sāyar!"

Says, "Yes, Neer!"

Says, "Do you think there is another pair of brothers named Sāyar and Neer besides us on this earth?"

Says, "Brother, our father may know better, but I haven't heard of any other Sāyar–Neer!"

Says, "And, that sounds like a woman's wailing."

Says, "Yes, brother mine! I too get some strange vibrations from that voice."

Says, "Yes, she definitely sounds like a mother of two sons like us!"

Says, "Brother, we must get to the bottom of this. Let us steal Lākhā Vaṇajhārā's *dholiyo*!"

And so, the two grown up princes Sāyar and Neer proceed to steal that ten-million-rupee *dholiyo* – the one with silk laces and diamonds the size of cotton bolls on every leg.

"My *dholiyo* is stolen" – Lākhā sends a complaint to the king of Morgaḍh. The king wants to know who the assigned guards were. He is told, the princes Sāyar and Neer were the night guards.

Says, "Get the princes here."

The two princes ride in. They admit to the theft.

Says, "Why did you do it?"

Say, "Father, we want to know one thing first. Is there another Sāyar–Neer pair of brothers on this 500 million strong earth?"

Says, "If there is, I don't know of them."

Say, "Then please tell us, father! Were we born to you or brought to you?"

The king's heart misses a beat. Surely someone that knows has told them.

Says, "Boys, you came to us but not born from my queen's womb. I found you in a basket on the bank of Gaṅgā-Jamnā.

Say, "Who are our real parents?"

Says, "Your father is King Chandaṇ of Loyāṇāgaḍh, who is now the king of Trambāvaṭi."

The two get on their horses and leave without even stopping to brush their teeth with *dātaṇ*. They arrive in Trambāvaṭi, grab King Chandaṇ's arm and stand him up.

Say, "Come on, saddle up your horse!"

Says, "But where am I going?"

Say, "We want you to identify our mother!" And, they tell him what is going on.

Says, "Young men, unsaddle your horses. Come, have some milk!"

Say, "We have sworn not to even brush our teeth until our mother is identified."

King Chandaṇ accompanies them to Morgaḍh. They all go and liberate Meṇaṅgari from Lākhā Vaṇajhārā's tent. But identifying her is a problem. She refuses to uncover her face to anyone.

King Chandaṇ suggests a way. "Boys, your mother has a lotus-shaped birthmark on her left shoulder. When sun's rays fall on it, the lotus reflects the rays in a unique way. That is her only sure-fire identification. Otherwise, there are too many people with similar looks in this world."

Say, "So what do we do?"

Says, "Have a window cut into her tent's wall high up. When the sun is appropriately high, let this woman sit down for a bath with her shoulders bare. If the reflected ray comes out, you know she is your mother Meṇaṅgari."

Here, Meṇaṅgari trembles with fear. *These kings seem to be working in collusion. What if one of them lays his hands on me?"*

Meṇaṅgari sits down for her bath covered with a single cloth. The high window lets the sun shine on her left shoulder and the reflection settles the issue. Her eyes are still lowered to the ground when King Chandaṇ goes in and gently holds her arm. A shocked Meṇaṅgari looks up to hear Chandaṇ say, "Don't be scared. It's me, Chandaṇ! And these are our Sāyar–Neer!"

The four become one, tears gush from their eyes.

Kood-kāvadiyā chooses that moment to appear there.

Says, "Meṇaṅgari! Ask me for anything you want. I am very pleased with you."

Meṇaṅgari says, "All I ask is that you don't show your pleasure to anyone the way you did to me!"

Kood-kāvadiyā says, "I return your kingdom back to you."

Sāyar–Neer say, "Father! We will come and see you. But, the king of Morgaḍh has been a father to us. We will not leave him."

Chandaṇ says, "Absolutely right, my boys! You must not leave him. Be good sons, take care of him in life, and consign him to fire when he dies!"

Sāyar–Neer say, "Father! Please permit us to whip Lākhā Vaṇajhārā."

Says, "Listen, boys! He is the one who brought your mother here, and made it possible for the four of us to reunite. We should feel grateful. In your place, I would get the state to forego the rupees 1,25,000 Lākhā Vaṇajhārā owes to Morgaḍh."

Lākhā Vaṇajhārā is thanked. His debt to the state is forgiven.

All return to Loyāṇāgaḍh. The men go and affectionately hug Bālu Ghānchā who had woven the basket that once carried the young princes. Bālu uses a *dātaṇ* for the first time in all these years. King Chandaṇ and Bālu Ghānchā sit down and share a meal.

Khāniyo

Two *umrāos* (noblemen) from Persia show up at the court of Dalli's[1] *pādshāh*[2] one day. The *pādshāh* treats them with all appropriate honors, and then asks: "Now tell us the purpose of your visit."

One *umrāo* replies, "*Jahāṅpanāh!*[3] We have brought these two gold statuettes, and have a problem for you to solve. Which of these two is the genuine and which is fake? Then, after you identify them properly, we have four other questions that we need answers for. Those questions are:

"Who is noble of birth, but of despicable conduct?"
"Who is low of birth, but noble of deed?"
"Who are the dogs of the royal court?"
"Who is the ass in the assembly?"

"We have gone around country after country with these gold statuettes and the four questions. So far, nobody has been able to provide the explanations. Every king has admitted his defeat in writing. Now we need from you either the correct explanations or the written admission of defeat."

Says, "Let me see those statuettes!"

Says, "Here you go, Sire!"

The *pādshāh* looks the statuettes over closely and is perplexed. The two statuettes seem identical in every aspect – appearance,

---

[1] Dalli: Delhi.

[2] *Pādshāh*: Emperor, *bādshāh*.

[3] *Jahāṅpanāh*: literally "the caretaker of the world", a salutations used for Muslim kings and emperors.

color, weight and purity – and he can detect not a sesame seed's worth of difference between the two. He looks and looks at them from all sides but finds no clue to which of them could be the genuine one and which is the fake.

The *pādshāh* sends the statuettes around to the learned – the *kājis* and the *pundits*; to the wordsmiths – the poets and the lyricists; to the businessmen – the traders and the merchants – present in his court. The statuettes pass from hand to hand, all around the court, but nobody can identify the original from the fake.

Then, the Persian *umrāos* say, "If that's that, *Jahāṅpanāh*, please write the admission of defeat."

The *pādshāh*'s face falls from his usual high of sixteen degrees to the low of one. *Oh no, we are going to lose this contest of intelligence to the King of Persia, and lose our face in front of the entire world!* The learned *kājis*' and *pundits*' faces hang down in shame. The big-name poets look humbled. They all look so pale that if you cut somebody, not a drop of blood will come out!

The Persian nobles rub it in, "*Jahāṅpanāh*, please document Dalli's defeat today."

The *pādshāh* says, "Patience, friends! Too bad my learned courtiers could not figure it out. But, it is quite possible that one of my citizens will. So, take these gold statuettes in a procession around the city of Dalli. Let our honored Persian guests ride atop an elephant and show the statuettes in every street of Dalli."

The visiting *umrāos* laugh within themselves at the *pādshāh*'s words. Even the courtiers believe that the collected wisdom within the court represented the boundaries of Dalli's intelligence. Isn't the *pādshāh* inviting more ridicule by suggesting that someone on the streets of Dalli can be wiser and smarter than the elite of the court!

The procession goes out the next day. The two Persian noblemen are seated in a howdah atop an elephant. An open *myānā* (palanquin) displays the two statuettes, and a man carries a platter with a *pān-beeduṅ* – a betel leaf stuffed with powdered betel nut, lime and *kāthā*[4] powder.

The man with the platter repeats an announcement on every road and every street: "Hear me, O citizens of Dalli! We need to know which of these statuettes is genuine and which is fake. Whoever has the answer can grab the *beeduṅ* (formally accept the challenge) and eat it. Someone take the challenge, provide the answer. Someone step up, protect the reputation of our Dalli city and preserve the honor of our Emperor!"

Listening to those words, Hemāshā and Motishā Sheth, the merchants, come out; so do Bhogaḷ Bhaṭṭ and Khokhalā Pandyā, the *bāmaṇs*. Miyāṅ Pepadeekhān and Hāṇḍeekhān are not far behind. All examine the statuettes. They look and look, and finally retreat to their houses – beaten and embarrassed. None is able to make out the real from the fake.

Then the procession arrives in *kājiwāḍā* where the *kājis* (the Islamic judges) live. The platter holder makes his announcement right outside the residence of the chief *kāji*'s house, "Is there anyone here who can identify the real statuette from the fake? If there is, come and grab this *pān*!"

A young boy hears the challenge and steps out of the chief *kāji*'s house. His name is Khāniyo. Khāniyo is a poor young man and looks unable even to drive a fly from his face. He steps into the street and says, "Stop, let me look at those little statuettes."

Everyone bursts out laughing. Nobody else dares to, but this ragtag, half-starved Khāniyo has the bravado to look at the statuettes! *No matter. Here in Dalli, every mustard seed counts as the same. So, have at it, Khāniyo! Don't ever say that you did not get your chance.*

Khāniyo holds the statuettes, looks at them every which way, and says, "May I take these inside the house for a while?"

---

[4] *Kāthā*: Powdered *Areca catechu.*

Says, "Yes, go ahead."

Khāniyo takes the statuettes inside the *kāji*'s house. A good look reveals tiny holes in both statuettes' each ear.

Khāniyo takes a piece of thin wire and inserts it in one statuette's ear. When pushed deep enough, the wire comes out of the other ear.

Okay! Now let me try the other statuette.

He sticks the wire into the ear of the second statuette. He keeps pushing it, and pushing, and pushing. The wire does not emerge from the other side but seems to go into the statuette's stomach.

A big smile spreads on Khāniyo's face. He comes out of the house, snatches the *pān* from the platter and puts it in his mouth.

"No! Stop! Stop! This is the *pādshāh*'s challenge *pān*, Khāniyo! He will run you through the oil mill for playing jokes with it, you idiot!"

While people are trying to stop him, Khāniyo calmly chews the *pān* and swallows it. His lips turn red from the betel juice.

"What have you done, Khāniyo! This is terrible!"

Says, "Terrible, ferrible! Let's go see *pādshāh salāmat*, and let me give him the true-fake answer."

The procession turns around. Khāniyo leads; a huge mob follows him; crowds are so big, there is no room to walk. The streets are filled with just one talk: "The *kāji*'s idiot servant Khāniyo has done the unthinkable. The *pādshāh* is going to have the poor slob's head for this!"

Back in the court, the platter holder announces that the challenge *pān* has been eaten. The *pādshāh* is elated. But, when the *kāji* learns that it is his servant Khāniyo who has taken the challenge, he scratches his beard.

The *pādshāh* asks: "W ell, *kāji*! We didn't know your Khāniyo was that smart and knowledgeable?"

Kāji's eyes are downcast and his eyelashes are practically digging into the ground in front of him! *Khāniyo doesn't have the smartness to break a dry twig into two; how could he do something this stupid?*

"Bring Khāniyo in!"

Khāniyo enters the royal court. But, the moment he steps in, his countenance changes completely. The face that always has flies buzzing around it is all of a sudden shining bright. He wasn't worth the rags he wore, but has now turned into something more valuable than gems. Fearless, he stands in the *pādshāh*'s court today. His master, the *kāji* has turned extremely pale. *God almighty! This Khāniyo is going to be my undoing!*

Pādshāh asks, "Khāniyo, did you eat the challenge *pān*?"

Says, "Yes, *Jahāṅpanāh.*"

Says, "Did you understand what the *pān* was for when you grabbed it?"

Says, "Yes, *Jahāṅpanāh.* It was to challenge the eater to identify the genuine and the fake statuettes."

Says, "Then tell me. Which is the real and which is the fake?"

Says, "*Jahāṅpanāh*, this is the genuine one." Khāniyo puts his hand on one of the statuettes.

The *pādshāh* looks questioningly at the Persian *umrāos*.

The Persian noblemen are flabbergasted. "He is right." Both nod their approval.

"And, Sire, this is the fake." Khāniyo points to the other statuette.

The *pādshāh* looks at the *umrāos* again. They nod again.

The whole court is in a state of shock!

But that is not acceptable. What if Khāniyo is just guessing and happens to guess right!

Says, "Khāniyo! You must tell us how you figured the genuine from the fake!"

"Sure thing, *Jahāṅpanāh*!" Khāniyo pulls the piece of wire from his pocket.

What is the wire for? Is Khāniyo just putting up a show! The *pādshāh*'s courtiers do not understand what is going on, but the Persian *umrāos* immediately realize that Khāniyo has indeed performed the real test on the statuettes.

Khāniyo picks up the fake statuette, inserts the wire in its one ear and shows it come out of the other ear. He holds it up for the *pādshāh*, the Persian *umrāos* and the entire court to see. Then he says, "*Jahāṅpanāh*! do you see what makes this one the fake? The person that hears something sensible, lets it in one ear, does not keep it to himself, and lets it out immediately . . . now, that person is a fake. That is not a real, a genuine person, no matter how good looking, well-clothed, bejeweled and otherwise properly behaved he might be."

Now, Khāniyo picks up the second statuette. He inserts the wire in one ear and pushes it in. An arm's length of wire goes in but does not come out from the other ear. Where all that wire went is anybody's guess.

Says, "See for yourself, *Jahāṅpanāh*! This is the sign of a genuine person. Anything this person hears does not get out but stays with him. Where? Down in his stomach. No gossip about others gets passed on, it gets buried within. This statuette is like the other in every way – in facial looks, in attire, in material, in workmanship . . . exactly identical. But, the difference is what you just saw. All people look alike. There is no outwardly difference. But, those that keep gossip to themselves are the genuine ones; and those that pass things on the moment they hear them are the fakes."

The *pādshāh* looks at the two Persian *umrāos*. The *umrāos* say, "Correct answer, Sire! We salute the solver. All our roaming has borne fruit. The world has found a wise man. Dalli city has much to be proud of!"

"I, too, salute you, Khāniyo!" The *pādshāh* rises from his throne, walks to the standing Khāniyo, pats him on the back and grabs his arm. Then he guides him back to the throne and gives him the seat of honor at his right.

The court rings with cries of "Bravo! Bravo! Well done, Khāniyo!" And the *kāji* that Khāniyo works for sheds tears of joy, "My Khāniyo!"

"Send for silken clothes!"

Clothes are brought in.

"A sword!"

A sword arrives.

The *pādshāh* ceremonially presents Khāniyo with the clothing and sword befitting an honored courtier. He also names him Khānkhānān (Lord among the Lords!).

The Persian *umrāos* say, "Now, Sire, we need the answers to the other four questions:

"Who is noble of birth, but of despicable conduct?"
"Who is low of birth, but noble of deed?"
"Who are the dogs of the royal court?"
"Who is the ass in the assembly?"

The *pādshāh* looks at Khāniyo, "My *khānkhānān*, shouldn't you answer these questions as well?"

Khāniyo says, "I will answer these questions, *Jahāṅpanāh*. But, not here."

Says, "Where then?"

Says, "I will answer them in the court of the Shah of Persia. But, only with the conditions that you pronounce me as your *shejādā*,[5] send me there with all the appropriate pomp and staff, accompanied by the standards and fanfare; I also need the permission to spend all the money I choose to."

Says, "Granted!"

* * *

[5] *Shejādā*: *Shāhzādā*, prince.

Shejādā Khānkhānān arrives on the outskirts of the capital of Persia one evening. Along is his entourage of some of Dalli's top *ameers*, and a whole caravan loaded with tents, palanquins and *myānās*, gems and silks, sweets and nuts, the choicest liquors and wines. *Shejādā* issues orders, "Listen everybody! We have to set up a whole tent city of our own here overnight. By morning, we need to be ready with a feast of food and drink, perfumes and oils, shawls and scarves, sashes and robes, diamond and pearl necklaces, silken turbans and all the finery! We are setting up a court to meet here tomorrow."

Morning comes. The Shah of Persia himself arrives with a procession and much fanfare. The whole capital city is in awe of this extremely wise and scholarly man from Dalli arriving here. The two *umrāo*'s emissaries have already spoken highly of the man that correctly solved the riddle of the statuettes. Now he is here in person to answer the four questions sets the city abuzz with great excitement and joy.

The procession approaches the camp . . . and almost faints with surprise. *Yā Allah! Wonder of wonders! This man comes to our kingdom as a guest . . . and sets up a realm of his own!*

Shejādā Khānkhānān comes out to receive the Shah of Persia and escorts him to the main *shāmiyānā* (the big tent). One look shows that an assembly room is already set up. There are assigned seats ready for every *umrāo* and *ameer*, bureaucrat and diplomat – all arranged by their court rankings! The food and drink, sweets specially brought from Dalli, carafes of sherbets and wine are all laid out. The illusion of the Shah of Persia being on a state visit to Dalli, and not the other way around, is complete!

The feast is done, and the court convenes. Gold and silver platters laden with gift articles start arriving. Shejādā Khānkhānān hands out gifts to all Persian dignitaries. Necklaces, gold chains, turbans, shawls, daggers of various kinds – something or the other is presented to each guest.

The Persians are dazzled and practically blinded by this one event.

Then, Shejādā Khānkhānān secures a promise from the Shah; *the Shah and his entourage are to have one meal a day – not only today, but every day – with us; in return, we will join the Shah at his palace for the other meal each day.*

Such mutual treats become a daily routine. Khānkhānān, the Prince of Dalli, continues to scatter his gifts and awards freely and generously. Persian *ameers* and *umrāos* flock to his court to receive his largesse. Not one of them holds back from this. Their noble tongues don't tire of singing the Shejādā's praises.

A month goes by like that, and the matter of answering the four questions is forgotten. The partying and razzle-dazzle are on everyone's mind. One day, Shejādā Khānkhānān receives the word that the Persian Vajeer's[6] exquisitely beautiful, incredibly intelligent and talented daughter desires to marry him!

Asks, "Is she in love with me?"

Says, "Yes, she is taken by your looks, virtues, knowledge and wisdom!"

Says, "Then I agree."

The *shejādā* and the *vajeer*'s daughter wed with great pomp and ceremony, and begin their life together. The two love each other very much.

The *shejādā*'s investigators have been going around Persia from day one. His quest for certain information has continued non-stop. One day, an informant comes and tells him of this courtesan who is the Shah's special favorite. She has a greater sway over everyone than the Shah does himself.

The informant says, "Shejādā, you must meet her."

On the other hand, the courtesan has heard much about Dalli's

---

6 *Vajeer*: *Vizier*, chief minister.

shejādā. How wise must he be to see through the statuettes' secret! Certainly worth meeting him just for that! And, he has such a big heart on top of that! He has come here to answer the four questions but is not doing anything about it! Surely there is a lot more there than meets the eye, muses the courtesan. She has watched him in procession from her balcony once.

Then, the *shejādā* requests permission to call on her! She replies, "Fortune must be smiling on me. It will be my pleasure to receive you!"

The two intelligent people meet, and decide to meet regularly. A deep relationship develops between the two. The *shejādā* visits her every day without fail.

He has now settled into a daily routine. He entertains the *ameer*s and the *umrāo*s, and showers them with gifts; lives his married life with the *vajeer*'s daughter; meets with the Shah's favorite courtesan every day, and is trying to put the pieces of a scheme together in his mind. Another thing he does is to cultivate a friendship with the Shah's young son. Soon, he has the boy eating out of his palms, and not wanting to separate from him.

One day, he goes to see the courtesan. Suddenly, for no reason, without saying a word, he gets angry. His eyes turn red; he pulls out a lash and swings it at her. *Fud*! *fud*! *fud*! He lands three hard blows on the courtesan's back, turns around and leaves without opening his mouth.

The courtesan just stands there without saying a word herself. The *shejādā* stops visiting her after that.

She tries to figure out why he would do that. Her pride is hurt but she decides to swallow it. *Something must have happened to enrage him; otherwise, a smart man like him wouldn't behave so. Whatever! Let it go for now, and just sit tight. The mystery will be solved some day.*

After letting two more months pass, the *shejādā* calls his *begum* – the *vajeer*'s daughter – over for a talk. "I need your help with something."

Says, "What?"

Says, "I am in a very tight situation. It is bad enough to make me resort to poison . . ."

Says, "Wait! What is going on?"

Says, "The problem is, Dalli has not sent me my expense money. I have sent messengers, but there's been no response from Dalli. I owe serious money, and cannot put my creditors off anymore!"

The *vajeer*'s daughter grimaces like she has swallowed castor oil.

Says, "What can I possibly do about it?"

Says, "Nobody else can help the way you can. Your father is the *vajeer* of Persia. All you have to do is to tell him that we are in trouble. He is sure to lend me the money immediately!"

The *begum* snaps even before the *shejādā* has finished: "My father would lend you the money? You use money like water, hand out expensive gifts every day; you want to hear people's praises and go to crazy lengths to get them . . . is all that my father's problem? No way am I going to ask him to lend you anything!"

Says, "Would you rather have me swallow poison?"

Says, "You swallow poison? Hah! Don't try to scare me! If you knew this time would come, why didn't you do something about it when you could? After all, you are the one that likes to throw money up into the air every day!"

Says, "All right! All right! Say no more for pity's sake, or the whole town will know. So be it if you are not going to ask your father. I will get the money somehow."

He leaves the *begum* and goes out.

After letting another week pass, he leaves for a hunt one afternoon. He takes the young prince of Persia along, but makes sure that no one knows that. He proceeds to his hunting lodge in the mountains away from the city. There, he eats a hearty meal, has the young prince also eat and both have a good time for a while. Then he gets his men to play with the prince and keep him occupied. He gives some instructions to his people and returns to the city alone. Disguising himself, he goes to a butcher's house.

Says, "Hey man, will you slaughter a fresh sheep for me? I will pay you well."

Says, "Sure!"

He carefully wraps the freshly slaughtered sheep in cloth, loads it on his horse and gallops the horse back to sneak into his tent city after dark. He starts digging a hole in the ground conspicuously enough for his *begum* to notice it. The slaughtered sheep lies on the ground, wrapped in cloth but with its eyes visible. Blood is oozing from the cloth bundle.

The *begum* comes and is aghast at the sight of all that blood, the bundle and the freshly dug hole in the ground.

Out of breath, she says, "*Khāvind*,[7] what is this?"

Says, "*Shhh*! Don't say anything. I have killed the Shah's little prince! Nobody must find out."

Says, "O my God! But why?"

Says, "To get the jewelry he wore. We are broke right now. Dalli has not sent me money. I asked for your help and you refused. What was I to do? I saw all that jewelry on the boy, and I lost my mind. I killed him and now need to bury him someplace. And, you need to keep quiet about this."

Says, "What? Stay quiet? You do the terrible deed, and I need to stay quiet, you idiot? I cannot believe you would sink this low!"

Says, "Oh no. I beg of you. Please be quiet!"

Says, "Hell no! *Nimakharām*![8] Betrayer of your benefactor! Killer! I will get you for this!" And the *vajeer*'s daughter starts screaming, "Someone help! He has killed our prince . . . for his jewelry! My

---

[7] *Khāvind*: Husband.

[8] *Nimakharām*: Betrayer of someone whose salt (food) one ate.

stupid husband has done this! Someone help!"

She runs screaming through the city streets and reaches her father's house. Meanwhile, Shejādā Khānkhānān dumps the sheep-bundle in the hole and fills it with dirt.

The news spreads through the city like wild fire and pandemonium breaks loose: *Catch that son of a bitch! Kill the black-faced villain! Grab him and torture him to death!*

The *vajeer* runs to the Shah of Persia. The evening assembly is in progress with all the *ameers* and *umrāos* in attendance. "The prince of Persia has been killed!"

The Shah asks: "What? Who did it?"

Says, "The Shejādā from Dalli!"

Says, "Impossible!"

Says, "Sire, my daughter saw it with her own eyes, and ran from there!"

Call her here!

The woman arrives and tells all in detail: he was flat broke, did this black deed for money and has buried the dead body.

Says, "Anyone here?"

Says, "Not one but twenty-one to do your bidding, Sire!"

Says, "Go, grab that *shejādā* of Dalli."

The order causes a flurry of activity. A whole army of soldiers takes off. They are followed by the courtiers, the *ameers* and *umrāos*. The Dalli camp is surrounded. The *shejādā* has instructed all his people, "Beware! Nobody is to say a word! Just watch whatever transpires." So, the Dalli contingent offers no resistance.

The Persian army arrests Shejādā Khānkhānān, trusses him up like an animal. The Shah's orders say, "I don't want to see the face of that killer. Take him outside the city in the morning and behead him in presence of the citizenry."

The day breaks. The same *ameers* and *umrāos* that enjoyed the Dalli camp festivities and accepted gifts from the *shejādā*, are now spitting at him. *You low life! So this is what you really were! You fooled us blind for four months, but the deceit has finally caught up with you!*

The *shejādā* keeps his head down and quietly listens to all that is being said. The unspeakable epithets fall on his ears. *No sweat! Nothing to worry about. This is exactly what I was expecting!*

And then they start out for the execution site! Guards in front, guards behind, and the tattered *shejādā* is in the middle. The streets are mobbed, crowds fill all available space. When a good spectacle is to be had, nobody needs an invitation!

The *ḍhol* drums play a martial *boongiyo* beat, the crowd is so thick that hearts grind against hearts. The *ameers* and *umrāos* poke the *shejādā* with their long sticks, and announce to the crowd, "We knew from the beginning that there was something wrong, that this man sounded hollow, that he was a fake, a cheat! We knew it! Yes, we knew that his trickery will be exposed one day."

When the rowdy procession nears the Shah's favorite courtesan's house, the noise reaches her ears. She looks out from her balcony and sees the musket-carrying guards ahead, more of them behind, and a tattered young man – his head shaven and coated with white lime, his face blackened with tar – in the middle. People are spitting at him, stabbing him with sticks and hurling curses at him.

The courtesan asks her maids, "Girls! What is going on here?"

Say, "Mistress, haven't you heard? That man is the *shejādā* from Dalli. They are going to cut his head off. The swine killed our prince!"

Says, "What are you talking about? Killed him for what?"

Say, "For his jewelry, my mistress!"

Says, "That cannot be right!" *Kaṭ, kaṭ, kaṭ* . . . the courtesan quickly goes down the steps of her mansion and stands in the middle of the street. When the procession reaches her, she raises her hand.

The Shah's favorite courtesan! Her word carries more weight than the Shah's! The procession comes to a halt.

The courtesan tells the commander in charge: "Stay right there. Don't advance even a step!"

Says, "But, honored lady! We are only following His Majesty the Shah's orders."

Says, "Doesn't matter, I order you to stay right there!"

True. Her orders override even the Shah's orders! She goes on, "Go, inform His Majesty of this, and convey my personal request that he grace us with his presence here post-haste!"

The Shah arrives. He is fuming. "Why have you stopped them?"

Says, "If you would bear with me for a moment, Sire. What crime has this man committed?"

Says, "He murdered my prince."

Says, "Shouldn't we be burying the prince first before beheading his killer? Why don't we keep him in prison so that he doesn't escape? Then decide what comes first: mourning the death or punishing the killer? Does anyone even know where the prince's body is?"

The Shah calms down immediately. "You are right. Why didn't anyone think of that? Someone go and find my son's body! Where is it?"

Minions run to find the prince's body. But, how were they going to find it? There was no dead body to find!

But, he supposedly did bury the body somewhere. The vajeer's *daughter saw him do so; she must know where it is. Call* vajeer's *daughter here!*

The woman arrives and triumphantly points to the place. "That is where he buried it."

Says, "Dig there."

They dig, and find . . . *O Allah! That is not a human body; that is a sheep!*

If you had cut the *vajeer*'s daughter at that moment, she would not have bled a drop!

Then where is the prince? Where is he buried? Where was he killed? Is there a witness? Where is the jewelry?

A lot of running around and pointless toiling ensues. One asks another, and he asks yet another. Nobody knows the truth. Some say they saw the prince at such and such a place the day before. Another points to a different place.

The Shah does not know what to do. He goes back and consults the wise courtesan. She says, "Have you asked the presumed criminal? Why hasn't anyone bothered to do that?"

Says, "But, of course! Again, you are absolutely right."

The *shejādā* of Dalli is sitting in the prison, looking worn out and in bad shape. Terrible in appearance, but smiling inside! He is asked, "Where is our prince?"

Says, "I have this hunting lodge in the mountains at such and such place. He is fine and having fun there. Go, check."

They bring the young prince back. Seeing him alive and well poses a problem: people don't know whether to laugh or cry! Everyone's faces are dark with shame.

The courtesan says, "*Jahāṅpanāh*, isn't it time you released that man from prison, brought him back to the court and apologized for his ordeal? If not, the Dalli *pādshāh* can be a formidable enemy! Besides, why don't you ask him what all this mystery is about?"

The Shah's court is filled to capacity. The courtesan sits behind a net curtain. The *pādshāh*'s *begums* are also seated in a veiled off area. The *ameers* and *umrāos*, officers and commanders, bureaucrats and diplomats are all in their places and can hardly contain their impatience. They are all eager to hear the Dalli *shejādā*'s explanations.

Then, the *shejādā* from Dalli rises and says:

"Great Shah of Persia! I came here four months ago to accomplish something. I am happy to declare that my work is now complete. I had come to answer your four questions, and my entire time here was given to looking for those answers. Everything I did here was geared towards that one task. I wanted to provide the correct answers. But more than that, I wanted you to actually see the answers. Your questions were:

"Who is noble of birth, but of despicable conduct?
"Who is low of birth, but noble of deed?
"Who are the dogs of the royal court?
"Who is the ass in the assembly?"

"The answers are all present here in front of your very eyes!"

"Let me take the questions one at a time. The first:

'Who is noble of birth, but of despicable conduct?'

"Behold the answer yourself, *Jahāṅpanāh*! Take my own *begum* – the daughter of a *vajeer*, born in a cultured, noble family. She said she was marrying me for love. She was completely aware of my practice of spending money every day as if it were water. Not once did she ask me if I knew what I was doing! But, when I told her that my money had run out, that Dalli had not sent my spending allowance, that the lenders were pressing to collect, that the only option I had was to end my life, that she could tell her father to tide me over with a loan, do you know what her reaction was? She chastized me: *Why did I spend money like it was going out of style? Had anyone told me to light up the skies of this foreign land with my largess?*

"Even that can be forgiven. But, when I tell her I had murdered the little prince, what does she do? She does not pause for a moment to think about it; she does not wait to see the prince's dead body; she does not ask me what I have done with the prince's jewelry. She just runs through the town shamelessly, screaming bloody murder! Without giving it a second thought she accuses her husband of vile crimes, and does not lift a finger to save him from death by beheading.

"So, *pādshāh salāmat* of all Persia! I submit that she is an example of a good pedigree, but a bad person in her conduct! Does that answer the first question – *who is noble of birth, but of despicable conduct?*"

"Yes, it does." The Shah of Persia reluctantly admits, and then hangs his head down.

The *shejādā* of Dalli presses on.

"Now, Sire, the second question was:

Who is low of birth, but noble of deed?

"The answer is this favorite courtesan of yours. When I first arrived, I heard much praise of her intellect and wisdom. I cultivated a relationship with her. One day, without a cause, without a word, I just pulled out a lash and swung it at her. *Fud! fud! fud!* My lashes landed on her delicate body; then I just turned around and left. I never saw her face again. What did she do about it? She just swallowed the insult and did nothing. Having known me for some time, she probably felt that this guest from Dalli was neither stupid nor a sadistic animal. *There must be a hidden reason for his inexplicable behavior, and that reason will be revealed someday* is what she probably decided and held her cool. Not only that, probably feeling the same way today, she actually stopped the procession that was taking me to my beheading.

"And, *Jahāṅpanāh*! When you and your wise *kājis* – the keepers of law and order, the oceans of wisdom – erred really big, it was this same courtesan that reminded you that burial of the dead should claim a greater priority! Had she not made that one suggestion that altered the scenario completely, you would have taken my head and would be regretting that with big tears right now.

"*Jahāṅpanāh*! This woman is a courtesan, considered low of birth and by profession. Yet, she has shown herself to be noble of thoughts and deeds. Does this adequately answer your second question, Sire?"

"Yes, it does, my friend!"

The court echoes with calls of "Bravo! Awesome!"

"*Jahāṅpanāh*, we have two more questions to go. Your third question was:

Who are the dogs of the royal court?

"Look around you, Sire! Look at the faces of all these people sitting here – the *khāns*, the *umrāos*, the *kājis*, and others. For four whole months now, these people have come to my place every single day, have eaten my food, have drunk my wine, have accepted expensive gifts from me and praised me to the heavens. But what happened this morning? My guilt is not even proven, and these same people spat on me, jabbed me with sticks, and said all manner of bad things about me. Not one of them remembered the favors I had done, or even sympathized with me. Every single one of them expressed his overflowing joy at my misfortune, and claimed he had seen through me right from the beginning."

"Now, *Jahāṅpanāh*, is that not an apt description of *dogs of the royal court*'?"

"It is. It most certainly is!" The Shah's was the lone voice to say that. The rest just sat with their faces pointing to the ground.

"So now, *Jahāṅpanāh*, that leaves but one question to answer! And that is:

Who is the ass in the assembly?

"If I had a choice, I would not answer this question. But, I have pledged to answer all four questions, therefore I must. I beg a thousand pardons for this insolence, Sire!

"The Ruler of all Persia breaks bread from one platter with a man for four months and has the feel of every nerve of this person's body. Then, without a thought, without asking him a question, and relying simply on the word of a foolish woman, he orders his guest's beheading. I call that person, The Shah of Persia, to be *the ass in the assembly*. I sincerely regret this insolence, and bow my head to you, *Jahāṅpanāh*."

The Shah rises quickly to his feet. He proclaims, "*Shejādā* of Dalli! Every word of your answers to our four questions is true. A hundred thousand shames on us!"

He steps down, walks over to the *shejādā* of Dalli and warmly embraces him. Then he escorts the young man towards the throne and seats him at his right hand.

After taking the Persian capital by storm like that, Khāniyo returns to Dalli and is received with the same warmth. The first thing Shejādā Khānkhānān does is to go and bow down at his 'employer' *kāji*'s feet.

Says, "*Mālik*,[9] my lord! I am the same old Khāniyo, and will always remain your Khāniyo."

[9] *Mālik*: Literally, owner; lord.